VIVALDI CODEX

Carey Maytham

Order this book online at www.trafford.com
or email orders@trafford.com

Most Trafford titles are also available at major online book retailers.

Print information available on the last page.

ISBN: 978-1-4907-5724-7 (sc)
ISBN: 978-1-4907-5725-4 (e)

Trafford rev. 04/22/2016

 www.trafford.com
North America & international
toll-free: 1 888 232 4444 (USA & Canada)
fax: 812 355 4082

CHAPTER 1

An enormous stone villa stood on the slopes of the Alps on the Austrian border. As usual snow lay all round topping the roof of the building and the fir trees a rich green beneath a heavy white sprinkling. The villa was situated on a gentle slope with an approaching road with thick snow everywhere. Now and again sleigh bells could be heard with parties of visitors the men laughing and women shrieking with mirth in the ice cold weather.

It had been snowing on and off for the whole day but had stopped now and the ground around the villa glinted cold and white. There was clearly a social evening about to take place at the villa that was owned by a middle aged judge, a pinched and strict man who lived there with his wife and only daughter Josina. His wife was seldom seen in the villa as she was sickly and had taken to her bed. The judge had little time for his daughter that meant she was left to her own devices when she returned from school a convent further down the slopes of the mountain.

She was left to the mercies of the servants a number that could be counted on the fingers of two hands. This evening the sleighs moved in to drop their passengers guests of the judge at a musical soirée. Judge Maesterich had given orders that his daughter be attired in beautiful clothing as she, he said in her mother's absence would have to act as hostess. The guests shed their greatcoats and parkas with snow shaken all over the hallway entrance of the villa.

A lackey was soon on the scene to sweep it all away. Cheers and laughter were on the lips of the guests as they made their way upstairs lit by candlelight to a large entertainment room at the top of the villa. On a podium at one side a group of musicians were slowly and carefully taking their instruments out of their containers and the violinists and 'cellists were rubbing resin onto their bows that they used to produce a good tone when performing.

There was also a piano and the pianist was striking the note of A so that the string players could tune up their fiddles and the 'cellos and double basses' theirs. Little tables had been placed conveniently around the room each one lit with single candles smoke drifting from them from the draught at the open door. Once the guests were seated there was talk of an enormous roast sucking pig to whet the guest's appetites.

It seemed that the little group of players would perform while the men and women were indulging in the meal. The guests numbered about twenty four men and women. Servants dished the edibles, roast pork potatoes and other vegetables and poured generous glasses of glühwein for all.

The guests that the Judge had invited were those with whom he had become acquainted while attending to the financial and domestic affairs of his household in the little village at the bottom of the Alpine slopes. The family with his wife seldom seen because of her infirmity had lived in the grand old villa since Josina had been born.

The Judge was by virtue of his calling somewhat narrow minded with his work at the local assizes, and was continually picking on his daughter. This caused Josina to be somewhat rebellious and the young girl drifted slowly from being as she should, an upstanding member of the family into a girl who fraternized with the handful of servants at the villa. The Judge wholly taken up with his work hardly seemed to notice her wastrel behavior.

One of the servants a lowly handyman of good looks but of humble birth had taken to making coarse comments in Josina's presence. In fact he had fallen for her physically as she was a most attractive seventeen-year-old still in her puberty. This evening Ernst the lowly chattel with whom she was becoming over familiar with, was doubling as a waiter at the social occasion. Josina in her innocence not really realizing the idiot that she was making of herself began flirting with Ernst. The guests found her behavior offensive and a leading woman of the town below whispered to the judge the about the atmosphere that his daughter's foolery was causing in upsetting the guests.

The Judge gave Josina a frown and spoke sharply to the Ernst the lowly menial. The two left off their rather public behavior and at the interval just before going on to the desert the orchestra too had a small break. This between time period was used by the guests to fraternize a little and soon there was a hub hub of conversation. The servants quickly cleared the dishes and brought on the desert.

Josina grabbed the opportunity to leave the entertainment room and instead of socializing with the guests as her mother had weakly from her sickbed begged her to do, she ran off to the kitchen to se what delicacies were to be served next and also to find Ernst. She located him behind a pile of dirty dishes. She said cheekily:

"And you have to clean up all that! I'm glad I don't have to do it." Coarsely he croaked back:

"You could do us a favor and help a bit," "Oh! No," she replied only too firmly. "They want me upstairs. My mother says I must be the grand hostess. But I'll see you in the servant's waiting room after the social is over."

"You will, will you?" Ernst answered knowing full well how their affair would go that evening.

Ernst had in his young male capacity of cynicism predicted correctly. The clattering of dishes and general hub hub of conversation was finishing and the orchestra was playing good night and farewell nocturnes. Ernst was waiting as he had told the flirtatious Josina and began to wonder if she was going to join him secretly as usual.

What usually happened at soirées like these was that her mother supposedly responsible for her daughter's conduct, had felt her sickliness come on as the evening progressed. She had tried to ask her husband to keep an eye open for Josina and see her to bed in time to rise for school at the convent. Judge Maesterich was just too socially involved to take any notice of his wife so Josina was left to her own devices.

The servants had begun to notice the time that she spent with Ernst, a popular handyman in rather a coarse way. This was where she was heading tonight - the servants' rest room. She knew she and he would be alone because the servants were only too keen to get home on a snowy winter's night and did not linger. Ernst heard the last of the servants and guests departing.

Silence fell. He heard a soft footfall on the wooden board outside the bare room with its two hard chairs and bed with just a rough mattress on it. He croaked audibly:

"Josina is that you?"

He knew that she flirted promiscuously for her age. He then saw the quaint little figure of Josina. She rushed quickly into the room and sat down next to Ernst. He said:

"I know what you've come for Josina. But it's getting dangerous. I heard your mother is asking about you."
"Oh! Don't concern yourself about her. She is abed by

eight in the evening and my father immerses himself in his work in his study where he ponders over the legal matters that he is concerned with for the next week." Ernst said:

"You and I are going to be found out and reported. The servants are talking about us and the news of our friendship is spreading in the village. Your father will have no mercy on me if we are found out and will confine you to your room. He has done so before for other reasons."

Josina took no notice of this and snuggled against Ernst's rough coat. "This is what you like isn't it Ernst?"

Her fingers touched his bare flesh and he breathed a sigh of relief. It made him feel good to bring a member of the family who were so hard on him at work, down to his own level. He had to control the girl though. All was quiet for another half an hour and then Judge Maesterich's sharp voice could be heard calling for his daughter.

It was not often that her strict old father went to the trouble of finding out what his daughter was doing at that hour of the evening after the soirée was over. She had not expected a summons from him. Ernst felt shivers of fright up and down his spine. The two cowered together as they heard the old man's staggering irregular steps descending from above into the now deserted kitchen quarters. His raised voice was heard, sharply baiting the two. He would get a shock when he saw the disheveled state he found his daughter.

He was not expecting to find her with Ernst. He was panicking because his wife was distraught with worry over their only daughter. The couple in their separate states paid the young girl little enough attention. When they did a drama was sure to ensue. For the last year the Judge, an ardent music lover had entertained others of the same persuasion to such evenings and the company had absorbed themselves in the music and admired the performers.

Josina had nowhere else to go and was not yet educated enough to appreciate the music so was left to the servants' wiles. She had been attracted to Ernst for more than a year now and he, living with coarse teasing from his lowly fellow workers had been egged on to pursue the relationship with Josina. They had after one or two encounters in the servants' rest room begun to react to the physical attraction they felt for one another. On his part Ernst took their love play half heartedly as he was basically a decent lad. Josina the more cunning of the two thrilled at his somewhat rough handling of her as she was growing into a rather svelte young lady. After three or four meetings the two had a passionate relationship. Josina always seemed to melt in and out of the rest room usually deserted at this time of the night.

It seemed that Ernst had scarcely begun to fumble with his lass, as the servants teasingly called her than all track of time was lost until Josina usually becoming nervous after a while at the possibility of being interrupted especially by her father, to Ernst's grunting assent put a stop to his clumsy hands' exploration of her body.

The relationship was still under control but Ernst was getting impatient with her. She had permitted so much this far that like any young man he considered it was right to take her bodily. She was resisting now on this particular night and was tense with fright at what was now bound to be a discovery of the affair by her father whom she was well aware could be very cruel.

The two terrified now on hearing the irregular footfall of Josina's old father as he shuffled down the bare wooden stairs to the basement kitchen quarters empty of staff who had left an hour ago. Josina whispered hoarsely to Ernst:

"My father is wearing ;his bedroom slippers that must mean that he is in his bedroom clothing too. He will be embarrassed to find us here and angry too. What can we do Ernst? Quick he is still quite far off still. You have just got time to leave from the basement back exit. Go now Ernst!"

Ernst was the instantly on the uptake regarding their now certain discovery. The door of escape was right outside the room where they were. Just as Ernst tried the door handle he found himself cornered as the outside door had been locked by the last departing servant. He could only hide in the shadows at the end of the passageway. The high sharp voice of the judge who was completely put out as far as his nightly routine was concerned could be heard calling to his daughter:

"You were not in your bedroom half an hour ago when you should have been my girl. I have searched the villa and the only place you can be…." here he threw open the door to the servants' waiting room not quite knowing who to find there. He continued: "is in this lowly room. Yes Josina what have you been up to?"

The sound of Ernst's boot could be heard softly kicking at the outside door in desperation at the confrontation he knew was coming. Her father snapped at her:

"You look a mess. Totally disheveled. What have you been doing? I know. I cast my mind back to my youth. There is only one matter to occupy you. You and a man have been embracing." His legal training never left him now.

"Is that the truth Josina? And where is you lover the culprit – you are aware that I know you have one? Who is he girl – can't you see that you are in danger and putting the whole villa out to gossip? And where is he this devil of a man.?"

Ernst was quaking in his boots. It would not be long now. Praise be he thought that he had held off the waif of a child Josina in a final physical act. They had been not far off from finally committing themselves to one another bodily.

At the sound next door the Judge again threw open the door from inside knowing there was someone hiding in the shadows. He stuttered half afraid for he knew it would be a young man who would be involved. He knew the effect the sharpness of his words had on people for had he not been in the courtroom most of the days of his adult life?

Ernst was cowering at the end of the passageway the only light coming from under the door of the servant's room where a guttering candle stood at the side of the rough mattress. The judge said to his daughter:

"Who have you been with this evening? Yes I know I was a young man once." He continued in his creaking voice:

"Who has been making play with your body Josina? I have heard vague rumors in the household but at first dismissed them as servants' gossip. I now see that there is some fabric as to the words being spoken amongst my staff. What have you to say for yourself Josina? Where is your admirer?"

He took the candle and went out into the passageway immediately setting eyes in the dim light on the unfortunate Ernst. The judge said:

"So you are the culprit!" The Judge's voice creaked with annoyance and embarrassment. "Haven't I seen you working around the villa?"

Ernst pulled his forelock in obeisance and pronounced:

"Yes sir I do the work of a handyman at the villa. I have been working here for three years." The Judge cut in:

"I'll speak to you tomorrow in the morning. I'll let you out. Go home now. It's quite possible that your employment here will be terminated from tomorrow."

Head sagging Ernst made his way out into the snowdrifts and stumbled his way home to his mother's chalet in the dark at the other side of the small forest of firs on the mountain Alps. He was the only son of a widow his mother who growing older now earned a pittance by taking in washing from the neighboring village dwellers. She relied largely on her son's income from his handyman's work at the great villa up the slopes of the mountainside. The poor old lady was shortly to hear her son's sad story.

She heard in a breaking of the silence in the room lit by only one or two candles the latch on the door being lifted. She was tense in her greeting to her son. She sensed immediately that there was something wrong. Of course out came the whole story. He had never held anything back from his dear mother. She was shocked that it was apparent that he would loose his place of employment and income. Instantly she promised that she would forgive him and that they should just hope for another place of work for him. She said:

"I am sure there are plenty of positions to be had in the village. One of the women that I do washing for says that her husband is a woodcutter and is keen to find a young man to help him, for a salary."

Ernst lifted his cowered head. There it was. He could always trust his old mother in times of trouble.

"Josina," the hated creaky voice of the Judge met her ears waking her the next morning. She had flung on yesterday's clothing and thrown some water onto her face rubbing it dry in all haste. She came slowly out of her bedroom. Her mother hobbled up behind her father.

The judge took Josina by the elbow saying:

"Now you come along with your mother and I to my study. There are a few questions I would like to ask you my girl. No doubt that rogue who was encouraging you in your misdemeanors last night has been at it for quite some evenings now."

When they reached his study Josina had not been able to say a word in her defence. Her father said:

"Sit down opposite me at my desk my girl."

It was seldom that Josina found herself in her father's study. She was finding the whole episode terrifying. Noting that she had not spoken yet her father attacked his daughter verbally:

"Don't sit there as if you were dumb. I am sure you had plenty to say to that handyman that I had the ill fortune to employ at the villa. He won't be back."

All that was running through Josina's brain were Ernst's last words to her the evening before, that were:

"I'll be back to fetch you tomorrow at midnight Josina. Be ready. I'll throw a pebble or two against your window to say we'll be on our way out of here."

How Josina hated what her father was putting her through and how she despised her mother sitting weeping in the background. If her mother would only pull herself together and take her part in the drama that was under way might there not be a happier outcome to the scene? "Father, mother," Josina pleaded, "this has all happened because it seems that neither of you has any time for me. I am left to the mercies of your servants when I am not doing my schoolwork. It is no wonder that I have fallen into their hands. There is no one else and I was lonely."

This seemed suddenly to have a ring of honesty to the old man who spent most of his time bringing justice to the courtroom scenes in the local town. In future then you can spend more time at your schoolwork and piano practice and see to your mother's evening meal and bathing and settling her into bed at night. Do you understand Josina? I do not want you fraternizing with the servants any longer."

Head down in unspoken despondency that lasted until lunch Josina was finally dismissed in deep disgrace by her father. His wife had confessed her inability to deal with her daughter's activities and because there was nothing else for her to do had again taken to her bed complaining about her asthma.

Although she had not one word to offer in defence Josina felt a fighting spirit within her. Before lunch she lay on the bed and thumped the pillows with clenched fists. She went over the last few month's in her relationship with Ernst until the final showdown last night. She spoke although she knew there was no-one listening who could answer:

"It's not fair! It's not fair! It's not my fault that I have no brothers and sisters."

Slowly tears began to flow. One of the chambermaids quietly entered the bedroom, and seeing Josina crying said:

"There now Miss Josina. I know what has happened. We all do all the servants. We all understand about you and Ernst." Josina sobbed:

"He's gone for good now. My father told him not to come back to the villa. Shall I let you into a secret Mirabelle?" "Oh! Yes, Miss Josina." The young girl not much older than Josina enthused. Josina whispered:

"He said he would be back! Tonight! To fetch me! You have always been a loyal friend Mirabelle. Don't breathe a word of this to anyone or your employment might be taken away also." "Right then my lady. Are you all calmed down now ready for luncheon? That's what I came here for."

At this Josina felt how hungry she was. She realized that she had eaten nothing the whole morning. Neither of her parents seemed to care as usual. Then later after dinner she amused herself halfheartedly though by strumming a little on her piano, all the time her thoughts on what Ernst had promised her before being confronted by her father.

"Be awake at midnight tonight. When you hear the soft rattle of some tiny pebbles on your windowpane you will know that it is I waiting for you outside. We are going to elope Josina my darling."

She gave a start as she recalled the words he had spoken to her. They had been loving caring words not like the servants teasing or her father's sharp utterances, usually at dinner. That was the only time they saw or spoke to one another. He had told her that she could look in at her mother's bedchamber at any time during the day but she declined to do this as her presence caused her mother to go into a fit of shaking. It would be worse today, her jittery reaction to the sight of her daughter after what had happened last night and this morning.

Josina's heart leapt for joy. She flew to the window and pulled aside the curtain. Her room was on the second story and it was pitch-dark outside but she could see the figure of Ernst below face pale in the starlight. So he had kept his word. He had seen her figure in the window. She gestured to him that she would be coming down. She had packed some clothing and toiletries and put the valise under the bed.

She now pulled it out. Her bedroom was not near that of her parents' but she knew that her door did squeak a little. Carefully she pulled it open and slid through the entranceway before it could make a noise. She had lit a candle and her heart was in her mouth. She could just hear her father snoring down the passageway.

All was quiet in the villa. She knew where the keys to the front door were kept. She opened the little box that held them and they rattled slightly as she took them out, but she quickly stifled the slight noises by enfolding the keys completely in her hand. Still there was no noise from upstairs. Carefully holding the keys that were on a ring she picked out the main key that she would need.

Her father kept the lock oiled so putting her candle on the little table near the door she turned the lock, opening it.

Soft flakes of snow were falling outside and Ernst stepped out of the shadows. The moon was shining at three quarter fullness and the stars giving off much light. Josina whispered:

"Ernst, oh Ernst thank you for keeping to your word. I cannot bear my home any longer. You know how it is here. It is quite stiflingly tense what with my father dealing with malpracticers all day long. He is getting old and was beginning to treat me like one of the vagrants that he has to give justice to. My mother did not come to my support at all. She is a weak and feeble woman."

"Hush love!" Ernst's words came through the still icy air outside. "I understand. Let us start walking to my mother's chalet about an hour's distance away. I have told her about us. She sympathizes but is sore afraid of the judge's ire should she be found to be harboring an innocent young girl. She too thinks that the circumstances at the villa are shocking for a young girl like you."

They had walked for twenty minutes now and far in the distance could see a faint light from a dwelling near the trees. Josina's face was pale and afraid peering out of her parka that she was wearing. Tiring a little now Ernst slowed down his hearty pace to match hers. The dullish candlelight on the window of the chalet became brighter and as they neared the little dwelling they could see a lone figure moving about through the window panes frosted with snow. It was Ernst's mother

"You poor dear," Ernst's mother began. "Ernst has confided in me your situation. It seems that no one at the villa took a proper interest in you. They'll be sorry mark my words, when they find you gone. You can rest up here for the night."

The woman although overlooking the danger that she might be putting she and her son in the elopement clearly had a soft heart. She continued:

"Heinke your brother is building chalets with the wood from the trees he is cutting down in the forest. We were talking about it only yesterday. Ernst I have spoken to your brother as I promised and he will let you have one of them set deep in the forest at no payment. You can probably help at first in your new abode." She smiled gushingly at Josina and then went on.

"Then you can look for work. Josina can help to win your bread by taking in washing." At these words Josina thought it was no use running away again. Her father would have no qualms about putting her in borstal if she went back now. Rather she and Ernst should disappear into the heart of the forest and do as Ernst's mother said:

"Rest now both of you. I have made up the extra bed that Heinke uses when he comes here and Ernst you can look for your brother in the morning with your claim to the free chalet. I have partitioned off one section in this little dwelling."

So Josina was able to undress and put on her nightwear and retire to fall asleep after the long walk from the villa. Fear gripped her as she lay awake in the unfamiliar bed. What had she done? But her desire for Ernst excited her. When could they be together alone again? She though now sleepily that they could take the two beds to the chalet that it was apparent she and Ernst would live in. As she fell asleep she felt glad that she had the sympathy of Ernst's mother in their predicament.

She awoke early to a dim sunlight shining into the chalet now frozen with the cold from the thick snow outside. It was clear that it had been snowing heavily in the early hours that night. Ernst was running his finger through her hair. She was about to speak but he put his finger to her lips.

"Quiet," he said. "My mother is still asleep."

She felt his fingers now ice cold searching for her breasts. It was a shock pleasant though and she found herself relaxing as her body made his hand warm. She curved her self like a cat stretching. Then there was a call from Ernst's mother.

"Put on the kettle for some tea Ernst and when it has boiled I will make our porridge. Later you can go to the town for milk and bread. I do have some lard left over from Heinke's boar kill, the wild pig that you prepared for me to roast. There is still some of the meat left over also."

The first voice that she heard after Ernst told her to hush was the slightly shrill voice of his mother: "Ernst,"

"Yes, mother," he answered. "You must go down to the village to look for work," she replied.

Ernst said trying to soothe his mother in the unstable situation they found themselves in:

"I'll be alright mother. I was out earlier this morning and spoke to Heinke. He promises to give - yes give at no charge, to me his latest built chalet that he has made the one right deep in the center of the forest. Josina and I will live there and like you Josina can take in washing to help find bread for us to eat."

These words pierced Josina's ears. Was this what Ernst had done to her? Then she remembered the times they used to have together isolated in the servants rest room at her father's villa. She lay thinking there must be more to follow between them. She was not sorry to have left her father and mother at the villa. Yes she had strung Ernst along finding for the first time physical attraction in his body. He was also good looking though in a rough sort of way.

She had a ferret like nature much in keeping with the demeanor and looks of her eagle eyed father the judge. Like him she questioned herself as to what would happen next. To hurry matters along she arose from the warm bed into the frosty air in the chalet and found what passed for a bathroom. There seemed to be no one about.

Having taken her clothes in with her, as she had learnt at the convent she gave herself a brief but thorough wash. Her dress was creased she saw with a sigh. It was not Mirabelle who had packed her clothes. She had. She put her nose around the partition scenting the porridge that was being cooked. It made her realize just how hungry she was. Ernst said:

"My brother is putting the finishing touches to our chalet in the forest. Out came Josina's words, fearful:

"No-one will find me here today surely. They will only miss me at supper having thought that I was at my schoolwork all day. The weather is coming over thick with snow today and tonight. I could tell from the thick clouds meeting overhead."

Lunch at the chalet was heated gruel and some dry rye bread. Ernst's mother unrealizing that she would be leaving the two alone said that she was going to try and avoid the heavy weather and fetch washing from the village early on in the afternoon.

When she had gone Ernst washed the dishes and the two sat staring at each other over the rough wooden table. Ernst had brewed up two cups of strong warm tea that Josina was grateful for because she was feeling the cold badly.

It was ice cold in the little chalet enough to curb their physical attraction. The discomfort caused Josina to speak:

"I am so afraid of my father finding out about what I have done. He is a harsh man and will not understand. I must do something to disguise myself if anyone comes looking for me." Ernst responded:

"I know my mother has a cupboard where she keeps old clothes some perhaps that have not stood up to the continual washing of them that she has had to do. Often her clients say she can keep the clothes if they do not take to the harsh soap that she has to use. I know many of these clothes are tattered and torn but she will be only too glad to let you have some of them that you could use as a disguise. My brother is expecting us this evening as he has put the finishing touches to the chalet, luckily over the last week.

There are beds and a table and chairs. I will have to put up wash lines because you will have to start work as soon as possible to supplement what income I can bring in."

The two sat staring at each other unbelieving of the temporary safety of the situation as it crept into their minds. They had known each other for a couple of years now so were contented in the manner of true youth to continue in the circumstances as they unfolded. Ernst said:

"I'll make another pot of hot tea." The thought of something physically warming cheered Josina somewhat as the last few gleams of wintry sunlight fell onto the table where they were sitting. The door was then heard creaking open and Ernst's mother Gertrude appeared with a large bag of clothes. She said:

"I found work for myself today with as much as I can carry. This will keep me warm for a few days now the activity of washing and hanging the clothes to dry." Ernst broke in:

"Mother Josina is short of clothing and I know you keep oddments of garments in your cupboard. Do you think that she could have some of them? She thinks it will help her play the part of a washerwoman."

He kept the true reason from his mother in his easing Josina's worry. Gertrude lavishly pulled some of the old clothes out of the cupboard. Some of the old garments had a look of old glory and some were in peasant style. She chose a few ragged peasant dresses that were quite tattered. They would do very well to disguise her deep in the woods where she and Ernst would live in the future. Then Ernst said:

"Quick now Josina we'll have to hurry to reach Heinke at the cottage by seven this evening. He has a sleigh and has promised to lay in some stocks for us for the next week. I will have to buy a sleigh from my own savings for us. I will have to pull it. He looked at the girl. "You are not heavy and we can buy the necessary food every now and again using it and collect washing for you to do."

Chapter 2

Ernst said:

"Farewell mother. I will stop in often on my way to and from work. Heinke says he has a few contacts for me in the town. You know that I did the work of a handyman at the villa. Well there is an aged woodcarver in the village who needs an assistant. Heinke tells me that the old man's eyes are failing and there is no one in his family that he can apprentice to himself in the woodwork he does. Heinke is going to make inquiries within the next few days. "Good bye Ernst," Gertrude answered continuing, "if anyone comes asking about you or Josina I will just say that your have work in the town but I will not say where." Ernst ushered Josina through the door saying:

"We will have a long walk to come to the chalet by nightfall. Tomorrow I'll take the sleigh and will bring your clothing that my mother has promised you. Then no-one will know it is you Josina the daughter of a judge who is a washerwoman, while I earn my living as a woodcarver's apprentice."

"Oh! Ernst," she panted at the fast pace that he was setting. "You have planned everything so well for us. I will work hard at washing clothes. It will be so much more fun to live like this than the awful life that I had with my parents. They mean nothing to me now or ever."

Ernst did not respond as he knew they must hurry now because Heinke was waiting with news at the chalet in the middle of the forest that he had prepared for them. It would be too late for Heinke to leave that evening so the three of them would spend the night at the new chalet. Just as night was setting in and the trees looming about them and with the animal noises in the darkness Josina began to feel frightened.

Then ahead of them along the path through the path they were following a faint light shone through the deepening twilight. It began to snow. Ernst took Josina's hand. They were not wearing protective clothing and they did not want to get wet. So reaching the lighted window near the door just in time he gave a sharp knock, keen for them to get inside.

The door opened and there stood Ernst's brother who greeted them warmly:

"Come inside quickly," he said. "The snow is gathering thickly, I could see by the sky. I have some brodwurst and glühwein. You must be starved. When did you last eat?"

Josina took off her gloves and parka and drew near to a heap of burning coals near a chimneystack in the chalet. The threesome ate their fill of the dried sausage and the glühwein warmed them. There were three beds in the chalet and Gertrude had seen to providing bedding for them. Thankful for somewhere to sleep they were asleep within minutes after the meal and in drifting off Josina thought to herself that these two youths were more like friends brothers as they were.

Upon wakening the next morning Heinke had some porridge on the boil and a little milkmaid from a chalet nearby that kept a cow had brought them fresh milk for the day. The first matter Josina attended to was to take the old ragged clothing out of the bag and to gird herself in old tattered peasant clothing. She had dressed in the bathroom cubicle out of Ernst's sight. Coming out she said:

"Do I look like an Austrian peasant to you Ernst? I'll just put on this bandanna around my head and put a pinched poverty struck expression on my face. Then if anyone comes looking for me I will be quite well enough disguised. I had a look through all the clothing that your mother gave me and there is no doubt that I could be disguised four or five times over with it all. Well, are you going to fetch some dirty washing for me to start work with, Ernst?" He replied:

"I'm going right away if Heinke is ready. We are also going to keep an appointment with a woodcarver that Heinke is going to introduce me to with a view to working for him. So we'll be gone the whole day. You will be quite safe here. I asked Grisella who brings the milk to pop in before lunch just to make sure you are alright. The chalet is only just completed and there are a lot of wood shavings and some dust lying around that you could sweep up for a start. We will bring back with the washing that you are doing to help my mother some of the strong abrasive cheap soap that she uses."

Innocently Josina could not wait to get started. The brothers bade her farewell for the present. All was quiet once they had left. Josina picked up a roughly fashioned hand-made bristle broom and began slowly to sweep out the sawdust and wood shavings from the floor of the chalet.

There seemed no one for miles. She looked in the cupboard where the food was kept. There was roughly baked loaf of bread and some wurst as well as some lard. Then she heard a soft tapping on the door. Unafraid Josina opened up to see a pretty peasant girl a little older than herself standing outside.

On seeing someone her own age, a girl and not one of the teasing petty socialites who attended the convent that she had escaped from Josina greeted the visitor cautiously. She was still afraid of being found out. She gave the girl one of her sly grins. Josina had nothing to fear though when the girl answered her question as to why she had come to the chalet.

"My name is Grisella. This is your urn of milk for the day. Heinke has already paid me. He is courting me you know. We are going to set a date for the wedding any day now. See he has given me this amethyst ring." Curiously she addressed Josina.

"Are you Ernst's girl? Where do you come from? I have not seen you around these parts, ever."

Not wanting to give away the secret of her upper-class birth Josina fobbed off the question by giving a very general answer.

"I used to live around the other side of the mountain. Ernst fetched me today. We are going to live together." The girl said timidly:

"Aren't you married?" Josina answered snappily:

"We don't believe in all that. So if you'll excuse me I'll get down to work." "Goodbye then," replied the amazed Grisella.

Heinke had not said anything about his brother having what Ernst must have - a lover. Josina took the tub outside as Ernst had told her and took it to a place nearby where there was clean snow. With a spade-like implement she began to scoop the snow into the tub until it was nearly full. Then she lit the fire where Ernst had left the wood piled up, under the chimney and lit the fire to boil a cauldron of water.

The she threw it over the snow in the container and it melted into clear water. She separated the clothes into heavy and light wear and put the underwear in first. Despite the hot cauldron the water was icy and her until now pampered lily-white hands, became slowly red and raw as she took the coarse lump of soap and began to rub the wet clothes together. Then she heard Ernst's voice. By now it was early afternoon.

"Hello there." She had heard the sleigh swish through the snow. She quickly stoked the fire with some wood that she found nearby and placed some of last night's gruel in a bowl over a grid on top of the makeshift oven. They found themselves eating together and as they ate Ernst remarked:

"Every day when I go out I'll see to it that I'll bring back food supplies coal and washing. I'll chop wood for the fire in the evenings. But Josina I have news." "Good news?" questioned Josina. "Quick tell me." He lowered his voice. She could see he was very pleased about something and was going to let her in on the secret. He shared with her what he had come by.

"Heinke has employment in town and has his ears open amongst the folk that he mixes with there to help me to find work. And he has succeeded. Josina I was given hospitality by a very old man, old to me at any rate, who after a welcome cup of coffee this morning asked me what I could turn my hand to. Heinke had told him that I was a handyman. He did not seem too concerned why I was no longer in my former employment.

I told him that it gave me great pleasure to mend various broken articles belonging to a household and that I particularly liked working with wood. Would you believe it Josina, it turned out that the old man was in the woodcarving business and that his only son had left the business to find work elsewhere. The two of them were finding themselves too much at loggerheads to keep the business afloat much longer. He said it was a lucky break for him that Heinke had heard his sad tale of woe and had asked him to introduce me to him. So it seems that I will be starting work with old father Grüssman as soon as tomorrow! Isn't that great news?"

"You will be gone for the day with the sleigh early in the morning then Ernst? You have brought me my first load of washing I see." "Yes we'll have to be up early to kindle the logs and coal for warmth and cooking during the days. Do you know how to bake bread?" "No Ernst." she answered. "Then I'll get my mother to teach you. It's not difficult. You'll learn quickly then we will have an ongoing supply of bread and Grisella will supply us with butter and milk. No doubt she was here this morning?"

"Yes," answered Josina. "I got quite a surprise, but a pleasant one. It seems that Heinke and she are married." Then she said a little sullenly: "That's not the way we live is it Ernst?"

"No Josina we did not have the chance. We are of different social backgrounds you and I. I am of humble peasant stock," here he paused then continued, "while you are of near aristocratic blood. It is strange that we find each other interesting but our recent situation has brought us together. I see nothing wrong with it do you?" He finished in rough peasant tones. She changed the subject. "I managed to make some soup with a shank of meat that I found frozen in the cupboard. There seems to be a crust of bread to go with it too."

The day drew in slowly and the light faded. Ernst busied himself chopping wood outside for the fire for when they would both keep warm and cook their evening meal. Over the coals that she had been watching off and on during the afternoon while awaiting Ernst's return she had heated the remains of the soup that she had made yesterday with some beans to sate their youthful hunger. Ernst wiped his feet outside the door and entered with a load of wood.

"Oh! Wonderful Ernst," Josina enthused. "That will keep us warm for the night." "Yes," he answered: "I have found an old grid lying outside that we can use to stop the coals from falling onto the floor. At least we'll be safe."

Ernst pulled rug off the bed so they could sit on it in front of the now cheerful looking fire after they had eaten. Startled for Ernst pulled her to him, Josina let out a question:

"What are you doing Ernst?" He replied in all seriousness:

"What did you expect us to be doing coming here with me? Josina?" He said her name expectantly. He knew from their past relationship at the villa that she would respond to the sound of her name. She relaxed against his sturdy chest. He drew her to him and began fondling her. She responded and their talking stopped. All that seemed important was what they were doing. Then roughly Ernst pulled Josina onto the bed and their lovemaking began in earnest. The chalet was warm now with the coals that Ernst had added to the fire. For the first time they came together and then found themselves lying exhausted side by side.

The only sound for a few minutes was the coals as they fell apart while burning. Then suddenly in the distance outside came the sound of heavy boots. Josina flew to the window while Ernst remained sitting on the bed. They had hastily pulled their clothes on. It sounded like a couple of men outside. Then there was a rough thumping on the door of the chalet with the words:

"Open up. It is the police here."

Ernst looked anxious and Josina was struck with terror. Ernst said to her:

"Don't worry. I'll handle these men. Just remember if they ask you to say that you are my wife and that you take in washing during the day. I will tell them that I am employed by a woodcarver in the town. Don't say anything if you can help it. They will have no means of identifying you and you look the picture of a poor housewife."

The thumping grew louder. In all indignation Ernst opened the door to an icy blast. Josina sat on the bed at the back of the chalet and could hear the men talking, Ernst quite angrily. With the remarks the police were passing Josina could hear that the conversation was becoming quite heated. She began to tremble as she heard the two men shuffling towards where she was sitting now one the chair next to the bed where they had lain together hardly an hour ago. Ernst was following them harping plaintively on the fact that he and Josina had agreed on. He said to them:

"Can't you see? This girl is dumb and retarded. I allow her to earn her keep here by doing washing and cooking as well as other household chores." One of the men quipped coarsely:

"And that's not all she does around here She works at night too it seems by the looks of things." He indicated the unmade bed. Ernst said protectively: "Lay off the girl. She cannot even speak in her own defence."

The men left her alone and she could hear them questioning Ernst as to his harboring any knowledge of a girl called Josina in the area. The officer of the law said:

"We are searching for the daughter of a local judge who lives in a villa around the other side of the mountain."

Ernst grew tense. He could not let Josina down. He hoped desperately for Josina's safety for she had told Ernst that if her father caught up with her activities he would most certainly send her to borstal, the institution for errant and unmanageable young girls. By this time Josina was looking scruffy and uncared for and had thrown on some ragged clothing. The two policemen had not thought to search the cupboard where she had pushed in her only good clothes to the back behind a pile of washing. Slowly the two men left off disturbing the household.

Eventually she heard the front door squeak closed. Ernst came up to her like a lamb for the slaughter. How could he have got Josina into this trouble? She ran up to him with quick little steps and put her arms around his neck. He tried with a half-hearted smile to free himself from her grasp but was unsuccessful. What he had told the gendarmes had clearly served to get her out of trouble. He said to her looking down onto her little ferret like face:

"I don't think they'll be back. You played your retarded and dumb role to perfection Josina. No one would have guessed that you were a Judge's daughter." She answered tartly:

"You pay me no compliment Ernst. This is my shabby look from now on. I will not be able to look even a little pretty for you in case word gets round about us. I'll have to play my part in full all the time."

It was clear that the feeling between the two of them was no more than puppy love that had developed in to an adult partnership in their behavior for them each night as they lay together. Ernst was a good-looking youth only just having reached twenty years of age, and the somewhat ferret-like looking Josina had only the passion of a young girl for him who was now her lover. For many months they were not disturbed by anyone besides Heinke and Grisella.

A young girls' friendship grew between the two young women. Every day Grisella brought milk in a small can for Ernst and Josina and butter also now and again. They fell to talking when Grisella came to the chalet. Josina expressed her fears to Grisella one day, harping on the same subject that she was afraid of being caught out by her father.

"I could not bear my family any longer. It was not only Ernst that took me away from my mother and father. I grew to dislike my father for his meanness and to despise my mother for her weak mindedness, always taking to her bed when my father behaved in a difficult manner." Grisella offered a sympathetic reply:

"How different my own family was. I can really understand how awful it must have been for you in your situation. My own mother was a strong minded and loving farmer's wife. My father was a kind-hearted man even though he was sometimes a little gruff. They were broken hearted when my sister and I left home to marry. I have often talked to Heinke about the ways things are between you and Ernst, that you are living together but not married."

Here Josina broke in. Her sharp tongue matched her looks and nature and she gave word to how she felt about the way her life was turning out:

"There is no way we can marry now that Ernst and I have eloped. I truly love him and would give the world to be married to him." "Wait,' said Grisella." The local pastor, a wonderful man who married Heinke and I would be only too glad to marry you and Ernst and I know that he would keep your secret."

That evening the two couples were talking together at Ernst's chalet. It had to be there because Josina was terrified of being found out. After all she was not even through with her convent schooling yet. Heinke suggested:

"Grisella, tomorrow you must go to Pastor Luke's house on the other side of the forest and tell him in confession how we are caring for my brother-in-law and the girl he loves. You must ask him to tell no-one and arrange with him a time when Ernst and Josina can be married."

"Oh! That will be wonderful Heinke," enthused Josina. "My father is not a religious person at all so it is unlikely that our marriage could come to his ears."

Grisella took the afternoon off from her household duties to see the priest in the little chapel higher up on the mountain. It was quite a climb and her cheeks were glowing by the time the Pastor opened the door of the adjoining living quarters of the chapel. He was a catholic priest and welcomed Grisella saying:

"What brings you to the chapel my child? Do you need confession with me? Perhaps that is so?" "No," she answered. It is about my husband's brother."

The Pastor said: "You look so worried. I fear for you spiritual welfare." "Very well Pastor." The two went into the inside of the chapel to the confessional.

Grisella managed to explain Josina and Ernst's elopement and the need for the two young people to be married. She said to the Pastor:

"It may seem that I am condoning what in God's eyes in a terrible sin but poor Josina was so unhappy at home. You won't give away their secret, pastor will you?"

They have committed a grievous sin of fornication that should be put right by their marrying," answered the Pastor. "I'll make arrangements as soon as I can for my brother-in-law and his future wife." Grisella said this joyfully and after a blessing from the Pastor set off down the mountainside to meet with and tell her husband the good news. Heinke said:

"You can let Josina into the plan for she and Ernst to be married. I saw Ernst in the village today. He said he is thoroughly enjoying his work with old Father Grüssman the woodcarver. I'm sure that Ernst will have much to tell Josina about what he does in the woodcarver's shop where he is now an apprentice. It seems that they are carving furniture table, chairs and commodes, as well as making wooden painted toys."

Yes Ernst was absorbed in his new employment as Josina heard that night during and after supper.

"I am happy as a sandboy cutting, carving, sawing and decorating wooden artifacts. I knew a little about it from my handyman days at the villa but this type of work is taking up all my time."

The next day after Ernst had set off for the village with some clean washing that Josina had done to be delivered. Grisella appeared as usual at the door of Ernst's chalet her face full of smiles. She could not keep it to herself any longer and burst out:

"I have arranged with the Pastor up the mountainside at the chapel that you and Ernst can be married there next Saturday." Josina stood stock still realizing the implication of what would now take place. She knew marriage vows were a permanent state of affairs. She knew only a little of what to expect if she was to bear a child but wanted to give such as might be born to she and Ernst a name at least. Their child must not be illegitimate. Now she would with taking Ernst's name be even more incognito in the alpine community.

Josina for all her faults as regards paying respect to her parents was a hard worker as she had been trained by her teachers the nuns as the convent just outside the village where until recently she had been a school child. She realized that to stay alive she and Ernst would have to spend their days working hard for a living as she knew her father did, even though as the months went by she realized that she did not even miss her parents; she was becoming a hardened young woman.

They had been married quietly a few weeks after setting up home together on the Pastor's advice. It was a strange situation to be in but no less strange than the home she had grown up in. She was happy to be mixing with other young in the form of Heinke and his wife Grisella. The two couples spent much time together. This Josina enjoyed. She said to Ernst one evening after he had returned home with another day's wash-load, hungry as usual as were they both what with the sharp Alpine air:

"Are we seeing Heinke and Grisella this evening?" Ernst answered:

"Heinke and I are very close my brother and I. Grisella he says prefers to be out during the day. She enjoys passing the time of day with you when she brings us the milk and butter." "Oh! But that's lovely to hear," responded Josina.

Marriage young as she was, was developing in her a warmth of character. The love she was experiencing from the other of these young was bringing out an affectionate nature in her. Heinke had some dice and they all spent many happy hours in the candle light of an evening playing games that the father of the two youths had taught them.

Being an only child and a girl at that had made her into a bit of a tomboy and they laughed and joked endlessly, partaking of a couple of glasses of glühwein while they enjoyed themselves over the luck of the throws of the dice and took bets with one another. Then reality struck. Josina fell pregnant. At first when she was sure she was expecting a child she drew Grisella in the chalet when she delivered the milk and confided in her. Grisella not yet having a child of her own said enviously:

"You are so lucky Josina. Now even if your father does find out where you are living as you said you were afraid of, there is nothing he can do because as we know and he must know a church marriage is a legal one also." "Yes," agreed Josina, "and I wouldn't want to go back to live at the villa anyway."

The newly married couple had to make do with separate beds that Heinke had made and given to his brother. One evening the two were sitting idly at table after Josina had cleared the dishes and had finished the kitchen chores after a usual frugal supper of bread and wurst. Ernst had brought some beer, pulling it up the gentle lower Alpine slopes through the forest to their chalet, and the couple sat partaking of some of it in front of the log fire.

Josina sipped slowly at the beer not really enjoying it then slowly gave her news to her husband:

"Ernst for a couple of weeks I have not been too sure but I am certain now. I am expecting our child."

Ernst steadied himself on his seat and came out with the gruff male response:

"I don't believe it. But if you say so it must be true. You did not keep it from me." "Yes," she answered. "I am telling you the truth Ernst. I have been talking over such matters to Grisella and she says she can't wait to be a mother. We will have to make our plans for the birth though." He answered:

"It will only happen in eight or nine month's time. I will ask not letting out our secret in the village, if there is a nurse who can be with us at the birth. You will have to stop doing the work of washing in a few month's time." She replied:

"Oh, nonsense Ernst. It will be quite alright for me to go on doing it, right up to the birth. We are going to need the extra money. Grisella though hard working as a farm girl can not give us milk and butter without being paid you know that." Then she changed her conversational tack:

"How is your work with old father Grüssman going? You are usually so busy collecting the wood and counting out the money for our provisions that you scarcely talk to me in the evenings. But then I am busy too cooking at that time. But my news is keeping us up later than usual tonight. What is it exactly that you busy yourself with in the furniture shop?"

Ernst stared at the glowing coals that the two of them were warming themselves with. She in her alert way was watching him and she repeated her question:

"What is it that you do all day?" Then Ernst spoke:

"Oh! I'm tired now but I will tell you that old father Grüssman has got me working on a rocking chair that an elderly friend of his has commissioned him to carve out of pine wood for his wife, Father Grüssman says, of many years. He says that the old lady is nearing ninety years of age."

Josina listened fascinated. Life she was thinking was becoming quite dull with only Grisella to talk to and greeting the odd folk who passed by, having cut wood for their homes to burn for log fires and cooking stoves too. The child grew in her womb and Josina grew more and more excited but also retained the calmness of an expectant mother. She continued to busy herself with the washing that Ernst brought to the chalet every day. It seemed that old father Grüssman was well known and liked in the town, so was able to give Ernst many contacts to collect washing for his wife to earn their keep.

The old man became all paternal when he heard that the young couple were expecting a child. Only sometime after a conversation he had with the young man concerning his past employment, he had said to Ernst:

"There is very little trouble in this town only amongst the business fraternity who bicker amongst themselves about the sales they are making. The judge is known to take an almost malicious delight in their troubles and arguments, slapping fines on them for the slightest reason almost encouraging their in-fighting This I suppose," the old man rambled on, "is to increase the contents of his own purse." Ernst had said:

"The judge is also a nobleman of the aristocracy so has claim to substantial government funds. Anyone would think he would be satisfied with that alone. But no he seems intent on worsening certain peoples' unhappiness."

Then later talking to Josina Ernst told her tactfully though how much her father was disliked by the townsfolk. She replied:

"It is no wonder he made me so unhappy. The servants at the villa although they had no other source of revenue were in awe and fright of him. He did have a number of friends amongst his own class in the palatinate who were all under the false impression that he was doing good in the community because he was encouraging honesty and fairness amongst the inhabitants of the town."

Josina pondered over these matters that Ernst told her about and was almost ashamed that it was her own father who was such a person. Her mother always sickly and almost a recluse she had very little to do with. Then she thought of the baby that was coming within the next two months. Ernst's mother had sent her some little garments for the coming little one as well as some of the basic necessities that she had kept stored for circumstances such as the young couple had found themselves in. Ernst had asked around the good folk in the town whom he was coming to know and had found a nurse who said that she would be willing to assist in the birth.

Secure in the knowledge that his wife could be cared for at the birth of their first child the couple counted the days until this great event in their lives. There seemed no fear of Josina being traced by her father the judge. From what the young girl knew of her father he was such a hardened and callous old man that he would not care if his daughter were missing and her mother was too helpless thus powerless to search for her.

Josina was happy enough in her own way. She had never felt wanted as a young girl so had quite tough feelings about her current state of life. It seemed better to her to be with Ernst every evening and to learn to cook. She found this latter occupation most fulfilling and with some encouragement from her new mother-in-law began to enjoy the task of washerwoman too. Her hands became rough and red from constant immersion in the cold water for there was sometimes no way of heating it. Sometimes she thought ruefully of the heated baths she had at the villa but knew that was all over now. She flung herself into this new adventure of a life. Then she was faced with her birth pangs and Ernst hastened to fetch first Grisella then the nurse both to comfort and assist Josina.

The young girl had on the advice of Ernst's mother prepared a receiving table with a warm blanket heated hastily at the right time over the stove, as well as a little cradle to receive the new baby that would want to sleep after the shock of being born. It all happened just as they had hoped with no traumatic episodes. Then they were all able to settle down for the night and Josina could begin her mothering the following day. At first she was too busy nursing the infant to do any of the washing that was piling up. Ernst brought up from the village the dirty linen. After a week or two when a routine was established in the little chalet Josina saw fit to continue her washing tasks.

During the days while she busied herself over the baby and the washing she began to wonder about the future of the baby girl. Music had been so exposed to her at her father's soirées that it seem part of her life she could not forget. She missed her piano lessons now. She said to Ernst one evening:

"All this work of washing that I'm doing. I am going to scrimp and save so that when Donella is older she can have 'cello lessons. She can attend the convent when she is older." Ernst said in response: "Yes it's good to dream about the future but there is a now to be attended to. Why is Donella crying at the moment?" Josina sighed.

Agitated now that their child was crying so lustily Josina took only a few moments to understand why Donella was playing up as she called it:

"Ernst can we not open the window at the other end of the chalet to let some air in? It's because it's so stuffy in here that Donella is wailing as she is," Josina said. Ernst answered, "No we can't do that, the air is frozen outside and we will all get sick if I do that." She begged, "But there are also cinders from the log fire floating in the air in here. Perhaps some of these are falling onto the baby's face. Can't you open the door just a trifle. Just for a little while then?"

Ernst walked over to the door and opened it up just an inch or two. Soon this made all the difference as the hot air inside was cooled just a little. Josina settled baby Donella for the night and the new mother and her husband fell into conversation:

"Did I tell you Josina that your esteemed father the judge has put an advertisement in the newspaper locally offering a reward to the person who traces your whereabouts?" Josina frowned in anger forgetting their present situation. All she could do in the following few minutes was dwell on the past unhappiness she had experienced as a growing young girl at the stone villa on the Alpine slopes way above the forest. She exclaimed:

"My father has no rights over me any longer. You and I are married with a family of our own. He can't touch a hair on by head even. He has no rights over me even though he might with his legal conivances try to get me back." She ended with a shudder. "He and my mama had little enough time for me when I was living at the villa. No Ernst this is my home now and I have never been happier. Are they going to do another search for me through the towns and villages? I do hope not. I will just reassume my rights as a washerwoman then. You can steer the police away from me, surely they will not be interested in a person in rags who looks poverty stricken."

The weeks passed in trepidation for Josina but nothing untoward occurred to upset the little family. Then the weeks turned to months and the months to years and the couple and the child, a toddler now, were left to their own devices. Josina became lean and fit from all the bending she had to do over her work. The young child thrived and Ernst became absolutely absorbed in his work of woodcarving finding it totally therapeutic as it was a creative way of staying busy all the day long.

CHAPTER 3

Ernst bent over the carved pine table that he was working on. It did not only have a flattened top and straight legs. The legs had been carved into a copy of each one curved at the top and straightened as they reached the floor. Also there was curved carving on the side of the table. Ernst was now busy painting in green and gold a pattern onto the patterned wood. The legs and other parts were also in the process of being varnished. This process not only improved the look of the piece of furniture but added to the attraction of the table by giving off a rich odor from the chemical.

Of course Ernst thought to himself the wonderful smell of the varnish would vanish in time with the ageing of the furniture. Ageing. His thoughts fell to those of his daughter now ten years of age. Josina bless her had scrimped and saved these ten long years to buy their little daughter Donella a tiny violincello so that she could begin the study of the instrument with an old nun at the convent school where Josina had herself been educated.

She had taken Donella there one Saturday morning shortly after her tenth birthday.

Josina had dressed the little girl in typical long stockings of white and brown leather shoes and a leather jacket completed the outfit. The small child had her father's curling golden locks that were tied back off her face with an emerald green ribbon matching the red in her clothing. Josina rang the all too familiar bell attached to its fraying rope well known to her from her own young days. Mother and daughter drew in their breath as a light pattering of footsteps behind the convent wall could be heard. A soft voice of Austrian dialect enquired before opening a large wooden door of the front of the building:

"Is that you Josina?" Josina had made an appointment with mother Armentia the old nun who gave 'cello lessons to all interested young girls. "Yes sister. Will you let us in? I have my daughter with me."

Silently the young nun with a fresh rosycheeked face opened the door. She smiled at the visitors and said:

"Mother Armentia is waiting anxiously in the parlor to meet her young pupil. She remembers you Josina, from your early days some ten years ago. As you requested she has promised faithfully that she will stop instantly any rumors of where you live now from reaching your father the town's judge.

Josina remembered some of the religious etiquette that she had learned while she had been a pupil at this same convent that she had brought her little ten year old daughter Donella to that day. She enquired in trepidation fearing that the nuns might somehow let her father know of her circumstances. She needed not to have been afraid of them though as the young nun introduced herself with the following words:

"Mother Armentia expressly asked me to usher you to the parlor where she is waiting to meet little Donella. She told me to let you know immediately that the visit is to be confidential in all regards. She knows of the reputation for strict injustice and hardness of heart that your father is known for in this town. She wishes me to tell you that she always had the deepest of sympathy for you as a young girl and always wondered how you could have endured living as you did while a growing girl."

By this time the three of them had climbed the stairs to the entrance of the convent. The young sister pulled at a thin rope and a bell chimed somewhere inside. Josina felt emotional now that she had returned after over ten years to the place where she had most of her schooling. An efficient tread of steps inside the convent could be heard and then the entrance door was opened to reveal another nun somewhat older who greeted the visiting couple effusively and hospitably. She said:

"Mother Armentia is right here for you. She opened a door to the left and a stately and dignified old nun could be seen on entering. Her gaze straight ahead fell on the young Josina and her daughter. The old nun said:

"May the Good Lord bless you both. Please be seated and we can discuss the music lessons that you wish me to give to this little Donella." At the old Mother Armentia's somewhat strident voice of old age Donella clung to her mother's side. The aged nun went on:

"I learned to play the violincello as a young girl in my father's house. I gave a few performances but soon with the guidance of our local priest I realized that it was my calling in life to enter the novitiate and commence life in a community of nuns at this convent. I have never looked back and have used my musical training to teach several young ladies to play the instrument."

Josina ventured in reply to the old nun's words:

"I will not be able to pay for school lessons as well as for my daughter to learn to 'cello." The old nun replied: "If that is the case we will charge only a pittance from you for Donella's education."

Mother Armentia was full of enthusiasm and conversation for someone that Josina could tell was well into ageing. Donella looked pale and frightened in awe of the old woman dressed, she thought quite strangely in white woolen robes with a high black headdress and tied at the waist with a brown knotted cord. The little girl had clearly never set eyes on such a person before.

It was becoming clear to the child that she would be seeing this person a nun quite often once a week :

"Just bring her to me." The words floated over Donella's head. The nun in an almost reprimanding voice said: "I will see you next week my child for our first lesson the cello here in the parlor. You see here is the piano on which I will accompany your playing."

Mother and daughter turned to one side to see the piano as Mother Armentia indicated to them. It was an old instrument and looked well used but greatly cherished and greatly cared for. Donella began to lose her fear of the aged nun sensing in her transferring of dependency from her mother to the old nun and the younger one who had sat in on the interview in absolute silence.

All the time Donella shyly tried to hide herself to one side of her mother. The old nun was obviously well able to handle little children and said with a curious warmth in her voice:

"Don't be afraid Donella my child. You will be well cared for during your lessons here at the convent. I am sure that your mother will escort you to school each morning and fetch you each day so no harm will come to you. There is nothing to be frightened of my child."

Donella tried to smile bravely. The interview then proceeded into a conversation about her mother and father as well as her grandparents. "Yes my dear strict silence about you and your parents will be observed by myself and my fellow nuns. While you were a scholar here it was well known the cruelty you suffered as a young girl growing up with such a difficult man as your father. Plainly speaking he had a hard time dealing with the bad folk he represented in the courtroom but as we nuns understood it he had no right nor reason to impose his hardships on you."

Josina was barely able to utter a word. The old lady had so much to say to the two of them. Josina had if truth be told felt the old sense of awe of a child towards her teacher that was the reason for her silence. Eventually when she felt Mother Armentia had vented her feelings about the state of Josina's family the old woman said:

"I think we should leave now Mother."

"Go with God then my children." She clasped Donella's two frozen small hands saying:

"You will be with me at this time next week my child. Goodbye."

The mother and daughter were let out of the convent door and began their long walk home. Josina talked to Donella as they went saying:

Do you think that you will like having violincello lessons with old mother Armentia?" Patiently she waited for and answer. She was continually forgetting what a little girl her daughter was. Josina focused her thoughts on the child noticing again how she had to run to keep up with her mother's strides. Donella panted her answer to her mother's curiosity.

"She does frighten me a lot the old nun. But I think she is a kind person. I liked it when she took my hands in hers. I think that I could trust her."

Her mother intervened seeing that her daughter was breathing heavily trying to keep up with her mother's pace. It was beginning to snow and Josina wanted to be home a soon as possible as the long afternoon was slowly turning chill. Josina said:

"I have arranged with mother Armentia that one of the nuns will pay you special attention while you are a learner at the convent. That is for the lessons in reading and writing that you will be doing every morning during the week while I do my washing that Ernst brings to me every evening. So. Now we are home. Fill the basin with water and I will heat it over the wood fire. Ernst has left some dried wood to start the coals for us to cook some sausage and potatoes to eat this evening. Go and wash and put on your warm nightdress while I make ready the fire." Donella said in a whining voice:

"I am so hungry mother." Josina chided:

"Go quickly and undress and I will soon have something ready to eat."

The child pattered off and no sooner had Josina got the coals going than Ernst appeared through the door, covered in snow. He enthused:

"That wurst smells good. Just what I feel like tonight. It's cold enough outside. He greeted his daughter fondling her head of golden curls so like his own. Josina pleaded:

"Do let us finish supper and then we can tell Papa what we did this afternoon. She had also prepared some gruel a sort of soup that they all gulped down hungrily and tucked into some rye bread and sausage afterwards. Josina told Donella to run off to bed. She knew that the little girl would sleep soundly as usual after the long walk to and from the Convent. Sitting down while Josina cleaned up after the meal Ernst enquired:

"Well! Did you arrange the 'cello lessons with the old nun?"

"Hush Ernst. Donella is nearly ready for bed. I will tell you a little later about it. She and I and old Mother Armentia had our interview this afternoon. She is a marvelous old dear that nun as strict as can be with her pupils. She would dearly love to give more children 'cello lessons as that is her forté, her strong point that is what she knows best to teach. She is tutor to the few senior girls at the convent as well that is how I know about her musical gift. She would be able for a small fee to tutor Donella at the 'cello.

Enough of that now though. It brings back hurtful memories of the past may own days as a scholar when my father would chastise me for the slightest indiscretion or careless remark. Ernst, you have no idea how unhapppy I was until I met you. I don't know how I stood it.

He was always picking on my poor old mother. He would have the upper hand with us both and we were defenceless. In the end my poor mother took to her bed feigning I am certain, illness. I despised her a little for not standing up to him but he was a difficult impossible old man. I tried on several occasions to cheek him but I found myself twisted up in my own words. So I took to mixing with the servants. They at best were my friends and more especially you when you became employed at my father's villa.

I always praise God for them all because as far as they could they always took my part when my father was exercising his cruel discipline over me. It was scant relief. When I looked for my mother for comfort she was never there. He stopped me from entering her bedchamber. I would be on the point of going in over and over again but he forbade me to go to my mother. I thought sometimes that she heard him chastising me, and I imagined that I heard her calling for me.

He did not allow me even to speak to her privately, that a growing girl needs. The only time I saw her was at prim and proper formal dinners where I had to make polite conversation. It was hard for me not to be rude to him but Mother Armentia and all the nuns knew what my home life was like. Sister Estella particularly made a point of comforting me as often as she could, and but for the nuns and my father's servants I don't know what I would have done.

I was not allowed to bring any of my friends home even. If I did they would fall under the severe judicial criticism that was what my father's life had made him, narrow-minded and mean.

Again one evening Ernst and Josine were conversing:

"We have a future though Josina," said Ernst "you have taken Donella to the old nun at the convent to introduce her. It will only take six or so years to train as a 'cellist. Then what we will aim for is to acquaint her with the conductor at your father's musical soirées to ask if she can gain some experience in the musical field by playing in the villa's little orchestra. This is an important plan; designed to be a secret from the child

Donella for the present. She is never to know of her family connection with the judge and his wife. Only later on in her life she might find out but by that time with they will in all probability be of such an age as not to realize or understand the significance of her relationship with he or his wife.

For the time being they do not seem to have made any further effort to find out what has happened to you. There is no necessity to do that for the moment. One day a week Donella can go to Mother Armentia for lessons on the 'cello."

Schoolwork passed as magically and slowly as only a child knows. Donella would make her own way to the convent gate and ring on the bell hung on the rope outside and Sister Estelle come out to fetch her for her schooling and the set afternoons with old Mother Armentia.

The old nun spent one lesson just showing the young girl how to sit on a chair with the 'cello straddled between her knees. It seemed to come quite naturally to Donella to grip the 'cello. Mother Armentia in between getting Donella to hold the 'cello firmly spent some time confiding in the young girl of her own younger days, of her successes in the musical world before giving it all up to enter the novitiate. She said in her now creaking voice for she was over seventy years of age:

"At the great college in the nearby town I also had to learned to play this instrument. I did well there and gave a few recitals with the town orchestra but my parents wanted me to give up the lay life and enter the sisterhood. I have taught at the convent ever since. I find the interaction between myself and the nuns soothing and comforting in what I found growing older was an evil world. You will have to work hard at your practicing so as to enable you to play in the Judge's orchestra."

The lesson was over. It was nearly the end of the week and Donella was weary of the convent and her studies there she knew until the weekend was over. She looked forward to the usual chattering that took place to celebrate the end of the week for all three. Her father was not home and as usual her mother questioned Donella as to how her classes especially the 'cello lesson had transpired:

"You always have something to tell me about how you are faring under Mother Armentia's tutelege. She seems full of stories about her performances as a young woman. What has she told you this week?"

Donella, she now in her mid teens answered:

"She must have been quite famous once. She told me how the audiences cheered and clapped after she had played the set sonata or concerto for the evening. Always she said bouquets of flowers fell at her feet after she had played for the evening. She told me that she performed once a week in the town hall. She is always praising me for my cello playing and says she is sure that I will be good enough to perform one day if I keep doing the 'cello exercises work she sets me every week." Her mother began to confide in her:

"Yes that is what we live with what I wanted for you. You did not know that you are really the granddaughter of nobility." In her early teens Donella gasped saying:

"How is that possible my mother?" Donella said.

"Do not tell anyone what I am going to tell you now. My mother and father were aristocrats who lived not too far away from here. But they were cruel to me especially my father. So I ran away to marry a handsome woodcutter your father."

At this point Ernst opened the front door to the chalet and shaking the snow off his head and shoulders heard the last of Donella's words, "your father," he said crisply straight in from the cold air outside. "Yes your father is back my girl." He went off to take off his parka. While doing this her mother put her fingers to her lips: "I'll tell you more another time," she whispered. To her husband as he came to warm himself over the now roaring flames she said: "I'll have our meal ready in a trice. Do tell me what you have been working on today!" Shivering still and trying to get warm Ernst spluttered: "The old man kept me right busy today."

She asked what he was so busy with that day considering that he seemed more hard worked and irritable than usual. Ernst came up with the story of his day.

"The old man has been asked to decorate a piano. I told him that this was not usual for a musical instrument. The old father insisted though saying that was what his instructions were to me, the one who had to do the paintwork decorating. I started doing the painting mid-morning today when I had got some sense out of the old man. I am doing a scroll pattern in reds and greens around the base and around the top of the instrument. It is very painstaking work as there is no way of taking off any unneeded splashes that might occur. So far we are both pleased with it. Well now what have you and Donella been doing this afternoon? The little girl is growing fast." Josina answered:

"It seems to be that this is the age she has reached when women talk to one another at great length. I have been explaining to her something of her background in her family, how you and I met and how cruel my own father was to me." Ernst rose wanting to speak but almost reading his mind she said:

"Hush! I intend to keep it from her the couple's name who were my father and mother. She must never know because I hope to put something of what I received as a child back into her parent's life. I have been feeling guilty about eloping with you Ernst even though I love you so much for understanding my circumstances. This "putting something back" into my old life is what I wish Donella to have. That will be by letting her musicianship on the 'cello reach such a peak of excellency that she can be taken for an audition with the conductor of the stringed instrument ensemble that meets at my father's villa and hope that she can be taken on as a 'cellist, performing regularly with the little ensemble at the judge's soirées. But Ernst I will never tell her that she will be playing at her own grandfather's home the villa. It will be a firm secret from her." Ernst responded:

"My mother heard from one of the local women that the judge your old father has been keeping up the musical evenings that he hosts once a week. She tells me that he is known too to be quite a dilettante and ladies' man. Apparently he lives in quite another world and his wife is just fading away unknown to all his lady friends."

When mother and daughter were together alone they talked much about Donella's parents. Without letting her daughter know who or where exactly Donella's parents were when she was little her mother Josina managed to tell her daughter much about her background. She concentrated at first upon her own life how intolerable it had been made by her father. She told here daughter:

"How would you have liked a mean, cranky, old man for a father?" Donella asked a little frightened by this: "Why was he such a nasty man mother? You are his daughter and you are a kind person." Josina replied: "This is because Ernst's family though poor have been so kind to me. Ernst is a loving father though only a lowly one. You know he works at wood crafting in the town below the forest. He has to carve tables, chairs, furniture and even musical instruments, violins, cellos and even double bases sometimes. The old father is from a family that has handed down the craft of wood carving for generations and your father is lucky enough to be employed by the old man.

You see Ernst your father is a happy man and when a person does creative work with his hands there is great satisfaction to be gained in life. And this happiness flows over into our life. I think my father had to work too much using his brain to think that is to consider justice and reward and punishment for non-offenders and offenders alike. He never put his mind to practical matters and that caused my mother's unhappiness and hypercondrical nature. I was never able to talk to her as I am proud to say I am able to talk to you my daughter." Donella said pensively:

"Where do these old people live mother and what is their name?" Josina said firmly: "I am not going to tell you that now not until you are much older and a mature woman:" Donella said then: "I feel quite ashamed of my grandparents from what you have told me of them mother. You too cannot be very happy doing the work of a washerwoman. I seem to have quite a mixed up family. The mothers of my school fellows at the convent school seemed quite flighty and nose-in-the-air by comparison to the kind of life you lead." "Never mind dear," Josina said lovingly to her daughter. "Ernst loves me and sympathizes deeply at the life I led as a young girl."

Time began to fly and Donella came out of her mid teens. She was constantly in admiration of her mentors the holy sisters who tutored her and her classmates so lovingly. The finances at the chalet where the little family that had made their home in the forest, began to dwindle. The only way to care for Donella seemed to be for the nuns to take her in as if she were an orphan. Donella co-operated with her parents in this plan. She had learnt years ago that the nuns at the convent were strict but kind. She had no qualms about being at boarding school. The years sped on and Donella was allowed home for special weekends to be with her family. She ventured to her mother saying:

"Mother I know now that I would like to enter the novitiate. The sisters are encouraging this amongst us girls but only a few of us have been persuaded to make this a goal for life. I am one of these. Do you think you will allow me to take my vows when I reach nineteen years of age? I have talked to Mother Armenetia about my hopes of joining the little community of nuns. She says that I will have to do the training novitiate course at the nearest big center. It will take two years and then I will do a teaching course at a nearby college and be qualified to take charge of a class of young girls as I was once. Oh! Mother please say I may! I feel the calling very strongly."

Josina was alarmed at this request. This was not what her parents had wanted for their daughter's future not what she and Ernst had planned at all. Josina said:

"Not meaning to be unkind Donella but your father and I had a slightly easier way for you to lead your life when you finish your studies." Donella begged:

"Please, please mother let me have my wish. I have almost promised the mother superior that I will be joining them. I am ashamed too of coming from such a poor home that the only future for me can be the novitiate. What else is there that I can do with my life?"

Josina cast her thoughts back to her own childhood. The ties were still there. She was still the daughter of the judge and his wife. She wondered if it was a case of absence makes the heart grow fonder. Was there not a way of giving back to her parents something that she had taken by leaving home and eloping with Ernst? That was it. She would in disguise go to the housekeeper at the villa, her father the judge's home and ask if Donella could have an audition to play the 'cello at the soirées given at the villa. No, Donella must be told that this was her future, not the novitiate.

Donella was now eighteen years of age. She was a quiet shy girl quite determined to become a novice in the sisterhood of nuns. These women had been her teachers while a scholar and had not hesitated to recruit young girls for the novitiate. Donella had been one of these. Trying to persuade her mother on one of these occasions Donella was putting her point plaintively though adamantly to her mother.

"Sister Rosetta is so kind to me. She understands how poor our family is and says I will have a better quality of life if I enter the novitiate. I finish my schooling at the end of the year and you know very well mother that I have nothing else planned to do at that time. I would desperately love to join the sisterhood." "Donella," her mother said firmly, "you are taken up with the glamour as it seems to you of what being a nun is like. You think it would be wonderful to wear their long white woolen robes with the tasseled cord around their waist and the bonnet headdress that humbly covers their head flowing over their shoulders. Oh, Donella it may seem an exciting prospect to you now but I am certain, my girl that behind all this glamour that is enticing you is a bitter life of hard, hard work with long hours of prayer and total dedication. You will not be allowed socialize in the normal sense and it will be a long time before you are allowed to teach the young girls at the convent yourself.

Don't you see that the hardship of being a nun would be devastating for you. I will put a better proposition to you my child. I had not spoken to you of it as yet but what I have in mind is to use what you love with all your heart, your 'cello lessons with Mother Armentia. That is to say you are a trained musician by now and can possibly join with a small ensemble to entertain folk of an evening now and again at the judge's villa. You would be paid a humble salary for performing I am sure."

Donella's mother had managed to swing her daughter's mood and wishes away from what she considered an unhealthy ambition. In the uncertainty of her youth Donella became intrigued by what her mother was offering. She loved playing her 'cello and Mother Armentia had produced an expert musician in the young girl. Her head bowed in disappointment at having her hopes shattered Josina could see that she had won the battle with her daughter.

Josina paused in her addressing her daughter about what her parents had in mind for her future as opposed to the dreams and ambitions of their eighteen-year-old daughter. She could see how brow-beaten and despondent was the influence she, a strong personality had on the more whimsical young girl. At that moment Josina could tell that Donella was a creative gifted girl who loved to play her 'cello as taught to her by the now ageing Mother Armentia. Donella raised her head slowly and Josina could see tears pricking at her daughter's eyelids. She gulped and wiped her reddening eyes. She said:

"Do I have to chose between the two, being a nun or being a 'cellist in an ensemble?"

Unlike her, Josina began to show compassion on her young daughter. With a warm show of sympathy she put her arm around Donella and said, trying to coax a response out of her:

"Donella dear you will have a few more cheerful and happy years if you continue with your 'cello studies for another few months and then we can approach the housekeeper at the nearby villa. We know this is where the little ensemble meets for musical evenings every weekend on a Saturday. Ernst has had to restore and repair some of the performers' musical instruments from time to time. That is also how we know about the soirées. I must tell you my girl that your father is all for your joining the group and possible being paid a small sum, even though to start with it might only be a mere pittance."

A few months passed and Josina in the meanwhile had approached the housekeeper at the villa where she had been a young girl. A flood of emotion swept over her as she walked up the pathway - yes it was an all too real a remembrance. Suddenly she felt a yen to see her mother whom she had hardly known while growing up, because of her father's mean nature. The ornamental lion's head on the wall outside the kitchen door of the villa sparked off so many memories of hobnobbing with the servants of her father's ancestral villa and final meeting and coming to start up a relationship with Ernst.

He was at the time employed as a handyman at the establishment. She approached the kitchen door and knocked. Time passed and a demure little maidservant dressed in black with a starched white apron appeared and muttered greetings She asked shyly what it was that Josina wanted. Josina stated her wish to see the housekeeper. Her heart thumped when the girl said:

"Miss Kempf is busy with the mistress of the villa." Josina immediately knew the servant was referring to her very own mother. The girl said:

"I will call her down. You wait there. She indicated an old much-used chair. Josina stared at the floor first realizing how great her loss of a home had been. How much had it cost her? In the middle of these thoughts the strident voice of the villa's housekeeper pierced her mind's activity. The pinched looking housekeeper was speaking to her saying:

"Can you please give me time to speak to the owner of the villa. You say that your daughter is offering her services as a 'cellist and that she is keen to play in the judge's little ensemble of musicians that meets occasionally for social evening soirées here at the villa?" "That is right," answered Josina wishing to make a good impression from the beginning for Donella's sake. "My daughter is trained professionally and has just this year finished her schooling." The housekeeper responded to this sharply:

"I happen to be aware of the fact that one of the two 'cellists making up the ensemble is leaving to play elsewhere and so there is a good chance that the judge will take her on. I will speak to him this evening and when you come back tomorrow then I will have an answer for you."

"Thank you kindly," said Josina and left the villa walking through the lonely snowdrifts on her way back to the warmth of the chalet in the forest.

Josina thought to herself: this will be a way of taking revenge on my father for the way he treated me so unkindly when I was still young. He will never recognize me now I have grown older and he will also never know who his granddaughter is in reality. I am certain of it. He will be paid back for his cruelty to me. I seems as if I did the right thing to elope with Ernst. No, I could take no more of the situation at the villa. These thoughts were with her until she opened the front door of her home.

Mellow sounds of the 'cello that she was used to by now greeted her. Donella put down the bow that she was etching out a melody with and in a humble way learnt as a convent schoolchild began to ask her mother what had happened that afternoon. Josina replied:

"I am to go back tomorrow. If I predict rightly you will be having an audition with the conductor of the little group of musicians. Quite soon! How do you feel about that?" "I am very grateful to you for arranging this," said Donella quite innocently. "It will challenge my ability to keep up my playing." The girl did not realize the pawn that her mother was making of her.

Chapter 4

Josina and Donella smartened themselves up in their dressing having washed before the afternoon of the audition with the conductor of the little orchestra. Josina said:

"We must hurry now Donella. You still have to gather your 'cello and music scores. You will have to have something to play to Herr Auberg. No doubt there will be a music stand on the podium where the ensemble meets for you to use. Frau Kempf has told me that the conductor is an able pianist. You can play with someone other than Mother Armentia surely?"

Donella answered soothingly for she knew how important the audition was although she really longed to be joining the sisterhood of nuns.

"Mother Armentia has given us a strict training and has told me about some of the musicians she has played with when she was a young girl. She has told me that I am a talented player and that music is something that all who have been trained to play can understand.

I am certainly quite keen now to go along with your and papa's wishes that I will have a successful audition. Josina said:

"Let us leave now. You have the piano accompaniments?" With you? Herr Auberg will be glad to have them I am sure."

Josina shut the front door of the chalet and the two set out for the fairly long walk across the mountain slope to the other side where the villa was. The sun was out and it was summer in the Alps. Grass grew abundantly and the slopes were covered with little Alpine flowers that shimmered in the slightly warm breeze that was blowing. To a stranger the two made an odd sight with Josina ushering her daughter along and Donella clutching rather clumsily at her 'cello and music case.

"Are you alright dear?" Josina asked. "You seem to be out of breath." Donella replied:

"It just seems such a long walk." The girl caught her breath. It seems that I never had to walk so far ever carrying my 'cello."

"Nonsense girl," Josina said sternly anxious to get her daughter to the villa in time for the audition. She had to judge the time spent on the walk from the only clock that they had in the chalet before they left. Soon though Josina was knocking at the kitchen door of the villa. Brisk footsteps from inside the building came to their ears. The door was flung open and the prim housekeeper greeted them.

The housekeeper for it was her, looked down her nose at Donella then looked at them in covert awe at Josina especially. Of course she had no idea that Josina had been a member of her household in the distant past, a past that did not fall into her sphere of life. She finally spoke

"Well my girl," she was very much the superior being in the situation as they found themselves in. She Frau Kempf had to be the go-between at the time and see that the young girl looked presentable and had all the musical accoutrements, her 'cello and presumably some suitable music scores that she could impress the maestro, the conducter of the little ensemble, with.

The servants inferior beings to the musicians looked askance at the ensemble and joked scornfully about the players. Of course they had to do all the menial tasks even wait on the performers. Fraulein Kempf spoke again all these thoughts going through head. She was not quite sure what she would say. The words that she came out with were quite kind nevertheless.

"Herr Auberg is expecting you" She put her index finger under the girl's chin. "A prettier piece of a young woman I'm sure I've never seen in my life." Then she looked seriously at Josina and said:

"Yes and she looks well brought up too. She hasn't said a word." Josina replied:

"Ask her how she feels about the interview then." Donella keyed up to perform for the young conductor, did not want to be effusive in front of the strict looking woman. She was entirely unaware of her connection to the household as was Frau Kempf. Josina yes, was quite aware of the true circumstances but was keen to see if things had changed since she was a young girl in the villa. She said:

"I will accompany Donella into the presence of our conductor, Herr Auberg. I know that she is nervous about it and would not like to let her be in any one else's hands but my own." Frau Kempf looked at her curiously saying:

"You have never been here before then?" She made this statement as she was aware that Josina appeared quite relaxed in what after all was the villa of her own right should the judge, her father, permit it. The housekeeper she could not understand. She racked her brains but could only remember a hint of having seen the young woman at the villa before. Perhaps it was because the woman was not wearing evening dress wear. Of course her thoughts rambled on. It was only mid-afternoon.

The young mother looked strangely relaxed in these rather formal settings. How could it be? Most visitors behaved in a stilted fashion with every word carefully thought out before it was uttered. Every nook and cranny was familiar to Josina as they walked up the stairs. It was a steep flight and they walked up in silence their thoughts fixed upon one another. Donella was taut with nervousness not knowing what to expect. As they walked the housekeeper said breathlessly:

"Herr Auberg is a young man. I would judge him to be only five years older than yourself, Fraulein." She was of course referring to the conductor or the little ensemble. She was a stern woman but like Donella's mother could see that the young girl was in a state of trepidation prior to the audition. Josina supported the words of encouragement saying:

"Yes don't be anxious dear. Mother Armentia has given her full support to your playing in the little orchestra that is if your performance this afternoon is acceptable to Herr Auberg and from the many times that I have heard you practicing at home he will be very impressed."

They had arrived at the door of the visitor's lounge. The housekeeper put her ear to the door to the auditorium and then spoke:

"They are not practicing at the moment it seems. They must be busy discussing their playing in some way or other. I'll knock. Are you ready?"

Donella nodded. The old woman knocked fairly loudly and after a moment or two's silence heard a young man's voice bidding them enter just as Frau Kempf pushed open the door gently. What met their eyes excited the young Donella. Three or four violinists, a viola player and a 'cellist sat in a circle together with some woodwind and brass players nearby. Obviously they were in the middle of being addressed by their conductor, known to Donella as Herr Auberg.

The leader of the orchestra the conductor was new to Donella. Herr Auberg sprang up from his chair in an effort at greeting the girl to show his enthusiasm and some manners in the situation. The little group of players were desperately in need of an extra 'cellist for the ensemble. Privately Herr Auberg thought from what he had been told about the young girl she was a most likely character to fill the gap in the group of players there being present only one 'cellist at the time. He enthused:

"Enter with pleasure Frau Kempf, you and your party." Turning to the young girl he said: "You must be Donella!" "Yes," she said." And this is my mother who arranged the audition with Frau Kempf."

This was the little group of three women with one of them having only two years to go before coming to full womanhood being nearly nineteen years of age. She was the one on whom all the attention was to focus this afternoon. Donella would not have thought so as she shrank back clutching her 'cello.

Josina gradually urged her forward to be in full view of both the conductor and the members of the orchestra. She could see the nervous smile hovering around her daughter's lips a sign that there was something of an extrovert performer in Donella's nature. This aspect of the sight of the lovely young girl immediately penetrated Herr Auberg's mind. Here was a player, if she was as talented as he had been told who would fit admirably into his elite little orchestra who would perform not only at the judge's villa but in the surrounding grand houses.

They were well known and popular in the community and earned a handsome living for themselves. Herr Auberg also encouraged his players to keep in practice by hiring themselves out to the town's greater orchestra that gave concerts during the week and played in the larger of symphonies and concertos for a regular audience of music lovers. Herr Auberg had sprung up from the chair that he had been sitting on when the door to the auditorium opened to the hoped for new player in his ensemble. He was finding the lack of an extra 'cellist most disconcerting now that the other young 'cellist player had left to start a family. The thought crossed his mind as he began to speak in a greeting. Would the same future take this new young 'cellist away from all the careful training that he was preparing for her? He spoke:

"Frau Kempf I am most enchanted to make your acquaintance." Then turning to Donella he said:

"This is you own instrument?" He did not speak loudly but quite warmly in welcoming Donella. Frau Kempf and Josina shrank back neither knowing too much about music and musicians. Josina's clasped hands tightened in tense expectation and hope for the chance of employment. This audition would offer her daughter employment now that she had finished as a scholar. Josina had sent a letter to the housekeeper requesting the possibility of a musician's post at the villa and as fortune would have it there was a vacancy in the elite ensemble. In answer to the maestro's question Donella nodded saying breathlessly:

"Yes my father ordered it to be created by the only stringed instrument maker in town especially for me."

Glad to have some common ground with which to begin the audition he continued:

"Sometimes my members of the little ensemble arrive late. As they come in I listen to them talking about their instruments. I hear them mention the old masters of the carving of the violins, violas and 'cellos. The name of the other 'cellist that you will be partnering is Kurt Weiss."

Donella nodded and breathed out an affirmative.

"Yes," suddenly shy of the young man who was surely only a few years older than herself. Noticing that the young girl was drawing back he tried to put her at her ease. He would give her a choice. So he said carefully after she had been introduced to the conductor:

"Would you like to show me some of the music scores that you have brought with you so that I can see what standard you have reached in your playing? Or rather be introduced and welcomed by the other players in the group?"

He indicated the little ensemble all attired in evening wear ready for the concert that they would be giving in about three hours' time. These players were relaxing now that their maestro was busy with someone new to join them.

A couple of the violinists and a 'cellist were tuning up their string pitches with the help of the resident pianist who was striking the note of middle A for them to gauge their instruments' level of sound. A viola player and an oboe player were practicing some of the more difficult sections of the quartet and quintet that they would be performing that evening.

They all looked quite busy with what they were doing. There was a little hushed chat ensuing with the single 'cellist. Donella saw therefore that she would be needed if there was only one 'cello at the time of the concert. Quite primly as Mother Armentia her teacher had taught her she said forthrightly:

"I think that I would like to meet your other 'cello player. I see there is only one other besides myself. He does not appear to be tuning up. I would like to ask him when he is from and inquire who his teacher was."

"Ah! – You would like to meet Kurt? He too has only been with us a short time. He came to us from a nearby large town where there is a music college. We can ask him to tell you his past tutor's name."

Herr Auberg ushered Donella up to the podium first. Donella with her head bowed humbly as Mother Armentia had taught her to move gracefully, smiled as she passed the little group that she would be playing with as she and Herr Auberg walked to Kurt's music stand.

Donella knew this was an important time in her life. She must make an impression not only with her ability to perform but with another aspect of playing in the little ensemble that of showmanship. There had to be a little bit of an actor in her stagecraft. This had been understood even directly pointed out by Mother Armentia at the convent. In the little yearly performances put on by the convent mainly to show the parents of the scholars how they were progressing artistically Donella had been popular and well loved.

She had taken an instant liking to the young ruddy-faced conductor with his blond curly mop of hair. He was brisk but she could tell that they both shared the emotional side of the music they performed as a group. He began again trying to introduce her to the members of the little orchestra. It was a sensitive task as it was clear they were all an intelligent and talented lot keen to show their mettle in the afternoon's practice session, not really concentrating on the personal side of matters when it came to being introduced to a new player.

They were not used to the new fledgling. Herr Auberg was trying to befriend them with her. As they stood beside Kurt he slowly lowered his 'cello after expertly finishing off some warming up runs and scales.

"Wonderful! Wonderful!" Kurt nodded sagely a smile at the corner of his lips at this praise. Herr Auberg confirmed: "Of course you are just as adept at this sort of run up to a practice session are you not Donella?" She replied a little nervously: "Yes what Kurt is doing is just like the scales and exercises that Mother Armentia the old nun who taught me to play my cello has put me through these last few years." Herr Auberg said sensing Donella's hesitancy. "Kurt perhaps you would like to lend Donella your 'cello for a moment or two and then we can both hear the sort of style she is accomplished at. Kurt said wittily: "Well all 'cellos are made in the same size so it will not make too much difference if she does a little tune up with mine or on her own."

Donella took a deep breath. It all seemed so strange to her. Little did she know her mother's secret that she was in fact a granddaughter to the old judge in the villa the establishment that hosted these musical soirées. She sat down. Suddenly her fingers seemed like wax relaxed and eager to show what she could do. It seemed as if her hands and fingers were working on their own. She did not feel as if it was herself who was controlling the members of her body.

Donella suddenly felt more than a little conspicuous in her traditional outfit that her mother had insisted that she wear for her audition. The older members of the group all looked so svelte in their evening wear with the young women in long black dresses and the men in black tie and tails. Her lederhosen and little leather jacket seemed so sparse by comparison and she suddenly felt embarrassed to be exposing a little of her bare leg. However she persevered and tried to relax.

Then she felt better and immersed herself in her run up of scales. She was warming up and felt once more her deep love of music and more than that of what she could achieve in her playing. She knew that she was talented Mother Armentia had told her so and as she remembered the old nun's praise she felt very confident. Then Herr Auberg was speaking to her:

"Ah! I can both see and hear that you are an extremely accomplished player. I will make my judgment about your joining our little ensemble right now. Donella I will be complimented and I speak for my group of players too, yes to have you play with us."

The conductor was obviously impressed with Donella who summoned up courage to speak in reply:

"I will be greatly honored in my musical life experience by attending rehearsals for the weekly soirées that I understand you hold here every Saturday evening."

She could not believe the news that Herr Auberg was accepting her in the little ensemble. She felt that she just wanted to hug her mother. This was her emotional response. After all it had been Josina who had encouraged her in her practicing always and who had suggested that she have this audition. What would have become of her if as she had wished she had entered the novitiate? She expressed her feelings as she rose from Kurt's chair.

"I will so enjoy playing with this wonderful group of players." Kurt broke in saying:

"You surely will. All of us are young not older than some twenty years of age. You will fit in here most conveniently. I was taking quite a lot of strain being the single 'cellist in the ensemble as Herr Auberg knows."

Donella smiled and she glanced quickly round at the other players who were enjoying the break while Donella was being auditioned. They were chatting and doing scale runs to pass the time, as well as sounding the more difficult phrases of the repertoire while they waited. The conductor suggested:

"I have heard what you are capable of. I am sure you are quite adept at sight-reading. Would you like to join us in a Mozart work that we are performing later this evening?"

Donella knew that this need to perform would come and overjoyed, nodded enthusiastically.

"We put a chair and music stand ready for you knowing that you would be coming in for an audition late this afternoon," said Herr Auberg and continued addressing Kurt:

"Kurt I gave you charge of the copy of the 'cello score for the evening's performance of the Mozart work. Can we have it for Donella to glance through? I am going to take the group through the work including Donella's playing with us."

Kurt had forgotten that he had the score but said to the conductor:

"Did you? Then I must have it, it must be behind the other three or four scores that we are working on." With fingers adept to his instrument he shuffled through the musical works on his stand. Donella's heart was in her mouth. Would he find it? Would it be there? Then Kurt spoke:

"Oh! Here it is right at the back. I nearly missed finding it. It was somehow placed inside the Beethoven septet that we have not rehearsed for some time. Donella breathed out:

"Oh! Thank goodness. That makes me very happy." Herr Auberg prompted:

"Let Donella look through it." Kurt handed her the music score. "Do sit down. Your 'cello you can rest against the wall. You must find it quite an encumbrance sometimes. Donella exclaimed: "No! Never! I love my instrument and hate to part with it. I am never happier when running my fingers up and down its strings making sure my scales are in tune so that I can play not only correctly but tunefully and artistically, to give pleasure to my listeners."

She sat down a little nervously. Herr Auberg said:

"I am going to start the playing directing from the conductor's dias. Kurt, you will keep an eye on Donella, see that she does not need anything that you can help her with. After all you are both trained 'cellists!" Here Donella broke in: "You will just give me time to resin my bow and to tune up my four strings?" "Of course," said the leader. Our pianist will at a sign from me strike your note and the one for the violins and violas too, although as you have heard by now they are nearly ready!"

He walked over to the dias in his young and spritely manner. The he said in a voice just audible to them all:

"We'll try the Mozart work again. Are you all ready?"

He looked questioningly at Donella. She smiled enthusiastically and then nodded. Herr Auberg lifted his baton and they all began playing. Soon Donella was playing out as gustily as her fellow performers. She never thought that she could do it, play in a professional ensemble. She had noted the key that the piece of music was in. It had begun in A major, but as she played the notes modulated to the relative minor key a few times.

Donella felt that Herr Auberg was paying her special attention. She felt encouraged every time that his eyes met hers in the performance of the little Mozart work. As she played her eyes also swept over the other players making contact for an instant or two. Suddenly she felt shy that she was attired differently to the other women players especially the violinists. Would they not be looking down on her, clothed smartly in her traditional Austrian tyrol leather jacket, colorful red skirt and long white socks?

She felt conspicuous. She thought as she played: how were her parents going to be able to afford an elegant long black evening gown for her? She remembered something that Mother Armentia had told her about being a musician. Her words came floating over the harmonies and melodies of what the young musicians were putting forth in this audition she was having. Yes, the thought suddenly struck her that she was still being tried and tested. But what had the old nun told her?

"Donella you must always remember that you are playing for the pleasure of others. In years gone by all musicians were regarded as servants."

A sudden pall came over her thoughts. Her father - he had been employed as a servant until something ominous had happened. She had picked up strands of conversation between her parents. From what she could glean there was a strong connection in her family to life in this strange villa. Her mother behaved in a cowed way when they came here, now for the second time. It was as if she was hiding something or wanted to avoid meeting someone. Who was it that Josina did not want to face here and why?

Donella had spent many hours with her mother while she was growing up, there had been no one else who could care for her and she knew her like the back of her hand.

Did it seem to her that Josina was familiar with this villa? Her eyes glided down the room to the hard backed chairs where her mother sat austerely with Frau Kempf. All these thoughts flowed through her mind as she read the music score by sight, bar by bar, the little Mozart composition that she was taking part in. It was easy she thought. It would be a simple matter she was sure to be taken on as the extra 'cellist in the little group. Yes, she knew that she would fit in.

Herr Auberg lifted then dropped his baton at the final chords and melodies of the work being performed. He paused as the notes faded away as the players stayed still in their seats. Head bowed he sprang off the conductor's podium and walked briskly up to the place where Donella had just finished playing to tell her how pleased he was at her performance with the others in the group. He burst out:

"Donella I have been playing you special attention this afternoon. I would like you to know that I am quite satisfied with your ability especially because you have been sight reading this work. I am wholly confident that you will easily manage the other works in our repertoire. In other words congratulations Donella. Your audition has been successful."

Donella felt her face flush with pleasure. She felt so out of place in her leather bolero and long socks. She felt the burning gaze of the women violinists. What must they be thinking in their elegant guise of the sort of background she came from. She mumbled her thanks to Herr Auberg embarrassed at being made to stand out before this sophisticated group. Herr Auberg saw her shyness and continued speaking:

"You just need a black gown to fit you in with the ensemble. Is that your mother waiting for you? I am sure she will see to it that you attend our next soirée on these Saturday evenings, all dressed up like the others."

To herself being at a loss for words while she closed up her cello in its leather case Donella thought: I can't imagine myself all attired in a long black evening dress. I am not at all used to that way of making my appearance. She had to offer some response so said firmly:

"What time should I be here for the Saturday evening concert please Herr Auberg?" He answered: "Our ensemble needs to join the guests for a bouffet supper before beginning the entertainment. Can you be here by six? We all meet together for some liquid refreshment before we eat then settle in to play for the guests. I do not mind if the listeners converse during the exposition of the quartets, trios and other pieces we play provided it does not become too much of an interference to us. The guests some regular, some new are aware of this and show us quite enough consideration."

The housekeeper was finishing talking to Donella about how to dress and what to expect at the soirée.

"Remember my young girl you are no more than a servant at these evening performances taking place usually every Saturday. You will have the privilege of mixing with the guests while they are enjoying the bouffet supper before the music begins and you may help yourself to such eats as your appetite allows you. Otherwise as you saw evening dress is the requirement. That is a long black evening gown."

At this point she handed Donella a slip of paper. Her mother took the paper away from her at Donella's blank look upon glancing at the missive. Josina said:

"Your father and I will see to this. This is an address in the town where we can buy your gown to be used at the soirées. My but you will look grand."

Then enigmatically, knowing in herself how really close to home Donella would be at the musical evenings she said:

"You will apparently then really be part of life at the old villa."

Mother and daughter trudged up the snowy track back to the chalet when the housekeeper had finished. Donella ventured then as they walked:

"And mother to think I will be receiving some sort of payment for my playing! Perhaps then it was a good training to have my learning to play on the violincello with old Mother Armentia that nun who taught me. Maybe it was better for me not to have entered the novitiate to become a nun." "Yes Donella" answered her mother quite sharply to her daughter. She stated quite firmly:

"There is far more to life than being shut away from the world in a convent. You may think it would be only for a few years the duration of your youth, but no Donella it would be forever! Right until you die! You surely don't want that!"

A little stunned at this blatant statement from her mother who after all had been the ministering spirit who had arranged for her to attend the convent as a scholar Donella said wistfully:

"But I so wanted to be like my teachers. They were so kind to me." Her mother snapped at her: "No young woman but we can't all have what we want in life. You know their beliefs and you can surely act that out in your own life without actually taking on the robes of a nun."

Josina and Donella arrived at last at the chalet and Josina went straight to the kitchen oven to put some of yesterday's soup on the boil. Ernst would be home shortly and was usually hungry. She put lard on some rye bread that she had sliced thinly. Donella went over to the corner of the one roomed dwelling and leant her 'cello against the end wall opposite her bed so she would be able to see it there as she went to sleep that night. Her mother asked her:

"What have you planned for this evening Donella?"
Her daughter answered:

"I'll have a hot bath now and then some supper
mother. Then I'll do a little tuning up and practicing, if
you and father will permit it. I won't be up late but the
audition today has made me enthusiastic about trying
my scales and exercises to keep my hand in starting from
today, also for the whole of next week so as to give a good
impression to Herr Auberg next Saturday at the soirée. I
have been invited to perform did you know mother?"

Josina responded gladly:

"You do just that while I tell your father about our
afternoon at the villa."

Both the older and younger women were busy with
their selfimposed tasks when snow was heard crunching
along the gravel pathway up to the chalet and the door
was swung open by Ernst. His immediate words were:

"What have you got on the stove tonight Josina?" She
replied: "I have cut up some left over sausage and added it
to yesterday's soup. It is simmering now.'

Her husband inquired, knowing that Donella had her
audition that day:

"How was Donella's playing at the villa? Were the
powers that be impressed? "Oh! Yes", was the reply. "The
interview was successful." Ernst felt a surge of pride
at this news. Just then Donella came out of the little
bathroom. She smoothed her clothes away and slowly
unlatched her 'cello from its case. Her mother had given
her permission to practice that evening and after greeting

her father with a smile she knew he would not mind her playing then. So she began her session with the mellow scales that she could produce on her violincello.

As she played with ears alert to the correct pitching of the notes, off and on she caught snatches of her parents' conversation. It seemed that it had been an ordeal for Josina. She listened more intently to all around her. A log fire crackled in the grate. Then she nearly stopped playing when she heard her father say:

"From what you tell me no one there today would have any reason to wonder about your connection with the owner of the villa." Josina replied:

"But I want Donella to know about her real involvement there one day." Josina could see that her daughter was listening to them, so tailed off these last few words.

CHAPTER 5

Donella was weary after the ordeal that she had gone through at her audition. She laid her head on her pillow and her thoughts sank into sleepfulness. Her parents' voices ebbed and flowed towards her as she rested. She tried to hear all of what they were saying. The phrase "to do with the villa" seemed to be the topic of their conversation and was being bandied about.

The two seemed to be at loggerheads at this subject. Who was connected to the villa and how? Both of her parents seemed from what they were saying to have familiar ties to the place she had been to today. Then she heard her mother say, as Donella moved restlessly in her bed:

"Hush, Ernst. I do not want her to know anything about it until she is older."

Donella had turned over in the bed and lay there hoping that what she had heard would be spoken about some more. But there was silence. They knew that she was listening and had heard the gist of the conversation.

Donella now knew that there was some mysterious connection between herself and the villa but she could not figure out what it was. Did it concern her mother? The tail end of the conversation had seemed to point to her. She had noticed that her mother had seemed on edge but had thought it was tiredness to do with the outcome of the session with Herr Auberg. Deeply mystified because she and her parents were very close she fell asleep. She would not dare to ask her mother about the reason for the conversation. She knew that her father had worked as a handyman in his youth. Had he been employed at the villa? She did not know how close she was to the truth.

She determined to ask her father about it the next day. He was far more lenient with her than her mother was and might well offer the solution to her questing spirit. As she fell asleep she heard her mother's words:

"She's bound to ask you about what was said tonight. You can tell her your part of the life played at the villa but please, please keep it quiet from her of my having anything to do with the people there."

Donella had fallen asleep at this moment so had missed hearing this vital information. She might then have understood a little more of the situation sooner than she eventually did.

Immediately upon waking the next morning Donella's first thoughts were upon the projected visit to the store in the town where the family were going to buy her black evening gown. Briefly her remembrance fell onto her parents' conversation the evening before. What she had heard made her feel a little uneasy.

It seemed that prior to being at the villa the Saturday before there was some tie between the little family and the folk who lived at the villa. Still young only just nineteen years of age she was in awe of her parents and would not be able yet to ask them about this relationship. She brushed those thoughts from her mind as she heard her mother call beckoning her.

"Are you ready Donella? Papa has the money all ready to pay for your new dress. He went to the bank yesterday to draw the payment for you knowing now that you will be able to repay him when you have settled into your working situation. From what Frau Kempf told me you will be paid handsomely for your performances. Your father and I will welcome the help as you will still be at home for the next few years. There is nowhere else you can live for the present. The three walked briskly down the road into the town and soon came to the store that sold women's attire. Her father said:

"I was here yesterday to find out if they had a suitable garment for you. It seems very smart wear for someone, a musician who is regarded as a servant. Did your mother tell you that as a musical entertainer you are regarded as no less than a humble servant?" She answered:

"Yes papa Mother Armentia told me that even if I was to earn my living by performing to an audience on my violincello in what she had taught me I would be considered as no more than this, someone who works for the pleasure of others. This does not upset me if that's what you are thinking. I am only too glad to give enjoyment of musical harmonies and melodies to people who really appreciate it."

Her father had now led them up to the counter attended by a woman severely dressed who would serve them in the projected purchase. The woman soon had a few differently styled long black evening gowns displayed for them.

"You must go to the back and try them on for fitting you," the woman added stiffly.

Soon after much dressing and undressing she was able to choose the most suitable dress. Her mother was helpful:

"You should take the one that you feel the most comfortable in managing your instrument."

Donella had a relaxing bath and Josina was ready waiting to accompany her daughter up to the villa on the Alpine slopes. Ernst for reasons long past could not face being at the villa longer than was necessary. He promised to fetch his wife and daughter by sleigh later on that evening when the concert was over. He would wait and look out for them in the throng. Josina realizing that until very recently musicians had been regarded as servants felt she too must undertake this role that evening.

She had arranged with the villa's housekeeper that she would help with the final stages of cooking and serving the meal that was to be given to the judge's guests. The housekeeper herself would not be there. Such evenings were given over to a Mâitre d'Hôte. Josina and her daughter were given a somewhat unfriendly welcome by this servant who clearly saw Josina's offer of help as something of an insult to his abilities as chef to the bouffet supper that he was hosting for the judge.

Days of long ago her childhood and early maturing years flooded over her as she busied herself in preparing the pride of the evening a small roast sucking pig. Josina ran to and fro handing out plates and napkins to the guests. And as they finished she took the debris to the kitchen. In a state of discipline of herself she realized that she probably should have been doing this in her teens instead of associating herself with Ernst. But Ernst had made her happy she thought shrewdly.

She wondered what the guests at the soirée would say had they known her real social status That was she was in fact the Judge's own daughter. Meanwhile Donella had found her seat in the musical ensemble and put her 'cello ready for the performance to be taken out of it's case when Herr Auberg and all the musicians were ready to begin the evening's entertainment. The unfriendly Maitre d'Hôte darted here and there now finding seats for the guests. They were a merry crowd and as it was near to the end of the year Christmas cheer abounded amongst them. Finally all were seated and the gush of conversation died down as the musicians took up their instruments and Herr Auberg rose to take his place on the raised dias from where he would conduct.

Donella was new to the occasion and felt conspicuous and conscious of the fact that all eyes were upon the ensemble.

Donella had kept her eyes upon the other musicians while they and the guests were enjoying a buffet supper. She knew that her mother was helping the servants in the preparation of the meal so relished even more what she and all the others were eating. As she stood to one side watching the housemaids taking the empty dishes from the now satisfied guests her thoughts fell onto the conversation between her parents that she had half overheard the night before. It seemed that there was some quite strong bond between her family and the people who lived at the villa. But who were they?

She had not yet thought to ask her mother who owned the gracious dwelling set quite high up on the slopes of the Alpine mountains. The guests were of all ages so the host and hostess must be very open minded in entertaining such a variety pf people. Some of them were not much older than herself itwas clear to her, and seemed to be quite well acquainted with the musicians. This must be a regular occasion for them all with folk from the community around them as permanent friends of the owners of this villa.

The six violinists looked alarmingly composed but she thought she was a good match for them also attired in a long black evening gown. How many 'cellists were there? She tried to deduce the number seemingly four of them with herself included. There were also a few players of wind instruments as she could see when the musicians started moving over to the playing area in front of Herr Auberg. The young male 'cellist whom she had met at her audition seemed to be taking an interest in her. He ventured:

"It seems that at long last this evening we can make a start with our entertainment. Did Herr Auberg give you copies of the works we will be performing this evening?"

Donella coming out of her shell at this communication from someone who like her had trained as a 'cellist, answered:

"Yes I have been going over the scores. The only one I found a little difficult was the Brahms. I see the work has been scored for a smaller ensemble than we are, not being players in a large orchestra."

The young man who introduced himself as Kurt confided:

"It is my wish and ambition to be taken on in the greater orchestra in the large town nearby here."

Donella who only as an inexperienced young girl was new to the nearby village where the convent was, abashedly looked interested in what Kurt was saying. They and the other musicians opened up their music scores on the stands provided.

Donella was experiencing a first occasion of performing on her 'cello to an audience. Herr Auberg was rounding up the musicians after supper was over and the guests now the gossip of the neighborhood was over were clearly highly anticipatory of the evening's promised musical entertainment. The steward of the villa with some underlings of the servants were hastily and unobtrusively setting the seating right for the guests. Gradually the flow of conversation became a mere whisper and those who were still talking brought forth a frown from Herr Auberg who was anxious to begin the concert. Kurt was ushering Donella over to their musicians' seats. He said:

"Don't be nervous. I could see from your playing last Saturday when you had your audition that you are a most adept player. Other players the violinists told me that they were most impressed. They are older players than yourself and are quite satisfied with you pitch and timing. As you know we string players have to be careful to keep in tune with one another. Herr Auberg told me himself that he found no complaint. Because I sit next to you in the ensemble he was anxious to know if you were pitching your playing with no difference to my own tuning in the piece of music that he tried you on.

I must say I had nothing to say in your disfavor." Donella replied breathily:

"Oh! Thank you Kurt I must say that it was quite an ordeal for me but you are really putting me at my ease. Though we cannot relax as performers can we."

Kurt smiled and together with the other players the violinists, 'cellists and the single double bass player, as the audience quietened, they resined their bows and tuned their instruments. There was a pianist who gave them the requisite middle A note to tune their strings.

A whisper went round the players as Herr Auberg said audibly to all present.

"We will begin with the Mozart sextet." Hastily the players shuffled their scores and within a minute or two were ready to commence when Herr Auberg lifted his baton. Donella was more excited than nervous, and enthusiastically her bow raced over the strings of her 'cello, keeping an eye too on Kurt next to her and her fingers thudded up and down firmly on the strings to produce the correct notes. Now and again she flashed a glance at the higher pitched violinists. Donella was happy at last and the thought whizzed through her mind that this was a life she could enjoy. No, she could never consider the novitiate again by becoming a nun and shutting herself away from the world outside.

She threw herself heart and soul into the melodies that she was etching with her bow in her right hand and the skilful running of her fingers of her left hand forming the notes she was playing in time to the up and down and across movement of Her Auberg's baton. She had noticed that the players in the ensemble kept glancing at one another as well as at the conductor to be sure that they all had the same beat. No, it would have ruined her life had she entered the novitiate. This thought flashed through her head as the langurous harmonies of Brahms' music drew to a close.

She felt enervated and elated as if she knew something was going to happen to make her senses reel. And they did. There was a gust of wind through the large drawing room. She noticed Herr Auberge's eyes lift from his conductor's score a frown clouding his face. She too looked at what he had seen. It was a man entering a most elegant and attractive personage, a most charming looking character more interesting looking than any of the other men there.

None of these so far at the soirée had entranced her as this man did. All in the auditorium heard him mutter apologies at interrupting the entertainment, that particular section fortunately was coming to a finish just as he had walked in from the frosty night outside. Snow still clung to him and he brushed flakes from his shoulders and chest. His attire she noticed was somewhat military. She was not aware of any fighting ensuing in the country being so involved in her playing and practicing for the evening. This was not to mention a complete involvement in her 'cello training while until a few months ago still a pupil at the convent set apart on the slopes overlooking a deep ravine.

Donella with her sharp musicians hearing caught the gist of what he was saying in apology to the steward of the villa. It seemed that he had been held up, he was saying in a tight voice:

"I was expecting news from the battle front from a servant whom I sent out to reconnoiter in the nearby town on horseback. The man informed me that he had been held up at gunpoint by enemy insurgent spies. The smoothness of his tongue and the lies that he told them about what his activities were all about enabled him to come out of the fray unharmed and he was able to return to my villa with the news that fighting was beginning in the far north of Austria."

The musicians came to an abrupt ending of the work of entertainment that they were performing a few minutes after the soirée had been interrupted by the arrival of the intriguing man who, judging from the whispers being mouthed by the audience of guests, was known as Über Luitenant Viktor Tazner. The women were squeaking in delight now that the music was over and they could turn their attention to this handsome but enigmatic young man who it seemed did not have a partner that evening.

The female guests fluttered their tongues over the fact that he was not only unaccompanied but that this seemed a permanent social state that he lived in. Donella too was charmed immediately she set eyes on him from the minute she put down her bow onto the music stand. In the moments subsequent to the finishing of the work that the ensemble had been performing Donella was able to rest her eyes from the group who had been enjoying the symphony that had been scaled down to fit the smaller number of players. The ladies and gentlemen were now rising from their chairs to enjoy a cup of coffee that the servants had rustled up surprisingly quietly. Kurt addressed Donella:

"Are you thirsty? I am. That was an energetic piece of music that Herr Auberg put us through. I do believe there are some snacks for us all too. Behind his shrewdness as a legal personage the judge is a generous man. He is partial to the ladies too I do believe."

Donella lowered her head in embarrassment at this confidentiality. She questioned:

"Where is he our host?"

Kurt who had attended many of these Saturday evening soirées was quite aware of who their host was, a judge. He answered:

"There he is darting to and fro between the servants and the guests ensuring that everyone is served and enjoying the evening. It is an important feature in his life now he is older and his soirées are well known in the community here. There is a rumor that he once had a daughter but that she disappeared under dubious circumstances connected with a hired hand at the villa many years ago. The judge is a cynical old man and I am sure that he knows where his long lost daughter is but is reluctant to disturb her living conditions." Donella was intrigued at this bit of gossip. The two 'cellists having put down their instruments were wandering up to the table at the side of the large room where coffee and delicacies were being served. Donella felt a pair of interested dark eyes fixed on her as she moved to take up her coffee cup and saucer. She would have liked to pass on a pleasantry of conversation but words failed her so intent was the man's contemplation of her.

Suddenly Donella felt alert to Viktor's gaze. He seemed to have the ability to rivet her own attention even while conversing with Kurt who said:

"We have a longstanding acquaintance, Viktor and I."

Viktor put in an assertive "that is certainly so. This is just as well as I am sure this will serve as an introductory go - between and let us two meet." He glanced meaningfully at Donella. It was clear that he would like an opening into an acquaintance with her. She felt her pulses racing and burbled out the words:

"I am just not used to meeting such an important person as yourself wanting to get to know me. I am after all only regarded still as a servant being one of the musicians." "Yes that may be so," responded Viktor, "but I noticed you immediately. How easily you seem to handle what I would call a most ungainly instrument. Does it not tire you?"

Enthused by the ease of his conversation and the soothing effect that it was having on her she answered eyes lowered not willing at all to deny the suggestion that he was making toward her she answered:

"Not at all." Her confidence was increasing as this man put her more and more at ease. She felt almost a sense of immediately finding herself reliant on him. How could this be? They had only just met. He switched the conversation towards Kurt having seen her embarrassment, continuing:

"As you can see I am all ready for the battlefront." He was in semi-military dress wear. Here Donella immediately realizing the meaning of his last few words, that there was fighting ensuing somewhere near broke into the conversation, suddenly afraid:

"Where, where is there fighting? My family do not know about it!"

Surely this wonderful man whom she had just met was not going to war - a war was transpiring somewhere? The reality of it was a shock to her. Was it possible that he might even be wounded? No, she dare not think about it. Worse, might his life even be at risk? The maleness of his role in the company present made it clear to Donella that this might even happen as his next words explained:

"These Frenchmen must be taught a lesson. They cannot meddle in the affairs of Prussia. This is a longstanding issue here in Europe."

The conversation buzzed on with Kurt and Viktor Tazner to the forefront in the talking. More of the male guests drifted towards this man who was in military uniform. Would he be able to provide news of the war against France that was apparently beginning? Donella was feeling a little left out with all this male company. Viktor seemed to realize her feelings as she looked desperately at the two female violinists who were standing to one side clearly longing to be included in Donella's group that was forming around her.

Donella's head was swimming and she felt out of her depth. She would take the plunge and try to approach the two women standing there. She turned to leave the now all male gathering. Viktor noticed this immediately and said authoratively:

"Don't go Donella. Let us two go in search of some wine and cheese and biscuits to finish off the bouffet."

Forlorn now Donella nodded and the two left the group of men who looked a little astounded at this social ploy. The group of men had begun to be noisy and presently quietened down with respect to their newly found hero who was telling them what to expect as Austrian or Prussian citizens when called up to fight in the army. Viktor's gaze flooded over Donella as they stood apart with their coffee slowly sipping it. Viktor read her thoughts:

"No Donella no one has taken special notice of us. It is just that I am wearing my army uniform. I must tell you that as I am overwhelmed to be in conversation with you, such a charming person as you seem to be. I am quite au fait with these soirées as have attended them for a few years now. All it seems in the waiting for this wonderful opportunity of meeting someone like you!"

He pauaed here wishing to see the effect of his words on the young woman who was scarcely out of school. Viktor sought a way of putting her at her ease as he went on:

"You love to play your 'cello I can see that. I am intrigued. Where did you learn your art? You are clearly most talented."

Now that the conversation was turning to a matter that she felt comfortable with as Viktor had intended Donella felt a little more relaxed. She answered with the primness that she had gleaned in her study with the old nun Mother Armentia.

"Yes. I have practiced very hard at my 'cello these last few years that I have been studying the art with an old nun at the convent I attended. Her name was Mother Armentia."

"Is she French? That is a French name." Viktor said quizzically."

"She is I believe," Donella replied. "Even though she is a nun at an Austrian convent she did tell me that her parents were of French extraction from the time of the Huguenot persecution. She was intending to be a 'cellist a performer and trained as such, but felt called to the sisterhood of nuns. She has taught many young women to play the 'cello she told me."

She felt Viktor to be more at ease and realized that her talking about herself to him had made him feel more relaxed. Not to be outdone Viktor began to tell her about the fighting on the warfront:

"Because I am of the nobility in fact of the baronetage I have been asked by the Prussian Imperial Court to take command of quite a number of soldiers. We do military training at the barracks now during the weeks. This has quite upset my routine as I liked to write before this interruption." Donella started. She was alarmed to hear that there was fighting in the country saying:

"Does this mean that you and your batallion's lives are at risk?"

Victor smiled, grimly though.

"We are at risk yes but the secret of warfare is to avoid being hurt or even killed by our skill in outwitting the enemy. Does that answer your question?" Donella looked relieved.

"I do understand yes. That makes me feel a little better about hearing about such ghastly actions taking place just when I was quite unaware of it." Victor continued:

"Yes it is one of the hard facts of life we all as adults have to accept it like it or not."

Donella turned away for a moment or two while theses ugly facts sank into her consciousness. She felt a little cheered when she remembered that Victor as she now knew him had told her that he was a writer. She quickly asked:

"You said you wrote. What kind of writing do you do?" Victor lowered his head humbly and admitted:

"I make an attempt at writing poetry." He noticed Donella draw in her breath sharply. She had always loved her poetry classes as a schoolgirl and here was someone she could share her interest with. Victor went on:

"Sometimes I struggle with my words but if I am patient they sort themselves out and I find all of a sudden that I have created a sonnet or else at least a four line verse." Donella responded:

"But how clever of you. I have always wondered how poets form their verses."

She said quickly to Viktor breaking the convivial but personal tête à tête that she and Viktor had formed together:

"I must go. I can see that Herr Auberg wishes the musicians to regroup for the second half of the evening's performance. I am keen to play again this evening. It is a Beethoven ensemble. You will love it." He replied with a charming look that she was already coming to know so well of his nature:

"Reforming then? Just like I have explained to you that we do in our military training!"

Donella gave him a frightened look. He was gently teasing her knowing that she had not the slightest knowledge of the barracks comings and goings that he was forced to undergo, He thought to himself as he watched her walk off to the musicians' podium that she must have had to undergo sever discipline not only as a scholar in her convent days but also as the musician that she was, a 'cellist.

As the little orchestra knuckled down to the waves of glorious the Beethoven music he tried to fathom out what it meant to play a musical instrument. He cocked his head from one side to the other also glancing rapidly at the rather older more experienced looking violinists. No, Donella had a mellower more innocent look about her that attracted him to her as male to female. He wondered if any of her family were attending the concert. She had seemed to be acquainted with her partner 'cellist Kurt, also a friend of Viktor's. Donella had told him that she had only recently had her nineteenth birthday. That made her really like a young bird who had just flown the nest. He sat back and closed his eyes but he could not escape the vision of Donella. The music drifted on with a heavy beat now, almost military – why did she have to think of that on this relaxing occasion? Meanwhile Donella was putting every effort that she could muster into the performance. She caught Herr Auberg smiling at her once or twice during the performance. She felt encouraged. It was strange she thought as she played that as a 'cellist she could lift her eyes from her music score on the stand, and be in visual contact now and again as they all played, with whomever of the other players happened to be looking in her direction. As she concentrated, the gathering was disturbed once again

The musical evening was again being interrupted. Donella new to such soirées anyway was very conscious of all that was transpiring around the small group of performers. The door at the back of the large room was being covertly pushed open letting in a blast of icy wind. From what Donella could glimpse while still playing on, a wisp of a man seemingly a messenger of some kind stood at the entrance for a few moments obviously wondering to whom he could give his message that appeared to be a scroll or a codex, some sort of cylindrical container. Donella could not see too clearly. She turned her attention back to the end of the Beethoven work.

What happened now was that Viktor Tazner, ever alert in the state of war that the country found itself in rose from his seat to intercept the man at the door. He said to the man whose head touched his chest, dumbfounded at the sight of the throng of guests, and who touched his forelock in obeisance:

"Man we are in the middle of a concert. You cannot barge in like this."

The music stopped and all eyes were now turned to the fracas that was occurring at the entrance. Viktor continued:

"Is it news from the barracks? Speak man." The man mumbled out his words:

"I have to deliver this codex of musical notation that I have to the villa Here take it."

He was holding a rusting circular metal canister in one hand that seemed to be very old. The scroll inside was coming loose as the rusty lid was being shaken open in the rough handling. He continued slyly:

"Those were the orders of my master who is a famous musician. I dare not say his name out loud for fear of causing trouble. I discovered the canister in his old attic. He is in danger, captured and held hostage by the enemy."

As the messenger was led away by the steward he thrust the canister into Viktor's hands and begged him to see that one of the musicians at the judge's villa would be in receipt of the painstakingly hand-written scores within the codex, saying as he did so:

"I trust that you will receive them, sir. I dare not tarry for I fear for my life."

The messenger was jostled out just as hurriedly as he had entered. Viktor now in possession of the music scrolls inside the codex, noted the name on one of the fraying pages, that of a famous composer of some centuries back. Curiosity was abating amongst the guests as the incident quietened and no one seemed interested in what had just happened any more. The ensemble was performing one more piece that Saturday evening but there was another coffee break before that. As Donella left the podium with Kurt she had a feeling that the man who had interrupted the gathering was familiar, but as she had been busy playing at the time could not look at him too closely.

Out of the corner of her eye she noticed Viktor elbowing his way towards her through the throng of guests. She noticed that he still held the scroll container in his hand. As he came nearer Donella saw that some of the inscription pages tattered at the edges, were nearly falling out of the container. They seemed to be yellowing and covered with musical notation carefully inscribed in black ink. Her curiosity got the better of her and as Viktor drew nigh to her she inquired:

"Where do those scores you are holding come from Viktor?"

She indicated the scroll as she could see that he was holding it somewhat distractedly, obviously more interested in her as a person. He replied, coming down to earth:

"Yes. This scroll of musical notation. I hope I did the right thing in accepting it from the young messenger. It is clear that the composer and giver of the scroll inside this container knew that there were musicians playing and entertaining at the villa tonight." Donella queried holding out her hand that he might give her the cylindrical box of compositions.

"But who is the writer of these compositions? They seem to be concertos. May I see? Yes here, the composer has written his name at the top of this work. Oh! This is a well-known composer in the country! It is Antonio Vivaldi! My 'cello teacher often mentioned his name. I believe she even studied with one of his pupils in her younger days! How exciting." Viktor said:

"The messenger asked me to give it to one of the musicians here. If you see fit you can give it to the conductor of the ensemble. The evening's entertainment is over now. The guests are all thanking their host the judge for his hospitality." Then Viktor changed the subject and asked:

"Where do you live Donella? She told him of her family's chalet in the forest nearby. She had not thought about it but then remembered that her father had told her that he would fetch her by sleigh once she was ready. She heard voices ringing out in tired tones as the evening drew on and the visitors began to wend their various ways home. She glanced quickly at the music scores in her hand and impulsively said:

"I must hurry to collect my instrument and music sheets. My father is sure to be waiting."

Viktor pulled himself up to his full stature and said with manly demeanor:

"You can tell your father that you have a friend who can see you home on the next Saturday that we all meet if he is in agreement."

Donella smiled wistfully. Viktor had said: "a friend." That meant so much to her having just left an all female convent school. A male friend! What would that be like? She had never had a deep friendship with anyone let alone her fellow scholars. She was an only child and anyway her mother had kept her hard at it in her music and other classroom studies. She came out of her momentary dream realizing what Viktor intended. She stumbled out an answer to his offer:

"Oh! I am sure that my father will be most grateful to be saved the trouble of having to come out to fetch me in this icy weather after his hard week's work."

Chapter 6

At a later time upon Viktor's suggestion Ernst answered a little surlily:

"I would be grateful then if you take my daughter home after the next soirée, Hertzog Tazner. Donella tells me that is your title and name. It would seem pointless that you lift her this evening seeing that I have come out with the purpose of fetching her. It would surprise my wife if anyone else brought her home this evening."

Donella's father spoke these words taking in Herzog Tazner's looks of adulation at his daughter's charming demeanor. She was standing there with her 'cello balanced in the shallow snow on the porch outside the front door of the villa. Her parka that her father had brought for her from the chalet was hunched up over her shoulders and her brighteyed face smiled winningly at Viktor, in thanks for seeing to her social needs that evening. Viktor had made an impression on her Ernst could see.

Viktor now made a pretense of seeing that Donella's parka was well pulled over her head hiding what he now knew to be a blonde mass of curls. He made a half-hearted attempt at putting an arm around her shoulders in gratitude too for her innocent companionship during the bouffet supper and coffee breaks. Certainly the two seemed enchanted with one another, but Ernst, her father who was a humble woodworker did not seem to notice the vital attraction pure chance had made for the couple. Viktor ventured:

"You need not fetch your daughter next week then. I am a free man with no commitments after the evening is over. It will not trouble me at all to escort Donella home on my own sleigh." Ernst replied:

"We'll take our leave then. I shall not see you again Herr Tazner until next soirée when Donella returns from the evening out. Let us leave, my daughter."

Donella rather clumsily with her 'cello climbed onto her father's sleigh. Her father began manoeuvering the sled and they were on their way Donella trying to hold on her parka hood for it was a freezing evening and late, as well as see that her 'cello was not bumped around too much. She was glad of the wooden case that her father had fashioned for her for the instrument. Her father steered the sled down the snowbound pathway through the forest that was lit through the bare branches of the trees only by the pale moon disappearing now and again with the stars in the clouds up above.

The week following was long and drawn out for both Donella and Viktor. Donella forgetting temporarily that she had not long ago keenly desired to enter the novitiate, became enthusiastic in her 'cello practicing. She went over and over her finger exercises conscientiously as she had learned from Mother Armentia, her 'cello mentor. The old nun having had famous teachers herself in her youth had told Donella that she had passed on to the young girl all she had ever known and had given Donella some of her old exercises carefully transcribed in her own hand.

Viktor on the other hand had to pass the week doing mounted military manoeuvers at the barracks outside the town. His platoon had been told that they could be called up at any time now. Fortunately Viktor's men were being kept in reserve to be used as a last resort if the French push into Prussia became too intense. Viktor although altogether masculine as a person was a sensitive man and welcomed this news from the battlefront. It would mean that he could attend the judge's soirées and partake of the enjoyment of the music and sociability provided.

More important to him though was his pursuit of the lovely young woman 'cellist in the ensemble, named Donella. He had absent-mindedly handed her the codex full of manuscripts of music notations by Antonio Vivaldi a famous composer in the locality of many years ago. The thought came to him as he dressed for the evening that he had done so because the messenger who had entered the room of guests and musicians the last

Saturday had covertly asked him to hand it over to one of the players. He had spontaneously chosen Donella to give the scores to. He wondered why and also what she had done with them. She was the type of young woman who would care for them with her life if necessary. He made a mental note being curious to ask her what she would do with them.

However it now had nothing more to do with him. Donella had in fact hidden the scores he had handed to her amongst her scarves and handkerchiefs in a bottom drawer of a chest of drawers that her father had fashioned for her, he being of trade a wood carver. The week did pass nevertheless and the two found themselves afresh in each other's company again. It was nearing Christmas and to them and the other guests' astonishment they were all welcomed by tinsel and coloured candles and lights, as well as an enormous Christmas tree most ornately decorated.

Viktor and Donella espied one another immediately. Donella had entered the drawing room where the evening entertainment took place. She was astounded by the show of tinsel and baubles decorating the large fir Christmas tree. She was a young lady who noticed her surroundings quickly wherever she was and the season's decorations nearly took her breath away. Viktor noticed this and quietly thought to himself that she had never probably, never experienced such a grand occasion in her young life before now.

He was touched by her reaction and wondered what price he would have to pay to break the ice of her innocence. Donella had immediately put up a barrier at being so overwhelmed by it all. Viktor said half looking at her and half glancing at what she saw:

"Donella I so want to see the occasion here this evening through your eyes. Clearly it is something very new to you." Donella caught her breath and answered:

"Yes! - Oh yes it is. We celebrate Christmas at home but in a very lowly way. My father cuts down a small fir tree branch and brings home some fir cones that he has found in the forest. He and my mother see that they are dried in front of our hearth fire and then my mother paints them different colors with paint over from my father's workplace that he brings home. I can't believe my eyes seeing the shining baubles – is that what would would call them?- hanging from this great big Christmas tree here!"

Viktor assumed a paternalistic facial expression at her telling of the way that she had spent Christmas as a young girl. Donella newly confident continued:

"Oh! And my father would take me with him to collect the fir cones. We only picked up the very best, the most perfect ones. We did not take those that the little woodland squirrels and other animals had broken so they could crack the nuts inside to eat."

Viktor was charmed to hear oaf she and her father's woodland adventures. He spoke:

"How I would love to go a-nutting with you in the forest nearby. I am quite sure that we would be able to collect as many nuts between us as all the little animals in the wood or even if you like enough of them to eat as there is in this evenings supper spread. Shall we go and see what the servants have prepared for us to eat?" Donella cast her eyes towards the table set along side of the room. They would have to be quick to taste what was offered. Herr Auberg had tapped Donella on the shoulder and Kurt had sidled over to Viktor and herself. Herr Auberg said:

"These eats are for the second interval that is as long as one hour before the closing entertainment. We are providing our little ensemble with this so that the guests will have time to eat and the servants will be able to clear the tables of the empty plates. These delights are only for viewing right now. Come along Donella. I can see that you are tempted by these foods set before us. Come and titilate an appetite in performing with us the work of Jan Sebastian Bach that I am sure you have taken great trouble in with your 'cello practicing at home." She answered wistfully :

"It seems we'll have to wait Viktor." This was the first time that she had called him by name and he felt his heart thumping inside him so enchanted was he by this girl. She did not seem to notice his reaction and with a farewell look at him for the moment was led away by Kurt and Herr Auberg. The latter was anxious to get the playing on the go as the evening was becoming late as it was. At last all the performers were seated with instruments at the ready and music scores open at the correct place. Herr Auberg raised his baton and the orchestra alerted to the sudden stillness of the guests and the expectancy of the occasion.

Soon the whole room of people both musicians and audience were swinging and tapping their feet to the music of the famous composer Bach. The players moved their bodies slightly to and fro with the ebb and flow of the piece that they were performing and the audience all smiled in delight at the cheer and suitability of the music to the Christmas season. Then the music was over and the enchanted guests looked at one another so stunned by the beauty of the performance that they had almost forgotten the eats provided for them. Victor ambled to the entrance to the performers' podium and while waiting for Donella to put her instrument in it's case until needed again congratulated Herr Auberg on the performance. Donella leaned her 'cello against her seat and with a little tripping movement made her way down to join Viktor who waited for her.

"Your 'cello is safe Donella" Viktor asked. "Oh! Yes." The young girl replied. "The playing has made me hungry. You would not believe the strength needed in my shoulders and arms to manage a 'cello. But I am tall and Mother Armentia said that I have a strong frame." Viktor snapped good temperedly: "I entirely disagree with the old nun your teacher. You look tired out and extremely frail to me."

A shadow of a smile lit Donella's earnest face. The Bach compendium had indeed taken a lot of energy out of her and she would need sustenance to see her through the Brahms ouevre. Herr Auberg had told her the week before that he had arranged the quintet for the whole ensemble to play together and she needed to keep her concentration going for the final work of the evening. Viktor ushered her through to the eating area. He intimated:

"I have had the pleasure of sitting down and enjoying the music that you have all been performing. I have attended a fair number of concerts in the town hall and have been quietly comparing them with what I have heard this evening. The comparison of tonight's performance rates highly in my estimation. I can see that Herr Auberg's little orchestra is a much younger group than the more older and experienced players in the town orchestra, but I see a great future for them"

What is your choice to eat now Donella? These little savoury biscuits look quite enticing. Oh! I see they are meant to be dipped in this array of sauces and dips over here."

They took a few biscuits and dipped and ate happily. The savoury entrées were giving Viktor just as much of an appetite as Donella had as a result of the heavy strain that the first two items of the musical entertainment had given to her so far that evening. When they had finished Viktor suggested that they try the veal sautées and potato wedges. He had been carefully looking ahead of Donella's satisfying of her appetite to tempt her with the eats available. He said:

"I do believe Donella if you are finished and have had enough of the veal that you can join me in enjoying some trifle, I think it is." She replied, relaxed now:

"I have never had such wonderful food in my whole life. At home I have to be satisfied with brodtwurst and rye bread or some soup that my mother prepares every day." Viktor said:

"Doesn't this look appetizing. I would say that it is just what you will need to keep you together in your thoughts to be able to concentrate for the last part of the evening. After all it is I and the other guests who have been able to relax at the sound of your playing. It is you and your ensemble who have been the busy ones this evening. I do thank you Donella."

Donella was gratified and smiled benignly. She countered:

"It seems as though this delicious meal is over doesn't it Viktor? It will stand out in my memory especially that I enjoyed it with you. Are you going back to your seat now?" "Yes,' he said. "I will just walk over to the podium with you first. I don't think anyone has noticed the interest that I am taking in you. That you are a center of interest amongst the young males here seems very clear to me. It makes me feel your allure even more so."

Donella and he slowly walked over to the front center of the auditorium where the musicians' dias was. Viktor took her hand in a friendly manner. Donella felt enchanted by this gesture and grasped his hand firmly in return. She felt drawn to this man and wondered in the total newness of the situation whether she would even see him again. Her head was swimming with emotion and she stumbled slightly as she walked past the four violinists all women slightly older than herself and sat down lightly on the chair that had been put there for her comfort as a musician.

Certainly the host of the evening whom she had seen but not spoken to had gone to much trouble to organize the event. He must be a keen music lover that was his calling, Viktor had told her. She tried to remember as she flipped the music score to the page that they were about to perform. Oh! That was it! He was of legal calling, a judge. She caught her breath.

Hadn't her mother talked about a relation who was a judge just the other evening, as she was falling asleep?

Her father had tried to quieten her mother then but she had been speaking vehemently against this person apparently a judge and in Donella's hearing. But why? What had her mother to do with any judge for that matter, let alone the man who was hosting this evening.

These thoughts rushed around Donella's head as she tried to open her score at the right place. She felt Herr Auberg's eyes on her and in a glance at him could see he was frowning at her. She was even more worried but was aware that he had great confidence in her and knew that she was an adept musician who would throw all aside that interfered with her doing her best in the performance.

Donella decided to fix her attention on her playing until the last part of the concert was underway and then while playing, and she knew the score well having practiced it thoroughly, she would let her subconscious thoughts wonder. She had heard her mother and father talking softly together just a couple of nights ago. Her father however seemed cross almost angry. Her mother had sounded anxious. He had been trying to quieten her. Why was this? Her mother had been saying over and over again:

"But the judge …" and "he is a wealthy man." What connection did her mother have to this judge? There was only one judge in the town and it was the man in whose villa she was appearing at this evening soirée. She would dare to ask her mother. The quintet was drawing to a close. Donella began to think how she would travel home.

The Saturday before her father on coming to fetch her by sleigh had met up with the inevitable male acquaintance of his daughter. He had not realized the intense interest that Viktor was showing Donella being of humble peasant origin. Slowly as she was feeling a little weary after the entertainment was over Donella checked that all her music scores were together so she could give them in to Herr Auberg just before leaving and receive the scores to practice for next Saturday.

Donella closed up her 'cello in its case and with a sudden surge of energy as she thought of Viktor who had offered to take her home on his own sleigh she heaved the 'cello up then as she rose and looked down the room. She did not have to look far. Viktor's eyes met hers and he quickly moved across the room avoiding as he did so several of the more socialite of the women who were keen to have some of his time. Donella breathed his name. "Viktor! At last the evening is over and I can relax."

Groups of people men and women gathered to applaud the musicians amongst them now, holding their instruments ready to make their way homewards. An appropriative voice shattered Donella's peace of mind as far as she and Viktor were concerned. Strident female tones came to Donella's ears before setting eyes on a demurely dressed guest with hair coyly piled on top of her head, but with a strict look about her. Donella wondered who she was. Viktor heard her address him:

"And who is this new female acquisition of yours Viktor?" and teasingly serious the same woman continued, "and you gave me to believe that you were my beau!"

Viktor looked caught out at her words. Donella was just so taken aback not even understanding correctly in her youth what the woman was getting at. She seemed to behave very familiarly towards Viktor. An old friend perhaps? Viktor immediately noticed Donella's awkwardness and sought to introduce the two women. The socialite acquaintance of Viktor's was clearly put out by the innocent looking Donella. Viktor, chin on chest in embarrassment offered a familiarizing of the socialite acquaintance to Donella:

"Donella meet Fraulein von Braun an old friend of mine. She is a regular attender at these soirées. As you can see Adèle, Donella has just performed on the 'cello this evening in the ensemble."

The older woman, clearly put out by the fact that by virtue of her ability to entertain musically Donella had at that moment more to offer in attractiveness than herself, adjusted her lorgnette quizzically and quipped:

"And just where my dear did you learn to play this cumbersome instrument?"

This friend of Viktor's spoke quite loudly when it came to Donella's answering her. Donella was by nature softly spoken although if opportunity called for it she could speak up if necessary. So she answered:

"I learnt to play with mother Armentia an old nun at the convent where I was a scholar until a few months ago."

The older of the two was obviously put out by the quality of Donella's education. Donella wondered who the person was. She was not going to be socially crushed under by her so turned from her and said to Viktor:

"You were going to lift me home on your sleigh, you told my father you would last week."

Viktor took the opportunity to extricate himself and Donella from the awkward social situation. Viktor kept his glances around him mostly on Donella and when she looked as if she wanted to leave stepped up to her and began to take the male domination role of ushering her out, saying:

"You remember from last week Donella when your father came to fetch you that it was decided among us that I should see you home. My valet will be here within the next half hour. It seems that my villa is on the way to the chalet where you live as your father explained to me so it will be no trouble." Viktor looked at his watch. "George is late this evening. I wonder what is holding him up. From what I have heard about the fighting in the north-east it could be that a messenger has come through to my villa from the front."

He looked at the beautiful girl standing in the snow the lamplight from the entrance glittering over her face. She did not know how desperate he was for her company that night to extend their relationship before going into battle within the next month or two. His life was at risk in the months ahead. For all the power of the Prussian fighting forces the French army was dapper and cunning and quicker on the uptake in the action that was taking place on horseback right at that moment though far away to the north. Viktor said:

"Ah, here is George."

A sleigh skidded to a stop right before the couple. The valet greeted his master and stepped off the sleigh.

"Will you help my lady friend onto the sleigh George? She has an awkward musical instrument to handle. I will climb on first so that I can give here a hand up then you can pass her the 'cello. Please hold it carefully when you hand it to her."

The guests departing around the couple were giving one another tired farewell greetings. Sleighs were leaving one after the other now. George started Viktor's sled moving and soon they were speeding down to his villa. Donella caught her breath in delight at the freedom the experience was giving her. Viktor said noticing her rosy countenance in her parka frosted from the cold:

"Would you like to come into my villa for a nightcap on the way back to your chalet? It is not late. Your parents will trust you to me I am sure. I know a made a good impression on your father last week."

Victor suddenly became silent as he watched Donella settle down on the sleigh as the servant maneuvered the vehicle faster and faster down the snow road. Donella was thrilled to be riding with Viktor and slid him several sideways glances.

They could not talk for a while until they reached Victor's villa. She had given him her unspoken affirmative that she would go with him into his home. He had an urge to make the young girl welcome in the place where he lived and that she see what he saw every day. It was a part of the sudden attraction that he had felt for her. She sensed his mood while riding on the sleigh and became vivacious smiling showing her lovely white teeth. He sensed her excitement but in a manly gesture for her safety on the sleigh ride put his arm around her. It was as if it would shatter him if anything should happen to harm his newly found friend.

Suddenly the sled skidded to a stop outside the brightly lit entrance of another villa. Donella looked questionigly at Viktor. Was this their destination? When the last of the snow particles thrown up on them from the sleigh's halt had subsided she said to him:

"This – this great villa – it's where you live?" "Yes Donella, ever since my parents were killed in an accident horse riding I have lived here. The villa belongs to me now. Do not be afraid if you see men in uniform around when we go inside. I took time off this evening to attend the judge's soirée. The military are here to discuss with me the training of soldiers at the barracks outside town. I have command over about forty to fifty soldiers some of them mounted cavalry.

Don't worry about that now. Here is one of my servants to take your accessories insides while you are with me. We will make ourselves comfortable in the lounge adjoining my study. He wanted her to know about himself.

"That is where I do my writing Donella." She responded quickly sensing the importance of his statement involving her. Softly she said to him: "When do you write Viktor? And why?" He could understand that she was interested and curious about his habits. He began to make clear to her the real reason behind his writing occupation and what he wrote.

"I will share my secret with you Donella. I write poetry."

She then understood his artistic handsome looks. All her life as a scholar she had longed to meet someone as charming as this man was to her. And he was a poet.

So the rather awesome Herzog Viktor Tazner was not only someone in real life a soldier, but also had an inner life of his own that of a poet. She thought back to those English studies when she and the other girls learnt poems by heart and pulled the wording of others apart so as to analyse their structure. She cast her thoughts back to the few Shakespeare sonnets she had studied and remembered rhapsodizing over the compact beauty and hints of their romantic substance. Now how marvelous to meet someone in the flesh who could conjure up in his brain the rhyming stanzas of poetry! It had always puzzled her how the lines of rhyming poetry were made up. Here was her chance to find out! She said slyly:

"Do you have to be inspired to write a verse of poetry Viktor?" She held her breath. Would he be annoyed at her curiosity about this very personal hobby of his? She followed up her question. Viktor lifted up his chin and looked down at the young girl quizzically and answered:

"It comes in a rush, just flows out of me. I found when my parents were killed in a riding accident that my bereavement of two people who meant the world to me heightened my senses so that I could not for long periods during the days after it happened express myself in normal conversation with those left at my father's villa, those were the servants. I could only write short spats of wordage that gradually realized themselves into verse after verse. I suppose it came from all the reading that I did as a young boy but the words just came tumbling out of my brain onto the paper I kept at hand before me.

"But why is it so with you Viktor?" Donella was determined to get to the bottom of this incident that had triggered Viktor's writing ability. Viktor took in the loveliness of her face made beautiful by her calling in life of being a musician. Could he confide the ongoing ill feeling that the accident had caused between himself and his former fiancée? Yes, he would trust this young girl.

"Donella," he ventured trying to capture her full attention. "I will tell you the full story." Her attention was now riveted on him. It was not only his tale but the man himself that had totally captured her imagination and taken her fancy. It seemed to her that by every thought of his causing the story that he told she was being captured into his mind. As he spoke she at first had her eyes fixed on his face but she gradually and then speedily began to listen to what he was saying. It seemed important that she understand from him that he was quite devastated by the recent death of his parents in a horse riding accident. His words began entering into her consciousness:

"....the ground was soft and Marina's horse must have made little sound impact as she cantered along the other side of the copse, from where my mother and father, also in the soft earth were trotting on their steeds. Of course they collided, the speed with which Marina was riding completely causing them to fall on top of one another without Marina coming off her horse or her horse falling. It was some time before Marina my fiancée could summon help but by the time the local farmers could assist in the accident it was clear that my parents, older people had not survived the ordeal. I received word of it at the barracks where the police traced me only a few hours later. As you can hear from my voice I am still getting over the shock."

Donelka summoned up as much compassion as she could muster and seeing his forearm resting on the arm of the chair next to her, she gently put her hand over his saying gently:

"How you must have suffered this last week Viktor. Is there no one close to you who can help you to bear all this pain? Your fiancée, perhaps?"

Viktor gave a sigh of desperation. It seemed that he would have to confide in this friendly soul more of the story of what had happened. He said bitterly now:

"You see Donella the police were not satisfied that the occurrence was just an accident. Marina my fiancée is under suspicion for having caused their deaths."

He drew in his breath sharply continuing:

"This is a small community and I would not like word to get out about what happened. It seems though that Marina knew that my parents were out riding and had set out deliberately to tip them off theirs mounts. I would not like word to pass around our little community about this. The police in the town have been in touch with me and made a thorough investigation of the incident but it seems that nothing can be proved in Marina's disfavor. The accident has left a nasty taste in a lot of mouths. It has come to light you see and I am confiding in you Donella that the death of my parents has left me a wealthy man. This is both in the inheritance of their villa and taking on of the title of a nobleman in this community.

Why the matter was investigated further was because Marina who is now my ex-fiancée was pushing for a handsome wedding gift from my parents. It is apparent that wealth and nobility were going to her head. My parents organized our meeting. Her family in my opinion now are nothing more than upstarts. They are not genuine blue-blooded people."

At this point Viktor halted in his tale of woe as he saw Donella give a start at this last statement of his. He wondered why for a moment then ceasing in his story, his curiosity aroused he asked her what had perturbed her. She answered at length:

"Viktor you have confided in me about your family. May I confide I you about mine? As you know we musicians are traditionally servants. Now you might very well not be so keen on keeping up our relationship when you hear what I have discovered about my humble parents. I was socializing with the servants at the villa belonging to the judge and happened to fall into conversation with one of the very much older housekeepers. I had noticed my mother talking in quite a vivacious almost domineering way to her on the day that I had my interview with Herr Auberg.

I questioned the old housekeeper who confided in me that she had remembered my mother from many years ago, as the judge's daughter who had disappeared without trace. She said though that it was common knowledge that the judge had his suspicious as to where his daughter was living with one of his hired hands, but was loathe to upset the situation she was existing in for fear of embarrassing his socialite friends. Viktor I do beg your favour when I tell you that I myself am the progeny of those circumstances."

Donella hung her head. At least she had found someone she could trust. Silence hung between the couple for a minute or two. Then Viktor spoke:

"Are you serious when what you tell me is that you are the daughter of a past servant at the judge's villa? And that your mother is in fact his own daughter?"

Donella felt anguish and pain at what she had admitted to Viktor. She had known about her humble origons only a week now having spoken to the aging housekeeper who had remembered her mother. This old woman had confided in Donella that rumor had it amongst the housekeeper's staff of servants that the judge had a shrewd idea of where his daughter had eloped to but was too mean of soul to take legal steps to get her back into his clutches. By the time he had known what had happened the couple had tied the knot and it was too late to take action. Then Viktor asked her:

"How does that make you feel Donella?" She replied:

"Well I did not realize what had happened as a very young girl and matters were eased as I grew up. The nuns at the convent just outside the town took me in as a boarding scholar and I saw only a little of my parents. Strange to say my mother though of those wealthy origins, accustomed herself to taking in washing quite easily. She was swept off her feet by my father although she, rumor had it, made the first amorous advances. Viktor spluttered:

"What a curios tale Donella. The nuns have though produced an excellently educated and well mannered young woman."

Donella slowly raised her drooping head and showed her white teeth in a shy though daring smile. Viktor took the opportunity and offered her a glass of warmed wine that he had laced with a dash of brandy. His parents had been light drinkers and he had a liking for it though he tolerated well the small amounts that he imbibed. Donella said looking coyly at the glass of wine offered to her:

"May I ask what this drink is? I have not tasted such a beverage before." Viktor had half turned away from her pretending innocence at the offer of the glühwein, genuinely hoping it would relax her. He found her a charming acquaintance at this stage even though to his high breeding her origins were questionable.

Chapter 7

Viktor was quiet for a few minutes while Donella a little cautiously sipped the wine that the servant had warmed for her enjoyment. She broke the silence as Viktor seemed not to have anything to say. In fact he was waiting to see the effect that the glühwein would have on his new friend. He was quite adept at handling social situations where strong drink was offered as his parents had been cheerful partygoers until their recent deaths. He missed them but always the drinking parties had worked on his nerves for they had expected a lot of him.

He had been a student at the nearby university and although being able to handle wine and beer the raucousness of the occasions, his father constantly called for him to be introduced to some new socialite an addition to his already long list of beaus. In the end he had to choose but his father had forced the choice onto him, a fiancée from a wealthy family from not too far away who had aspirations of a title of nobility for their daughter. The villa that Viktor's family lived in was in constant need of repair and there was an extravagantly large number of servants to be paid. This was in addition to Viktor's student fees.

At this time Viktor was also enjoying a glass of wine and cocked his ear as she spoke, eager to hear her comments about the way he was living and his circumstances:

"Now that is very sad what has happened to your parents. I know that I love my mother and father and how I would miss their support especially in my 'cello studies. I used to work so hard at my practicing in the school holidays when I was at home as a youngster. My mother used to tolerate even the most audacious squeaks and squawks made by me while I was becoming more and more adept at my 'cello." Viktor broke in:

"Yes I have made it my business to judge the expertise of you musicians while I have been attending the judge's soirées. I was overawed I can tell you not only by the fluency of your performance but also by your gracious looks."

He paused half expecting Donella to respond immediately but the wine was relaxing her and making her languid. Then she said: "Oh! Oh! You were admiring myself and my playing at the judge's last soirée. I had a particularly bad evening that night as it was very cold and it took a long time for all the musicians to warm up and give a bright performance.

The evening was becoming cold outside and the couple was savoring the moments as they passed before

Viktor escorted Donella back to her chalet. At length Donella said in a whisper as she really was exhausted by the events of the evening, both her playing in the orchestral ensemble and their sojourn at Viktor's villa afterwards. This included her appraisal of the recent events in Viktor's life with the loss of his parents and the breaking off of his engagement to Marina under suspicious circumstances. She said:

"If you don't mind Viktor I think we had better leave for the chalet. Am I correct that you said you would escort me home?" "That's right Donella although I am loathe to break up this tête-à-tête we are having. I can tell you it is the first time I have been in intimate circumstances since the exit of Marina from my life. I must admit it that is, if you don't mind filling the gap she left. You are a most charming and elusive replacement. Just knowing you with both your gentleness and effervescence as a musician make you a most adequate partner. May I venture the words, long may our union endure!"

Donella was looking misty at his words scarcely able to take them in. However she was bent on leaving now suddenly concerned that her parents would be worried about her. She snapped herself together saying:

"Yes I must leave now Viktor."

They had been totally relaxed in one another's company yet wary of the dramatic effect they were having upon one another. "Yes," Viktor said, "when we leave on another Saturday and we can meet here again. I have not much longer to spend in this villa as the military authorities have put me on roll call to join the fighting with my platoon in about two month's time." They rose from their chairs. "Fighting, who are you fighting against Viktor?" "It is those darned Frenchmen. As you know I am of Prussian noble birth and we are a proud race. My people are not standing for the molestation of the French on our borders. The whole army has been called up to resist. There is longstanding animosity between our two nations."

The two did not speak to one another after leaving Viktor's villa and on the long sleigh journey back as usual back to her parents' chalet. Donella was wondering what sort of reception she would receive from her mother and father, arriving home much later than usual. She made up her mind not to tell them where she had been. It was late nearing twelve that evening and everyone was tired. Her father ushered her inside scarcely noticing who it was who had brought her home. He said gruffly

"Time is drawing on now Donella. You must get to bed. Your mother and I particularly wish to speak to you tomorrow morning before you begin your 'cello practicing. You know that we do not like to interrupt you one you have started that. It is because if something your mother found, in your cupboard today. Good night my girl."

As she was falling asleep that night Donella racked her brains as to what her father was referring to. No, she did not feel guilty about anything. Surely she could not have displeased her parents? Forgetting about it she awoke to the sound of her father stoking up the living room coals to warm up the chalet for the day. Her mother was already dressed and was preparing breakfast of rye bread and lard, and coffee for the three of them. Then Josina spoke:

"I was tidying your cupboard yesterday Donella and I came across this." She reached across to the standing drawer nearby the table and produced the timeworn canister that Viktor had been given by the curious intruder who had entered the judge' soirée meeting a couple of Saturdays ago, as it seemed a yokel who had forced his way into the auditorium. She remembered that he had carelessly given the container to her. Now to think about it, the man had resembled her father. Had the item been stolen? Stolen from some wealthy person's attic?

But no surely this was not so? Perhaps it was chance or good fortune that had happened. She thought back to her meeting with Viktor. Yes. She had told her mother about Viktor and she had described Viktor to her and Josina would have told Ernst her father all this. Or was all this her imagination playing tricks on her?

The scroll, being handled now was stained with yellowing age around the edges and was also fragmented at the sides and shedding dust. It was a strange item but on opening it she could decipher musical notes written on staves of the manuscripts, seemingly for one instrument and orchestra. It was quite a thick roll of vellum and seemed to be in the form of concertos written for solo and orchestra. Her mother continued:

"I have shown the parchment manuscript to you father, Donella. It seems that the composer of what is inside this canister is Antonio Vivaldi. It is very old, as old as two centuries. The manuscript is very delicate and seems to crumble easily. It must be very valuable too. Your father is angry with you for letting it lie in your cupboard. He says that you should take it to the monastery outside the village because the monks will know its value and will take care of it. Do you want to speak to your father about it or shall I tell him that you will do what he suggests?"

Thinking of Viktor then, the male acquaintance that she had made at the judge's soirée she wondered if he had remembered giving it to her. At the time he had been busy organizing the sleigh for their ride home. No, he must have forgotten about it. It had been such an unusual occurrence. Even while playing her 'cello in the judge's entertainment ensemble she had looked up from her music score and seen the stranger enter the room and thrust the parchments in the container into Viktor's hands. Viktor had said nothing more to her about it so she had presumed that the giving of the container had been entirely unexplained and unexpected. She answered her mother:

"No, I am a little afraid that father will be angry with me if I do and that will upset me. He seems to be becoming very temperamental these days. It is not my fault that the vellum manuscripts are in my possession. It was given to me to look after at one of the soirées. I could see how delicate it was so was being so careful with it that I forgot to return it to my friend. See, even now it is tearing at the edges. I will wait until the weather clears today and then I will make the journey on foot to the monastery. Have you got any bag or holder that I can carry it in so that if it does begin to snow the parchment will not become wet and damaged any more than it is?" Her mother answered:

"Yes I thought of that. I have a sack that I received some washing in that will do nicely to protect the parchments in their canister. What are you going to do while you wait for the weather to clear?" Donella replied:

"If it will not disturb you I will get on with my practicing. I cannot leave my 'cello alone too long as the muscles in my hand will stiffen and I will not be able to perform as well as I should at the soirée tomorrow evening."

Donella had become very concerned as the day went on, about the possession of the vellum parchments. As a young girl scarcely out of her teens she was scarcely aware of it's importance and value. Her parents had realized that it was urgent to get it into some sort of permanent safe keeping and on discussing it, her father was unreasonably angry with Donella she thought, for handling it so carelessly. He had ordered her to take it to the local monastery. He said to Josina after telling her that he had taken to stealing for their bread and butter :

"I have complete confidence that the monks there will know what to do with it. Have you asked Donella how it came to be in her possession?" At this statement he looked sideways at Josina in an almost underhand way. She replied:

"She told me that a unkemptly dressed stranger barged his way into the judge's soirée last Saturday evening in the midst of a performance of the ensemble she plays with. She could not help noticing because of the disturbance his entrance caused.

Her acquaintance Viktor Tazner was roughly handed the parchment. He could not understand why this was so, he had been standing at the back of the room when it happened. Donella told me that he was finding it an impediment to hold while he was organizing the sleigh to take he and Donella home that evening so he gave it to her to hold and then forgot about it. She slipped it carefully into her music case and only took it out later the next week. She told me that she was aware of the fragile state it was in and had handled it most gingerly." Her husband responded:

"She must take it to the monks just as soon as the weather clears a little today. She can wait until this afternoon if she has to do her 'cello practicing this morning. I must leave now for work:

Drifts of this conversation came to Donella's ears as she looked through the music scores that Herr Auberg had given her to prepare for the next Saturday. Was she imagining it or was her father sounding guilty, even sneaky? Could there be a connection between the intruder into the soirée and her father? Her mother had told her he was at loggerheads more and more with old Father Grüssman now and her father was in danger of loosing his employment. Hadn't the person who had lurched his way into the judge's soirée resembled her father? She could not be sure for she had been concentrating on the music she was playing at the time.

She glanced quickly through the window to see what the weather was doing. It could go either way. It could worsen or even lighten up. She threw herself into her morning 'cello practicing with a will. Lunchtime came and there were iron gray clouds in the sky. Her mother said:

"Whatever the weather you will have to go to the monastery later on today. Your father is pestering me about it now. Here, I found an old sack that you can wrap the codex in. It will protect the parchments inside the container.

At this point the door of the chalet opened and her father stood at the entrance brushing snow off his parka. As he slowly adjusted himself to the warmth and cosyness of the inside he remembered that he had to chastise his daughter about the vellum manuscript in the codex. An angry look flooded his face as he stepped into the dwelling. He spoke:

"Donella I told you mother last night that you must take the old music scores that you have in your possession down to the monastery and give it to the monks there for safekeeping. We could be in serious trouble from the authorities if it is found here. You know how the local municipality like to inspect the chalets from time to time. If the parchment is found lying around here there could well be unpleasant inquiries."

Josina broke in to the conversation trying to appease her husband:

"Donella was about to leave Ernst. We were waiting for the weather to clear it has been so bad with all the snow during the day. You must have seen how heavy it was outside. It seems to be clearing a little now but not much. Is it possible that she can leave it until tomorrow, her journey to the monastery? It will be a lonely path to take after all the snow today. She might even loose her way and there could be fresh falls even from now on."

Donella struck the dividing chord in the conversation saying:

"I'll fetch my cape and go immediately father. If I leave it any longer it will certainly be too late to go at all."

She quickly donned her hooded cape and took up the sack containing the flaking music scores that Viktor had inadvertently handed her those few evenings ago. Was she doing the right thing? She would have to obey her father so reluctant to go out into the cold she set out after bidding her parents farewell. It was still light outside with a gray sky flooding what last of the rosy glow the sun had left on the horizon. She hastily took her direction.

The heavy snow during the day had completely blocked up the pathway through the woods. The trees mostly firs still had their winter foliage and they cast dark shadows as she walked anxious now about finding her way. The sky was quite clouded over but she made it through the woods before the light on the horizon just visible through the trees dimmed completely.

Snowflakes again began to slap her face as she neared the edge of the forest and they began to fall thickly onto the already hidden path. She found she was stumbling in the masses of snow lying in front of her. Suddenly her foot hit an emptiness below her through the whiteness in front of her. She immediately thought: I have put my foot into a fox's hole or even a beaver's next. She moved her foot beneath her. No she had not hit a stream. It must be the hide of some animal. She sank deeper into the mush of snow.

There was at first nothing to grab onto to lift her out of the hole. The faint yellow pink glow in the sky was slowly disappearing. She clutched the sacking folding it over and over so as not to let in any moisture. She looked around her in the now darkening forest. She looked in what she could remember the direction she had been heading in and could see some stars on the horizon. How to get out though?

She began to scrape at the snowdrift with the hand that was not holding the sacking. She caught onto a stunted root. Hoping against hope she grabbed at it and tried to pull herself up. Just then she heard the squelching of footfalls approaching her in her predicament. It was apparent that someone was coming near to her. With what little breath was left to her in the icy weather she summoned up the semblance of a scream for help. As the person came near in fright she saw that it was an old woman dressed all in black with wispy untidy gray hair escaping from underneath the hood of her cape over her head. A voice croaking in the near nighttime mist met her ears. She heard the old woman near to her say:

"Who is it? Who is down there? Donella screamed at her:

"Don't come near here madam! It's snow covering a fox's hole that I have fallen into. A voice came to Donella's ears:

"My child I will try to help you. You are lucky that I came upon your plight. See I am wearing two cloaks for warmth. I will take one off and use it to pull you out." She cackled on chiding Donella for being out so late.

"Thank you, thank you old mother!" Donella gasped. The good old woman gave what Donella could just see for the woman's senility, a baring of the toothless gums, meant to be a smile. She croaked:

"You be on your way my child. It's late enough as it is and you should be home by midnight." Donella said confidingly:

"I'm on my way to deliver a parcel to the monks at the monastery. I'll be all right. The stars will light my way back and, is that a half moon that I see rising over there?" The old woman cackled:

"Go on with you now. I'm on my way myself." Donella panted:

"Thank you again old lady and to you heart felt thanks for rescuing me."

Donella's outer garments were soaked but she could not discard them. The clothes nearest to her skin were dry enough. Thank goodness her mother had made her dress up warmly. She could see the outlines of the monastery a black shape against the sky ahead of her. At least she knew that she was walking in the right direction. The monks must have heard her, for then flooding the building came a dim lighting of the building by candlelight, she thought for the monk's evening prayers. She was right. As she came closer she could hear the almost monotonous plainsong chanting of vespers being sung. She approached carefully. If they were celebrating their evensong, she wondered how long they would be at it. Perhaps she should wait.

Shivering in the cold she waited a while outside the high surrounding walls.

Then it became unbearably cold just standing in the snow. She walked around the wall covered with lichen, moss and tufts of snow. She was looking for an entrance door where she could at least knock loudly or even there might be a bell. Soon she came around to a large wooden entrance door. As luck would have it there was a bell-pull and she would not have to hurt her knuckles by thumping on the door itself that she could see was iced over.

The rope of the bell that she was about to pull was tattered and frayed and uncomfortable to the touch. She drew in a freezing breath and pulled hard. A melancholy clanging hit her ears. She had been hesitant about pulling the rope afraid it would break it looked so tattered. She had thought that the icy frost clinging to the bell pull might clinch the matter of it fraying completely. Then where would she be?

The monks inside had stopped and then again started their chanting again after the bell had sounded. It was clear that they knew someone was waiting outside so Donella knew now that she would receive some sort of response to her summons on the entrance bell. She was right. Above the sound of the singing inside the monastery and the gushing of the falling snow the chanting came more loudly to her ears as the door of the monastery grated open. It too must be iced up she thought.

The evening was drawing on and becoming colder. She wondered if her apparent approaching benefactor was afraid of a possible molester for the monk who was coming to open the great door to the outside was walking very slowly. It seemed an age to wait and standing still as she was with only her inner garments being dry to say the least feeling most uncomfortable. A tiny ray of light was now moving closer to her outside the door. The welcoming monk must have a shaded lantern or candle. She marveled that he had in fact been so quick to come out.

She surely could not have been waiting that long. The little light was visible even though the monastery windows were shedding a stronger glow behind the approaching man who was nearly at the door. She heard a gruff greeting but she knew any sound she made would not be heard. Surely he would open up the door. She heard a rusty lock being turned with what sounded like an equally rusty key. The door grated open. It was obvious that it was not often used, perhaps once a month for food supplies to be carted in.

A cowelled head peered around the door covering a young pinched face. The figure of a monk made its appearance. Donella was struck with fright seeing the man's long brown robes with the golden brown tasseled cord worn around his waist.

Both persons it seemed did not quite know what to make of one another or what was expected one of the other. Brother Paul, for that was his name was wondering what the abbot would say if he offered this girl temporary shelter on this frozen evening. What had she come to the monastery for? He racked his brains before stammering out a question to Donella.

"Who are you my sister? What is it that you want?"

His words were jittery and stumbling with amazement at the damp forlorn sight of the poor girl. She held her breath wondering if this young monk was the right person to give the carefully cared for manuscript to. He seemed quite as nervous as she was but she stuttered out the words:

"This is a Franciscan monastery? Am I at the right place." The young monk responded somewhat more eagerly now that she had broken the ice so to speak.

"Oh! Yes! My little sister we are a monastery of twenty monks here. Will you venture to take some shelter for an hour or two to explain why you are here in this inclement weather?"

Donella was perplexed as to what to answer, what to do at this invitation. Then she took courage. Perhaps she should be speaking to someone older, a senior of his. She did not think that he would realize the importance of her mission. At last she now had an entrée into the monastery. She was sure they would be kind to her if the young monk took her inside:

"Yes, yes. Could I come inside for a moment? I would like to give something to someone older than yourself. That is with no offence meant to you."

She looked at the young monk earnestly and questioningly. What would his reply be? It was not long in coming.

"But of course my sister. Brother Andrew will be only too pleased to cater to your needs. We never turn anyone away from this monastery. I will take you inside. Come with me now."

She stood inside the gate to one side as Brother Paul firmly latched it. She felt shut in and claustrophobic but it seemed that he wished to help her and be kind. Their feet squelched in the heavy snow as they walked up to the front door of the monastery. It appeared then that another of the monks was waiting for them as the entrance door was opened slowly.

Another older monk made his appearance. He was clearly the head of the monastery and was concerned about the young monk who had made a foray out into the snow to see who the unexplained visitor was. He had a red but wizened old face and as he spoke showed a compassionate manner. He said slowly in a querulous but pained voice;

"My young brother who is this little sister that you have brought into our monastery? Is she in need?"

The young monk began stammering out what he had been told by the young girl that was not as yet much. He said:

"It seems….. it seems that she has a valuable parcel to give us for safe keeping here at the monastery. She has not yet explained to me what it is or how she has come by it. Perhaps Father Andrew she will not be afraid to tell you about it because I can see she is very nervous. I do not think that the thunder and lightening outside now are making matters any better. The old monk summoned up words to ask her why she was here:

"Come now my daughter, surely you can say what it is that you have with you? We will not hurt you my child."

At these words of comfort from old Father Andew Donella lifted her bowed head. Suddenly her shyness was gone and she ventured forth in a tumble of words:

"My friend the Herzog Viktor Tazner was given this scroll of music manuscripts at a soirée held at the Judge's villa where I am employed as a 'cellist."

Some other monks had now gathered around protectively and the number of the company of brothers was again making Donella nervous. One of them said:

"Ah! The Herzog Tazner! I know him well. We have met often in the village while I was gathering provisions for the monastery. Another broke forth:

"A scroll of music? But where has it come from? Who gave it?"

Old Father Andrew frowned benignly at this commotion. Donella spoke amongst the group of brothers:

"An unknown person gave it to Herr Tazner who gave it to me for safekeeping. My father discovered that I had it and bade me give it in at this monastery as he is of the opinion that it is valuable. We do not know what to do with it otherwise. The old monk spoke while the thunder rolled and lightning flashed outside.

"My child you have done right to bring the manuscript of 'cello concertos to us at the monastery. The monks now and in the future will see that it is kept safely here until it is needed once more. I do fear for you safety at present as the evening is drawing in and it seems that there is a storm brewing with a heavy snowfall outside. We can let you have an oil lantern to light your way home." "Yes," responded Donella, "I live in a chalet in the middle of the forest but thank you for the loan of the lamp to see me on my way. I am not afraid of the storm outside." The old monk said with warmth and compassion in his voice:

"You are very brave my child. Brother Gustave will see you out and on your way." Another of the monks handed her a shaded lighted lantern.

Oh! Thank you brother," she said. "If you will let me out I will be going. "Come then my sister," said the young monk, "the sooner you are on your way the better because time is fleeting now."

She left the monastery then as the lightning flashed and the thunder rolled again and again. She took her bearings from the monastery from where there was a dim light as she looked back now and again using the lantern to light her steps. The snow was thick but she managed in the courage of youth to find her way through the forest.

The leaves of the trees were falling now that it was winter. The storm began to abate. Now and again the wick in the glass covered lantern began to flicker but luckily it stayed alight and soon the glow lighted her to within sight of her father's chalet. She let out a sigh of relief and stumbled the last few yards her fingers ice cold holding the lamp that Father Andrew had lent to her.

Her mother must have had her ears cocked for any sound of her returning daughter. She had begun to worry fretfully when the storm had hit the area where they lived. She and her husband had begun to spar with one another with the worry of their daughter out in the thick snow. Josina said defensively:

"I had no option but to let her go to the monastery. The weather was so unpredictable the whole day."

Donella's mother and father waited anxiously. Josina was finding that Ernst was becoming very crabby of late. They had always hit it off together but he was finding his daughter's practicing on her 'cello quite tiresome. This was especially when he came home in the evenings after a day's work crouched over his woodcarving that old father Grüssman who was his employer required of him. Josina had noticed this happening gradually over the last few years and especially that he was taking it out on their daughter. Josina had quite literally had to hide herself from people as she and Ernst had at first never married but had stayed together as common law husband and wife. Josina also feared discovery or at the least interference by her father. At the present recent time waiting for the return of Donella out of the snowstorm he became positively bad tempered saying:

Why did you let her go out even? You must have seen that the weather was threatening. I am taking no responsibility if she is in danger." Josina was for once near to tears as the minutes ticked on and Donella did not return. She said nearly sobbing:

"She must be coming home any minute now." She was right. The couple heard the sound of the door handle turning from outside. Josina breathed a heavy sigh of relief and said to Ernst:

"Do not be harsh with her please Ernst. It is not her fault that she had to take the manuscript to the monastery. You were the one who asked her to go." Ernst answered gruffly pleased in his way that Donella was back safely:

"It was not that I was cross about it. I just felt that she could have chosen a more auspicious time of day to do the errand. Not at a time of day when there was thunder and lightning and pitch blackness outside. Josina lowered her head beaten again by Ernst's words as was becoming a habit of hers only to lift it again to welcome her daughter:

"Donella! Oh! My darling girl. You are back safely. She did not at first notice the lantern that the young monk had given her to light her way through at first but her father did, and immediately picked on her in his exasperation at worrying about her safety.

"Where did you get that lantern?" Donella answered head down:

"One of the monks lent it to me". Ernst chided then.

"It must be given back to them the soonest possible."

CHAPTER 8

As was becoming a habit with her Donella put her head down in shame. She had been very fond of her father as a young growing girl but could not understand the ongoing vituperation that he was showing towards her mother and herself. Josina had confided in her daughter that she feared for his sanity. Donella comforted herself at the remembrance of her mother's words of just the day before:

"I have persuaded your father to see the local doctor. He is constantly losing his temper with me and for your sake Donella your father and I must stay together. I have nowhere else to go nor have you. I dare not go back to my father's villa. I know the judge will never take me back after what I have done in leaving my home with one of his hired hands. My only choice was to persuade Ernst to see the doctor. He is being entirely unreasonable and is talking of leaving his place of employment. That will leave you and I as the sole breadwinners here at the chalet. It would mean your father would have nothing to do all day and all our nerves would be shattered if this were so. You have your 'cello practicing and I have my washing and housekeeping but we would have a pittance to live on. I fear that he is very ill."

Donella thought again about what her mother had said and hoping that her father would calm down in his questioning about the lantern decided to explain patiently how it had come into her possession. She ventured showing her fear of her father:

"You know that you told me that I should take the vellum manuscripts to the Franscican monastery on the other side of the forest so that it might be in their safekeeping?" Her father interrupted her quite ill temperedly:

"Yes, yes Donella. Did you do as I told you? You do not always listen to what I say nor does your mother. This makes me very angry." Donella answered afraid:

"Often I am at my 'cello practicing and trying to concentrate when you speak to me. It takes me quite a while to realize that you are asking me something." Her father responded angrily:

"Your 'cello. Always your 'cello. You should be busying yourself around the chalet and helping your mother."

Josina felt relieved when she saw that her daughter had returned safely and both Donella and her mother shrugged off Ernst's bad tempered reception at his daughter's return. At his question as to where Donella had found the lantern she was still carrying the girl realized that she must put out the light within the lamp. This her father ungraciously helped her to do. The evening was growing late and all those in the family felt ready for sleep after the upset.

As Donella snuggled into her pillow thankful to her mother that she was home and dry her thoughts fell on her experiences earlier that evening. What was the young monk's name whom the Abbé had ordered to take the scrolled manuscript from her? His friendly ruddy face had made a deep impression on her. That was it. He was called Brother Paul by the old Abbé. It had been a nightmare experience for her, a young girl inexperienced in life, to find herself surrounded by the group of monks all solicitous for her welfare as was of course their calling in life.

She tried to imagine what Brother Paul had done with the manuscript he had taken from her that was the reason that she had made the journey through the snow and across the forest to the old monastery. The last words she had heard the Abbé say to Brother Paul were:

"Take the scroll up to the attic and find a safe place to put it. There are shelves up there with copies of the music for the organ that we use to sing to in the chapel. Try to see that it does not become mixed up with our own books of organ music. Put it on the top shelf where it will not be noticed. We will see to our new possession another time."

Donella remembered his words clearly and made a mental note of them so as to ask Viktor the next time why he had the manuscript in his possession but all he had replied to her was:

"It was quite unexpected that I was given the scroll of musical notations. I had no idea who the little man was who flung open the door in the middle of the musician's performance at the soirée." Donella remembered her answer to Viktor at his statement about the scroll. She had answered:

"It seemed to me that he was a valet, some sort of servant. Maybe he was given charge of it and had heard that there were musicians playing at the judge's villa who would know what to do with it." She drifted off to sleep worried at the likeness of the person Viktor had told her about to her own father.

When she had awoken and dressed the next morning after breakfast she was greeted with a barrage of criticism about bringing the monk's lantern into the chalet.

"What else would I have done to light my way home through the darkness of the forest in the late evening?" She answered her father as reasonably as she could. "Brother Paul only wanted to help. I can take it back sometime soon. I am sure the Abbé does not need it urgently."

Her father's ill temper was increasing day by day and as her mother had confided in her:

"He is becoming almost irrational. We used to be such a friendly couple but I think the fact that we were once only common law man and wife has pulled apart his reputation in our village community and people are whispering about us. He is becoming cruel to me verbally because of this and the thought has come to me that I fear for his sanity. This has been continuing now for the last few years and is worsening. He is unwilling to see a doctor about it but I am keeping on at him to take this step. I am trying to appeal to the last vestiges of his good nature that I knew once as a young girl. I even suspect from what he has told me about his daily activities that he has taken to stealing."

Donella immediately thought: was it a stolen codex that the intruder who could have been her father had given to Viktor? Her mother continued.

"He was never like this before but now blames me for our situation." Josina took a deep breath. "I must confide in you Donella that I was a child of the judge at the villa where your father worked that was how we met. My own father was as mean as mustard. He would not allow me to have friends and I was forced to hobnob with the servants at the villa for company. When I eloped with your father he did not even bother to find out where I was living. If he did make enquiries I was not aware of it."

Donella was shocked to hear this tale of woe but asked her mother:

"I suppose you do not want me to say anything to anyone about our connection to the Judge? I can understand that. Sometimes he makes an appearance at the soirées. He is altogether very gracious to his guests but must be covering up a great lack in his personality. He is an older man now." Josina said:

"Over the years I have built up a regret for leaving what was a luxurious life at my father's villa. It has been hard living a life of poverty with your father a humble woodcarver. He knows this and blames me for the circumstances we find ourselves in. He has never known what it is to be wealthy as I have you see Donella." Josina finished by saying: "I hope all that I have confided in you is not upsetting you Donella."

Her daughter replied listlessly. She did not know what she should answer to her mother's concern about the bare facts that she had revealed. On the one hand she felt immensely proud of the news that her grandfather was in the legal profession actually at the peak of his calling, a judge in the community where they lived. On the other hand she could not reconcile his high standing with the lowliness that was her father's status in life. Not only his status but the fact that it was apparent that he was slowly losing his mental faculties and her mother was having the utmost difficulty persuading him to see the local doctor about his failing health. He had though agreed to keep a doctor's appointment about the matter the following week. He had been upsetting everybody with uncalled for behavior. Josina settled down to keep her hand in at her 'cello for the afternoon until bathing and dressing for the evening. Later on she heard her father grumbling most unpleasantly:

"Josina I find it most inconvenient that I should have to transport Donella to the villa on the sleigh. Can't she arrange with friends or members of the ensemble where she performs for a lift?" She heard her mother's clear voice standing up for her. Donella had her heart in her mouth. She needed the lift to the villla. "I did tell you Ernst that she has an acquaintance a nobleman friend of the judge's family, who has offered to lift Donella to and from the soirées. You turned this down and now you are complaining about it." He replied:

"Herzog Tazner, I know. You know very well that we or I at any rate are not of the Herzog's social standing. I do not want our family to be involved with the likes of him. It is not our place."

Clearly the couple, Donella's parents had an unbalanced social relationship of long standing that was causing Ernst's illness. Donella's father nevertheless provided the sleigh for the ride to the villa with bad grace. Fortunately just then Josina saw that Donella was ready to leave as her husband waited impatiently. Her father drove the sleigh in an act of sulky energy to the villa where Donella was playing with the judge's hired ensemble that evening. He did not speak to her while they were traveling.

Donella caste her mind back over what her mother had told her about their relationship with the judge at the villa. She gave a start once again as she realized that the mean crusty old man who appeared from time to time during the Saturday evening soirées was none other than her grandfather. She wondered that he had made no attempt to trace her mother who was his daughter.

It seemed that after Josina had eloped with her father he had deliberately cut all ties with her. She also could not understand what had happened to her grandmother. From what little her mother had told her the old person was sickly and kept to her bedchamber while Josina was living at the villa. Donella imagined that in all probability she had passed away even, for amongst the guests at the soirée's interval she was never spoken about nor did she ever appear with the Judge her grandfather who hosted the evenings.

They were soon at the villa and her father left with bad grace after dropping her off. Donella trundled up the stairs to the auditorium with her 'cello. There were a number of minutes in hand while those who had already arrived waited for the latecomers. Herr Auberg stood on the podium studying his conductor's music scores. Donella scanned the guests for a sight of Viktor.

Her heart jumped then as after a while when watching the entrance she espied him coming through the door to the guest lounge with all the elegance and tastefulness of manner that she had come to expect from him. She bit her lip. He was a man of the aristocracy. What could she ever be to him, a young girl of humble birth even though her grandfather as she now knew the judge to be, was clearly closely known to him.

She had her looks yes but had scarcely time or place in the chalet to pamper her appearance with powder and paint as could clearly be seen amongst the coquettes frequenting the soirées. Donella clung to the fact that the few fleeting glimpses that she had of herself in a cracked old mirror belonging to her mother told her that she was young anyway, and was a pretty girl. Did she even dare to think of herself as a beauty?

She was ready. She tried to think how she could keep her father's bad temper from upsetting her. She did not want to give a poor performance as a result of his attitude, one of resentment towards her on the way to her grandfather's villa. Her grandfather! The old Judge, as her mother had after all her years of girlhood now told her! Josina had not had the time, and Donella could understand it, to request from her daughter what she now knew was to be kept in confidence. She was aware that she was not allowed to divulge her relationship to her grandparents or not just yet.

It seemed that her father was dimly aware that Josina had invited Donella's confidence in the matter and was behaving in an unbalanced way because of it. She thought that the first stage in reconnecting the relationship and she wondered if that was even the right thing to do, would be to enquire discreetly as to the presence or rather lack of it of her Grandmother.

They arrived. Sulkily her father turned and left. Donella made her way to the little orchestral area and turned her mind to her music scores in a quick concentrated look. The other musicians were all ready to wait for the guests to finish arriving and then to attend to the appearance of the dapper and sprightly Herr Auberg, their conductor.

As they waited the 'cellists whispered, though audibly to their counterparts about their readiness to cope with the more obtuse passages in the music they would perform that evening. The violinists and other instrumental players did likewise. Soon the shuffling of feet and soft anticipatory wave of chat died down. Herr Auberg was in command of the evening. Then it seemed like no time at all that the first part of the concert was over. The players fingered and felt the crispness of the new scores as they prepared for the next part of the entertainment. It was interval and Donella's eyes concentrated as she relaxed slightly, and then fell on someone who held her attention immediately. Yes, it was Viktor. She saw his sleek dark hair shining beneath the chandelier. As she looked at him she did not notice the expression on his face at first but saw his neat cravat and the flowing white shirt with leather jacket that he was wearing. She noticed his elegant black leg wear and polished black boots. Then she set her eyes again on his facial expression.

The sound of the Mozart music that Herr Auberg had just conducted for them in rang in Donella's ears. A typical musician her eyes were everywhere from attending to her conductor's final control of the last beat of the music before interval started, to her fellow 'cellist who sat next to her and to the score on the music stand before her. She glanced too at the small group of violinists and as they all sat aback with the closure of the piece of music she felt free to search out Victor in the audience.

Her heart fluttered. Now it was not she only who was looking for Viktor. No he was already holding a steady gaze at the lovely young girl. She blinked her eyes still not ready to take on the social occasion that was before them all now at the interval. Her mind was leaping ahead to the next work of music to be performed. She questioned herself as her gaze settled on Viktor. Would she have done enough work, enough practicing to give full value to what she was being paid to be part of the Judge's employed music ensemble?

Still Vikor's face remained immobile. It was up to her to rise from her seat and join him. He was tacitly from a distance asking her to do this. As she rose she saw a grotesquely clad woman approach Viktor. The woman seemed to be dressed in violently clashing colors with an extraordinarily elaborate hairstyle. On second glance as she neared Viktor the woman, she realized was only dressed up for the soirée. She wondered. Was it a form of jealousy at the attention the other socialite was paying Viktor at present that she seemed to stand out so in her thinking? She saw Viktor rise and come towards her.

"Donella!" He said almost breathlessly. "How overjoyed I am to see you again. The older woman produced a fan and interrupted Viktor's attempt at the conversation with Donella and before the young 'cellist could say word said:

"I am sure these musicians know very little about what they are doing. They do not seem to be in touch with reality at all!"

The woman addressed Donella with such spite that the young girl was dumfounded. Viktor felt obliged to enter into the conversational fray. The atmosphere he felt was becoming somewhat nasty. He had passed the time politely with the socialite who was now forcing herself he felt, into his group. The violinists were beginning to whisper amongst themselves. Viktor could just hear that they were lining up to cross swords with the interfering guest who was building on her first assertion that the musicians knew very little about what they were playing. She said:

"See Viktor these performers are too afraid even to vouch for the fact that it was Beethoven music that they were playing!"

This statement that was inherently foolish made Donella's face burn. The young 'cellist could not contain her feelings any longer. Just before she spoke she saw Vikotr's intense gaze swing form the instigator of the furore to herself. He was about to speak but saw that Donella was in control of the situation. She pronounced in what was for her a loud voice:

"Didn't you know it was not a Beethoven work but a Mozart concertina that we were playing?"

At this point the female guest put her foot in it even more and complained pouting in an ugly manor:

"Why has the Judge not given us some program notes to follow so we guests can have a better idea about what we are listening to? Am I to be just left to guess?"

In a fury Vikor could see, Donella stated:

"I would have thought that anyone who attended such gatherings as these knew or at least could recognize such music as we play in this ensemble. Mozart works are widely performed throughout the neighboring palatinates and most people can recognize his works."

The woman who had taken up the cudgels against Donella now started a high flown conversation with another guest regarding the display of eats. As it could be expected now from this woman who had been in the audience she was criticizing the way the delicacies were being presented on the tables. To every one else they looked delightful. Viktor ushered Donella away to fetch plates for themselves, saying:

"She is too wealthy and high born for her own good. I wish she would leave me alone. She always attaches herself to me on these occasions."

Viktor put an end to the gathering for himself and Donella. The young 'cellist hastened to set her music scores into their case and fastened up her 'cello securely. Viktor had insisted on lifting her home on his sleigh. She made her way off the orchestra podium to where Viktor was for the moment standing alone. Before their bête noir the female guest could get near him again and hold up their leave taking he lead Donella out into the snowy night.

It was magic to Donella to feel alone with Viktor in the darkness lit only by a few lanterns swaying in the hands of the servants of the Judge who was showing the guests out. Viktor took Donella's 'cello while she climbed onto the sleigh her ankle turning painfully as she tried to press her left leg into the snowy mass to find the pressure to lift her body onto their means of transport. Viktor said as he put the sleigh in motion:

"We are away Donella. How relieved I am to be out of that stuffy auditorium now."

She raised her voice over the wind, responding:

"Oh yes Viktor! The socializing we had to do to please our host was becoming quite odious. I was deeply hurt by the female guest who questioned a musician's knowledge of music. Of course I have never studied at a music college so perhaps do not know as much as some mature music lovers."

Viktor cut in sharply supporting her feelings:

"She had no right to speak as she did. I found her most offensive too. I thought you reacted most bravely, a young girl as opposed to her maturity. Then ever alert Donella cried:

"It looks as if we have arrived somewhere."

The sleigh bells had been gently ringing all the way back to Viktor's villa that was their destination. Thick clumps of fir trees surrounded the elegant old villa lying lower down on the Austrian Alps slopes. The sleigh bells stopped but their arrival had been heard by the waiting servants, three of whom came out to welcome the couple and take away the sleigh for the time being.

Viktor and Donella tramped through the snow and were soon ensconced in the warmth of the interior of the villa in the comfortable guest room. The laughingly brushed off the snowflakes from their clothes and the snow particles disappeared into the colorful rug on the floor. Donella watched as they dissolved deep in thought so there was silence between the couple, Viktor wondering what she was so pensive about.

Both of them seemed reluctant to break the peace that had settled between them in Viktor's luxurious guest room. Viktor's deep voice broke the atmosphere that they had created for it seemed that Donella was never going to speak. Viktor felt then that he had to take the manly option and begin a means of communication between them.

"You are so quiet Donella. It is not like you. You were so outspoken towards the Judge's guest who tried to take the upper hand with you. You do know that she was jealous don't you?"

She nodded still not saying a word. Viktor continued:

"That woman has been dogging my footsteps for weeks on end new. I have been trying to shake her off but was unsuccessful until tonight, a climax when you spoke your mind to her. It was a release to me. Donella?"

Viktor came up close to her and put his index finger under her bowed head lifting it gently

"Oh! Viktor!" Donella's voice was emotional.

"I hated to take an upper hand in the situation but I was so insulted. I come from humble origins you know. It pained me to have to speak out. And in company too. I could have lost my employment as a musician in the ensemble if she had complained to the Judge. Viktor I would like to confide in you. You have taken such an interest in me, you have been so kind."

Viktor responded she could tell he was a little hurt

"Is that all I am to you Donella? Just a kind person? Just someone to confide in?"

Donella countered urgently needing him to understand what she was getting at. She burst out:

"My mother told me last night that the judge is my own grandfather. I was not supposed to repeat this to anyone but cannot keep the truth to myself. You will want to end our relationship I know when tell you that she also told me that my father was an impoverished handyman in the service of my grandfather with whom my mother eloped. They were married though. It seems that my grandfather had a coverted awareness of the whereabouts of his daughter, the little chalet in the woods where she lived with my father but was reluctant to interfere."

Viktor took her hand and held it tightly not replying immediately. She followed these words saying:

"I suppose now that you know the truth about my birth you as an aristocrat in this palatinate will wish to end our relationship."

Viktor spoke for the second time since their arrival at his villa.

"That is exactly the opposite of what the attitude of the nobility have towards those of, shall we say lesser breeding than themselves. You have been excellently educated Donella, by the nuns and that together with your musical training makes up for anything that your parents may have done."

Feeling Viktor would understand what was happening to her Donella uttered miserably:

"I was an outcast even among my fellow scholars. Word got out about the fact that my father was of nearly peasant origin and that my mother was something of a mystery woman, someone they could not make head or tail of. My parents were at least married. The only person who treated me kindly was the old nun who gave me my 'cello lessons once a week, Mother Armentia. She could be very strict but always had such patience with my strivings in my 'cello practicing. She was the only friend that I had at the convent. It is she I must thank for my ability to earn the pittance that I do in the Judge's music ensemble."

Viktor had been listening to her but was taking delivery of two mugs of hot chocolate at the same time. As she finished confiding in him he said;

"Well you have another friend now Donella, myself. And I hope I can be more than that even to you also."

Donaella's heart thumped as she took cognizance of Viktor's last words. What could he mean? They sipped the hot chocolate drinks slowly and then sat back quietly together on the couch that was lined with silken covering. Viktor slid his arm around the back of the seat thus showing Donella, and she had noticed this about him, some appropriation of a beautiful young girl. He asked her:

"Are you unhappy at home then Donella?" She answered despairingly:

"My mother I am angry with for putting me in the position of a half breed. She is kind enough to me but I know she wishes to use me to reinstate her own position in her father the judge's household. He has long since washed his hands of her. This is because she has fears that my father is loosing his mind and she will have to turn him into a sanatorium. His mental health is deteriorating and she is fearsome of having no income to live on.

Viktor broke into Donella's tale of woe concerning her family:

"It sounds as if your family is going through a really chaotic time. It seems as if your father is losing his mind." "Yes," answered the young girl, "and I feel so guilty because all our family's life I have had to practice on my 'cello. My teacher, old Mother Armentia would not have it any other way. I fear the constant sounds that my instrument makes has driven him to insanity. I have told my mother this but she says he has consulted a doctor in the village and will have to be permanently hospitalized in the near future. He does not know this as my mother fears the anger he might show when he is told. She has also confided in me that she is desperately short of money to keep the household running and it will be even worse when my father is in the sanatorium. She says it is not only me who is responsible for this but the fact that she and he are from two different classes of people.

I am paid a pittance by the Judge my grandfather for my services as a 'cellist in the little ensemble that he employs for his Saturday evening soirées. He is completely unaware that I am his granddaughter. I know though. Do you think he would help us if he knew our predicament Viktor?"

Viktor looked perturbed at what Donella had told him but came up with the words:

"My family has known the Judge for many years. I even remember visiting his villa when I was just a young boy. He has always been rather a mean and cynical person, less so of course when he was younger. I can recall the upset he was caused in his life when his daughter disappeared. From what you tell me Donella, his daughter who eloped with one of his handymen servants is none other than your mother. It seems that she is in dire straits now.

Her father the Judge is an extremely difficult and most eccentric old man quite unapproachable in fact from what I hear. He would be absolutely against a reunion with his long lost daughter." Donella asked Viktor:

"Would he soften his attitude do you think if it was made known to him that I was his granddaughter?" Viktor replied to this:

"He is far gone in his older years. I think he would only be vaguely aware of you if you made yourself known to him as his granddaughter, yes " He continued:

"It does seem Donella that life has thrown us together at a time when both of us are enduring severe sadness and difficulty. Mine is the sadness of having lost both my dearly loved parents so tragically but yours is the difficulty of venturing out into the big wide world to earn a living, alone. I will be so upset if you have to leave the Judge's musical ensemble to find work of a more important nature, such as in the town orchestra somewhere not too far away at least. It sounds to me that your father's health also is permanently impaired. It will just be a matter of time I suppose before he can be admitted into the sanatorium."

Donella found tears pricking her eyes at the sympathy and understanding that Viktor was showing towards her.

"Yes I know," she began in response to what Viktor had said, "and then how will my mother collect to washing that she does for the townspeople that she works at for a living? I suppose that my uncle could help a little. I cannot bear the thought of leaving Herr Auberg's ensemble. To begin with it would mean that I would never see you again, Viktor."

Viktor was moving towards her to take her in his arms but pulled up short at her emotional outburst cajoling a little in the situation:

"Do I mean that much to you Donella? Even after meeting so few times.?"

He was taller than she was and he looked down on the face puckered with sobbing. He said trying to put their togetherness in lighter vein, being a man:

"All is not lost Donella. Even if you are forced to leave the musical ensemble I will make sure that I know where you are performing elsewhere. If so I am certain someone as talented as you will easily find a post in the nearby town orchestra. It is not many who have the training that you do or as I can tell from watching and hearing you playing at your 'cello, are so talented."

Donella pulled herself together at Viktor's compliments.

"So I'll always be able to see you Viktor?" Suddenly he put his arms around her the first physical move that he had made towards her. Her lips melted as she felt her mouth searching for hers. After that passionate embrace Viktor continued:

CHAPTER 9

"From what I understand from the usual guests at the Judge's musical evenings he is passionate about the entertainment that he gives on a Saturday evening with his hired ensemble. His wife is ailing seriously in her health and never appears socially. As you might know he has been retired from his judicial practice for a couple of years now and never mentions the fact of his daughter's disappearance. It is rumored that he is quite aware of her whereabouts but is too bitter about her relationship, last heard of in common law marriage with a former servant of his, to make any contact with her. He does not know that you are his granddaughter."

Donella responded to these facts with a telling what her mother knew, imparted to her a couple of evenings ago. Her father had been working late and she and her mother had been having supper together. Donella explained:

"My mother told me of my father's impending placement into a sanatorium on the outskirts of the town.

She told me that if he was not willing to be admitted the doctors were going to use physical force to see that he was taken in at the hospital." Her mother said desperately to her daughter:

"What is wrong with him do you think Donella?" Donella's face was a blank. Josina whispered confidentially:

"It is apparent that he is suffering from a recently discovered disease of the brain. It has been affecting his thought processes for nearly a year now. I am suffering badly from his worsening cruelty, and it appears from what I can see that he is losing his sanity! He has told her that he has apparently been stealing by putting himself as an imposter offering to clean out attics. I think that is how he found the Vivaldi Codex that you lodged at the old monastery on the other side of the forest a few months ago. I think Ernst was afraid of being found out as the monks confirmed it could be very valuable."

Viktor sympathized with Donella:

"You must feel caught right in the center of this situation. How awful for you. He changed his tack saying:

"Do have some more of the wine. I am pleased that I am the one to whom you can tell all this to. It must have been weighing on your mind heavily. I too have a certain amount of manipulation in my family, from my parents for quite a while before they died. My ex-betrothed had manoeuvered herself through them into the relationship with me as my fiancée. She pandered to my parents who persuaded me to become engaged to her.

She used her ability for gaining the confidence of older people in the situation that happened as far as I was concerned. After they died tragically I was able to fob her off. You see I would have done anything to please my father and mother I was so fond of them."

Viktor came up short in his telling of his personal life. Why would Donella be interested even? He felt deeply physically attracted to the young girl and pitied the plight of her poverty. He mustered up the words:

"You are so beautiful Donella. I cannot keep my eyes off you when I am with your. You golden hair, your lovely face and your entrancing body drive me to distraction."

Donell's hair was pulled back with an old velvet gray ribbon that she had bought at a little costume shop in the nearby village. He had noticed it and said, suddenly shy of her presence:

"You make such a wonderful picture to me Donella. I will never forget this evening. May I untie your hair? You have made such a success of your life with your 'cello playing. I can tell that as Herr Auberg the conductor always seems to have extra time for you after the performances on Saturday evenings!"

They were suddenly shy in each other's presence, a couple of innocent young people. Donella certainly had no idea of what would ensue between them. She only knew that Viktor understood her, the way she had grown up at her 'cello lessons with old Mother Armentia that she had practiced for with such diligence, her time at her 'cello taking her out of the miserable poverty that she had been raised in. She said, instinctively wanting him to touch her:

"Loose my ribbon then Viktor. It feels tight and uncomfortable anyway. She felt Viktor's hands on her neck as he felt for the velvet. She noticed that he had turned the lamp low. He forced her gaze into his as he fumbled with the piece of velvet holding her hair in one place. She said:

"Do not let me lose my hair ribbon. It is all I have to keep my hair neat on these Saturday occasions."

Viktor responded urgently:

"Is that all you can think of at a time like this Donella?"

He pulled the velvet roughly off her hair. They were sitting together and his hands tugged at the straps of her black evening gown. Soon they were lying together on the couch, burning with desire for one another that they gratified for a while. Donella then pulled up short from their love making. Viktor slowly eased himself from her mystified at her gesture, she said:

"No Viktor. We musn't do this. He tensed at her voice. She fell in a heap on the couch as Viktor rose and began to pace the room near her. She said to her:

"I feel poetry coming to me at my feeling towards you Donella. You didn't know that I wrote poetry did you, girl? Oh! I think I did mention it to you." She replied from the cowed collapsed state she found herself in on the setee:

"I would not have thought that a humble person like myself could inspire such a proud and handsome man as you to compose words of elegance!" He answered enthusiastically:

"That's just it. Our very opposites in life contrast sharply in my brain. My parents would never have approved of what I see as a match between us, you in your lowly circumstances of doubtful parentage and my self being of aristocratic birth. But my mother and father are now dead."

He ceased from his talking as a bitter expression crossed his countenance for a few minutes after his advances towards her. Donella looked up at him knowing as she did so how he felt about his dear parents and how they had met their death in the riding accident. She said:

"Then it is my good fortune, while sympathizing deeply with you over their demise that I have your attention towards me Viktor. I am beginning to cherish what you feel for me. If you were to go away or if I was not able to see you Viktor I don't feel that I could bear it. Viktor ceasing in his pacing up and down, was listening to what she had to say. He said, hesitantly knowing that what he was about to tell her would cause her distress after what she had made known to him about her feelings.

"I will have to go away Donella. I was at the barracks this morning for my military manoeuver planning and my battle front superior informed the training troops that we will be leaving for the French border in a matter of two months. Donella do you see it? We have only a matter of weeks together before I leave for the north with my mounted battalion. Will you give me this time, these precious moments to be together? Will you?"

Viktor suddenly tensed his body at her reaction to what they had found in themselves, one towards the other. They tacitly agreed that it was time to halt. There would be other times like this they both knew. Donella suddenly proud of the allure she had obviously shown to Viktor tossed her hair back and her hands trembled as she searched for her velvet ribbon. While she held up her arms to catch up her long hair in a gesture so graceful that Viktor could not keep his eyes off her, he began to pace up and down on the thick woven rug.

What they wished they could say to one another hung in the air between them. Donella did not dare to be the first to speak. Instinctively she felt that the words should come from Viktor. Then he stood still and sat down next to Donella's now sedate though slumped figure on the couch. Her head was bowed. Viktor seemed to sense what she felt. He spoke with a clear confident voice:

"Please don't feel that I have taken advantage of you Donella, just because I am an aristocrat and you tell me that you have a humble peasant birthright. You know from your schooling at the convent that no one holds this against your. You have been educated to be a graceful young woman skilled at your musical instrument. You even earn your living with the use of it. All this in itself puts paid to your humble parentage. I certainly do not hold it against you. I respect what you have achieved in life."

Here Donella raised her head at his encouraging words. Typical of a young woman she was mystified as to the reason for her attraction. Her voice fell on Victor's ears clear as a bell:

"But where is this all leading us Viktor? I will not be able to be seen with you socially because of my background should you even want that. I have not even the clothes suitable for being seen with you even as an acquaintance." Viktor interrupted this flow of words saying humbly:

"And you would even consider being seen with me if you have the correct wardrobe? Donella I will see to this for you." Donella replied with verve at this offer, trying to summon up a reason for a dignified response:

"I will never be able to explain that away to my father and mother!"

She drew herself up at a loss to know how to respond to this offer of care. She had never experienced such luxury as it was clear to her that Viktor lived in. Suddenly she came to a conclusion and daringly as she thought at the time, summoned up courage to answer to his offer of this world's goods to her. She said:

"Viktor we must face up to the fact that you and I come from two very different worlds. Although the nuns at the convent where I was raised set their standards for me you have no idea of the poverty that I have lived in. My mother has told me that she wishes to use me to reinstate her relationship with her father the Judge at his villa, where am employed on Saturday evenings as a 'cellist in the little musical ensemble that you and I know so well.

She is desperate for me to do this but I have not the faintest idea of how to go about this. She needs the money you see. My father she has told me is at any time now going to be admitted on a permanent basis into the sanatorium for the mentally ill on the outskirts of the town. She and I will then have but a pittance to live on. She is sorry now that she was seduced by my father, my father's handyman. They are constantly at loggerheads and she has confided in me that the doctors are going to force his admittance to the hospital. What can I do?"

She ended this statement of her feelings on a hopeless note. Viktor as a nobleman felt immediate compassion towards the young girl to whom he was so attracted and came up to a solution to her problem. He had realized that her father was a commoner but had no objection to this as his family had been acquainted with Josina's family, that was Donella's mother's, for as long as he could remember. This was the reason he had been one of the guests at the Judge's soirées. He began, trying to sense out her feelings at what he was about to suggest to her:

"Donella you must affirm to your mother that she will be in dire need of financial help, help that only you can provide for her."

At this Donella looked even more dejected. She said softly but firmly:

"But how Viktor?" He replied equally firmly:

"You must tell her that you are taking on the work of a servant maid at a friend of her father's domicile. That means, here at my villa

This prospect at first appeared daunting to Donella and she managed to respond to Viktor's offer:

"Yes, my mother is desperate to reinstate her relationship with her father although he never had any time for her while she was growing up. Her mother was sickly but could not be bothered to help reinstate her at the villa after she eloped. He had no control over his daughter you understand." Viktor said:

"Don't worry about that. I am sure that the old Judge's heart will be softened when he realizes that you are his grandchild. Just to see the entrancing sight that you are – Donella – will be enough I am sure to encourage a patching up with the threads of his relationship with your mother."

"How will that even be possible Viktor?" She said. "Donella I have known the Judge since I was a child. For all his cantankerousness he still had friends of his own generation and if I visit him and make mention of my late parents, he will know immediately who I am" "Will you then make clear to him who I am, his granddaughter long unbeknown to him?" Questioned Donella. Viktor replied easily:

"He had always shown respect towards my family. He is getting on in years now and will want to see an heir to his vast estate. Both you mother and yourself were young once too so the crusty old man's heart will be warmed at the knowledge of your existence that I will impart to him." Donella asked:

"When will you tell him?" Donella challenged" Viktor replied:

"I do not think that I should have one special meeting with him to do this. I will approach him casually sometimes over the next few months at the Saturday evening soirées, and introduce him to you. I won't tell him at first who you are. He has an active mind for his age and will be able to place you as the new 'cellist in his ensemble."

Donellla pointed out worriedly to Viktor:

"It is not myself who is important in this hoped for family reconciliation. It is my mother. She is going to be near destitute with my father's illness. Will he help her do you think?" Viktor said:

"He still holds a grudge against his daughter Josina but I perceive that you would be a key figure in the reinstatement of financial and other help to your mother." Viktor continued:

"We can surely plan it so every problem we are experiencing between us comes together in a solution. You and I know how we feel about one another. These times we live in are very permissive. Your Grandfather need not know that you will be living here. He need only know you are my fiancée. Yes Donella. My fiancée."

My mother will never agree to that Viktor." Donella replied. So Viktor came up with a solution:

"You can tell her that you are being employed here as a housemaid. That situation ought to satisfy both she and you father. She needs the extra money that I am more than willing to provide for you and your papa was a servant himself so can have no qualms about the situation. The Judge will accept his daughter's new status as your mother and will not realize that you and I will be living in the same villa. I need not clarify our relationship as regards your mother and I am sure she will not have the gumption to tell him your and my relationship, that of a handservant, that is all she will know about it anyway."

Donella replied dumfounded at these schemes Viktor was making on her behalf.

"But Viktor you do not mind that I am really of humble origins with my father being only a handyman? I am constantly aware of it especially now that he has a strange illness that will cause him to be hospitalized." Viktor replied:

"No Donella my love. A true nobleman has nothing against those of inferior birth to himself. You had the very best of schooling. You must tell me about it. We will have all the time in the world once you are settled in here. If your grandfather the Judge realizes that you are his daughter's offspring you being such a beautiful young girl I am sure it will go a long way to melting the old man's heart. He will not go into any detail requiring from you only to know your status here as far as your mother is concerned. It will only serve to boost your mother's reinstatement in her father's household in the long run. She will probably be allowed to live at the Judge's villa able to care for him in his old age."

It seemed to Donella that Viktor would never stop speaking. She was so perturbed by this sudden new relationship that she scarcely took in what he was saying. As the husky dogs that would pull the sled began to bark outside needing the warmth of their kennels for the night, Viktor again took Donella's shoulder this time needing her to understand his plan. Afraid of the renewed physical attention that evening Donella stuttered out words of co-operation with his plan. She felt at a loss of making a decision about her future. Viktor spoke slowly:

"Donella you must do this for me. It is for everyone's good." She answered:

"Viktor I feel that I am being a pawn in this situation. I have no money of my own I give everything that I earn to my mother." He replied:

"That is why you must come and be here Donella. I will make sure your mother is remembered for what your father earns when he is finally forced into the sanatorium for his health's sake. That is of course if your mother's father refuses to take her back into the villa."

The circumstances were now becoming almost unbearable for Donella. She felt tears running down her cheeks. She would have to go along with Viktor's plans. Donella was attracted to him and the thought of being near to him on a day to day basis was turning her heart upside down. Both of them were coming down to reality as the dogs' yapping became more urgent. Viktor again took the upper hand and snapped out the words:

"We must leave now Donella! Your parents are waiting for you."

He took her arm. She moved quickly to snatch her cape and take up her 'cello. The two were soon seated on the sleigh. Viktor shouted to the huskies that were obedient to his commands. The snow was thick on the ground but the stars shone brightly above in the night. Donella's frightened face stared ahead as they approached the forest and it grew dark overhead among the trees. Then Viktor was kissing her as she tried to get indoors before her father came out to meet her. She was becoming more and more afraid of Ernst's mental state. Donella clutched her 'cello to her after she had disentangled herself from Viktor's arms. The door to the chalet opened slightly to receive her back home. Her mother ushered her in saying:

"Quiet Donella. Your father is sleeping". Donella whispered, thankful that Viktor's sleigh was sliding nearly silently away into the forest.

"I have good news mama. One of the guests at the soirée this evening has offered me work as a housemaid at his villa."

Josina gave a start at this news a possible change in her domestic situation that was becoming more and more unreliable. She said lightly:

"Hush my girl. We can talk about it in the morning."

Donella put her 'cello in it's place, washed quickly and hugged the bedclothes to herself as she fell asleep that night savoring what had happened between she and Viktor that evening. She awoke to the sound of her father who was as usual these days behaving aggressively towards his wife. It was apparent that Josina had told Ernst that Donella would be leaving. Donella, aiming to quieten the family upset quickly dressed and put in her part into the fray. Putting her wishes into the fracas, she broke in hearing that her mother was winning and getting the better of Ernst. She said:

"Father you must realize that very soon you will have to be admitted into the sanatorium. You know that the doctor is insisting on this. What can mother do alone here? I will have to help and this is the only way. The nobleman who will be employing me has told me that my mother might even be reinstated into her father the Judge's family."

Josina took the opportunity of Donella's father being told this news and spoke emotionally:

"It will be a solution to our financial problems. Ernst butted in showing his increased unreasonableness:

"What financial problems? You know I support you both Josina!" She answered:

"You know that you are becoming more and more depressed and irritable. Your employer you have told me is already complaining about your bad temper at work."

At this Ernst cowed by these statements that he knew were true, came up with his response:

"Alright then. Donella can pack her clothes and accessories and I will take her down to her new place of employment early next week."

After an awkward weekend with the couple and their daughter trying to pursue their separate tasks to keep their lives going in the chalet Ernst and Donella were packed and ready to leave for Viktor's villa, and Ernst for the sanatorium where he had been admitted, much to his displeasure. On the way he cruelly told Donella, and spitefully that he was only too pleased that he would not have to tolerate her practicing any long and muttering:

"I am certain that your continual scraping at you instrument is partly the cause of my breakdown. I don't know how your mother tolerates it." Donella tried to defend herself stating:

"Mother Armentia did not find my playing tiresome. She always praised me in the efforts I made. The conductor at the Judge's Saturday evening ensembles had also told me that he is quite satisfied with my part in our performances."

Ernst grunted to himself and there as a lapse into silence as the two dogs laboriously pulled the sleigh across the slopes to Viktor's abode. Ernst's final words to Donella as the sleigh pulled up in front of the villa where Ernst and Josina understood their daughter would be employed:

"It will pull your mother down a peg or two to realize that you are going to be employed as a housemaid. Do you good too to get stuck into menial tasks. He added pathetically: "It is what I have had to do all my life. You can support your mother for a change."

Donella was only half listening to her father now gathering up her accoutrements as a couple of men servants appeared to help her inside. It was obvious to them both that she was expected at the nobleman's villa. Then she saw Viktor was standing outside the grand front door of his domicile head bowed in thought at first and then when he saw the young girl who had so charmed him at his grandfather's soirées he earnestly raised his eyes to view the pathetic sight of Donella alone with her few valises and 'cello. He spoke:

"Donella! You have arrived safely at last. I have been anxious about you every second today until this minute. How are you?

Donella was near to sobbing with the way her father had treated her on the way to Viktor's villa, not to mention the change in her circumstances at her very young age. At the pathetic sight of the young girl standing in the snow whom he had come out to welcome, his heart warmed towards her. He was curious though as to the reason for her tears and asked:

"What has upset you Donella? I was hoping for a joyous reunion with you. Is it a family matter? Do come in out of this icy chill in the night into the warmth of my villa."

Donella in a state of isolation from her family clutched at Viktor's kind invitation. After all as she suddenly realized this dual role that she was to play with him in the future. As far as her parents were concerned she was being employed as a housemaid at the villa to supplement her income as a 'cellist in the Judge's musical soirées. With Viktor she was fulfilling a role of future wife unbeknown to any other of the aristocracy in the palatinate. Viktor was a learned young man having studied at the nearby university and he was entranced at the fluid skill of her actions as a 'cellist.

His parents had recently been killed in a riding accident, with his ex-fiancée a scheming woman under suspicion for this tragedy. He was now solely in charge of the villa that he had now inherited and had made this decision regarding Donella's accommodation. This was particularly because of the position that she found herself in regarding her supplementing of her parents income. She was very nearly an abandoned soul, where else could she go? He felt guilty too having led her on in their relationship.

Viktor helped the young woman with all her bits and pieces. Seeing how strained she looked he bade her put down her possessions and sit down a while. When he had brought her a glass of glühwein that she gratefully accepted then he asked her how she felt:

"My head has cleared a little now," she said. "My father had the last cruel say to me as we rode here in the sleigh. Do you know Viktor that he told me that I was nearly an illegitimate child. He and my mother were married though when I was born. My mother wants to ingratiate herself once more into her father's villa, using me as a go between. You said that your family were longstanding acquaintances of my grandfather the Judge. Do you think that he will welcome me as his grandchild? Or take my mother back after what she has done?"

Viktor was silent at this outburst of the unfairness and unkindness that Donella's parents had treated her with. After she had finished speaking her mind to him they were both quiet for some moments as tears welled up in Donella's eyes. She stuttered out some words in self defence at the social position that she had admitted herself to be in. Viktor did not appear to be moved by her reaction but said to her:

"Yes! Yes you are so like your grandmother. I can remember visiting your family with my own as a child. The Judge and his wife were always hospitable and friendly when they were younger. I used to enjoy being with their family."

He put his index finger under Donella's chin lifting her face towards his as he moved closer towards her and said softly:

"Yes I can see the likeness that you have to your grandmother. She was a motherly woman for all that she was married to the somewhat sharp and cynical Judge.

My mother was a pianist and both couples adored music, both performing and listening to it. I was always in awe of your grandfather on those visits. He was an arrogant man typical of his class to be found in this region. How your grandparents had such a longstanding relationship I do not understand. They are as different as chalk is from cheese.

I think that the Judge finally got the upper hand and made your grandmother just take to her bed with his dominating personality. She finally succumbed and died only a few years ago. He is now a bitter old man especially in the knowledge that his daughter defied his wishes and eloped with one of his handymen at the villa." Donella chimed in:

"That was my father. He has now had his final comeuppance. He is going to be admitted to a sanatorium for the nervously ill within days. What can I do Viktor to save my poor mama from destitution? She is desperate and sees no future in the life that she is living. I will only be able to help her a very little."

Viktor soothed her:

"I will see that your mother receives an allowance each month. It will only be a little because you and I are at present putting up a front that you are being employed as a housemaid here. That is what she agreed wasn't it?" Donella nodded eagerly and added:

"My mother told me she is hoping that my status as a musician in the Judge's household will gradually cause a reconciliation between she and her father."

Viktor looked pensive. Donella was coming to know him more and more as the soirées passed. At this particular time as she was making known to him what her mother was wishing her to do for she and her father. She understood that Viktor was thinking how he could help her poor dysfunctional family. Then he spoke:

"I came to know the Judge, your grandfather well as a growing boy. My parents' and your mother's although quite apart in age were well acquainted. When he was younger and less cynical as he is now he not only enjoyed music but also reading. My own father was well versed as a student of the arts in his younger days also. I seem to remember that the two older men studied at the same university near here. You must have heard talk of the institution?" Victor's glance flickered at her asking for an answer.

"Yes I did hear mention of the place now and again during my school days but did not take much notice of it. Will you help me Viktor? I am desperately worried about my mother. She dearly needs to be reinstated in her father's villa. You seem to be on good terms with the old man."

Viktor did not answer immediately pondering how he could help this entrancing young woman who seemed in dire need of family counseling. He had willingly taken the first step of allowing her to be accommodated at his villa, she also assenting to this so he said:

"I can help but this will all take time. You have told your mother that for the present you are doing a servant's work. Well, a musician in the long ago was considered as a servant. Perhaps we can get around this little white lie when you appear to your grandfather when we make known your true relationship to him. That is if we decide this at the time so as to put your mother in a more favorable light as far as the old Judge is concerned."

Donella was beginning to look more hopeful even enthusiastic. She was a little tense, knowing the plan that was unfolding would mean some hard work as a musician.

CHAPTER 10

On the last occasion of her being at her parents' chalet, Donella talked out her family situation with Viktor as time went on. Viktor was taking more and more of an avid interest in, and responsibility for Donella's well being. Josina was let into the secret of her daughter being ensconced at Viktor's villa, not just as a servant but as Donella could only explain it for the time being to her mother, as a companion to the bereaved young aristocrat.

She was also told of Viktor's close acquaintance with Josina's father's family and how Viktor hoped to help reinstate her with him at the villa. Donella explained that she would use the opportunity of being a musician already chosen to play with the evening soirée ensembles. She told her mother:

"I already feel more confident at these social evenings especially as Viktor has plenty of sharp retorts at the spiteful and jealous remarks made about myself and my playing in the little orchestra. These are mostly from aristocratic older women who attach themselves to Victor and I when we are partaking of the eats provided at these social evenings." Josina said lovingly though sharply:

"You must pander to these socialites Donella. They are our livelihood. That is until you can make it known to my father the Judge exactly who you are. It will come as a shock to him hopefully a pleasant one with your graciousness my daughter. If you can ingratiate yourself with Viktor's connivance in the cynical and bitter heart of the old man it will be all the better for us all."

Donella was hopeful for her mother's welfare now and seeing how anxious she was over the whole strategy enthused:

"It will be with Viktor's help and words of tact that this plan can succeed. When the old Judge sees how well both you and the nuns have cared for me he might well turn a blind eye to your prodigal nature, mother. Both Viktor and I are well aware of the background of my very birth and existence in this village. He will do all that he can to have a hand in reinstating you in the villa of your youth especially as my father because of his strange illness can no longer take responsibility for you or I.

The following Saturday soirée at her grandfather's villa again came around. She was now ensconced in Viktor's domicile her mother having given her permission to be there because her father had been hospitalized. Donella was preparing for the evening ahead in the lush accommodation that Viktor had made available for her in the form of a room of her own. Her own bed would be made up for her by a serving maid every morning with a coverlet something that she had never had before, an eiderdown.

At her father's chalet she had been used to only rough sheets and blankets. These bed sheets were of a soft silken nature. She had laid her clothes out for the evening including the only dress that she possessed, a black gown reaching to her feet worn especially for the evening ensemble performances. She moved to the beautiful polished wooden dressing table that stood opposite the bed. On the vanity table stood a mirror something that she had never set eyes on before.

Curiously and half afraid she sat down on a cushioned seat at the mirror and looked into it. What she saw almost frightened her. She had washed her hair that evening as usual and had dried it not thinking at all of her appearance a habit that she had formed at the convent. Suddenly she became very aware of her body, her face certainly now as she peered into this item of furniture obviously meant to enhance her own attractiveness. She looked and realized how she must appear to Viktor comparing herself to what she only knew of other women, those she had known in her schooling and the heavily made up socialites frequenting her grandfather's soirées.

She stepped back and held her breath as she looked. At this moment there was a knock on the bedroom door. It was Viktor. She was wearing a rough woolen gown that her mother had bought for her some years ago. Viktor stepped inside looking puzzled. To one side on the bed that she had not noticed lay a colored item of clothing of soft hues. Viktor came to her having picked up the garment. He said:

"Surely this will make our evening together more enchanting? Wear it Donella." "Now?" She said questioningly. He looked at her earnestly responding a little tightly at her doubt as to his meaning. He put his hands out and gently took off the old brown woolen garment that she was wearing. She stood for a moment as she thought, thankful that she was still clothed beneath the gown and conscious of Viktor's nearness and of her exposed limbs. She said panicking:

"Viktor I will put on this beautiful gown some other time."

She draped it over her lissome young body. At the exposure of her body quite innocently on Donella's part she felt an increase in her attraction to Viktor. She did not understand what she was feeling but knew instinctively that there was some purpose to the way Viktor was behaving towards her. He was making it quite clear to her that she was important to him. He turned on his heel after she said:

"I must prepare for the evening Viktor. You will leave me alone now?" He answered before leaving the room: "I will see you downstairs. We can enjoy a glass of wine before we leave for dining. I have seen that your 'cello is carefully put away for this evening. You did right to ask if you could practice. Any time you need to keep your fingers supple please feel free to use the piano in the study."

Donella was relieved to hear this as Viktor had been taking a lot of her time in his close attention to her. He left. She quickly bathed noticing the luxuriously scented bath salts and soap placed at useful points for the evening's washing preparation. She slipped on her tight fitting black gown noticing as she did so some other dresses lying on the chair. They were obviously there for her use as she should choose.

She darted over to them and held one or two up to her body. Yes it seemed that they were the right size. They were silky and attractive. Feeling less attractive in the more austere black gown she eased her feet into her shoes and quickly bound her hair. Seeing some lip gloss on the vanity table she carefully rubbed it onto hr lips. Her lower chin sank as she noticed in the mirror the picture that she made. Not nearly attractive enough for Viktor she felt.

She opened the door quickly and began to make her way down the thickly carpeted staircase. Viktor had said that he would meet her downstairs. She looked about her for him and then heard a door open from the landing below the stairway. It was Viktor. He said:

"You must be frozen in that dress. Here is an ermine cape for you to wear. It belonged to my mother. You must have it. There is a fire burning in here in the lounge and we will dine later."

They walked into the lounge together. Donella held her breath in excitement at the forthcoming meal to be enjoyed with Viktor. She exclaimed with her hand to her mouth in her humility:

"Viktor! I have never in my life seen or enjoyed such luxury. I cannot believe that this comfort and glamour is meant for me! Compared to this I was living in poverty, near destitution. My father could not have cared what became of me but I know my mother wished for better things in life. I know that she regretted leaving her home the judge's villa with all his wealth but had earned her father's displeasure by eloping with his handyman servant." Viktor replied:

"Do sit down and relax Donella. My servant will call us for our meal in a little while. I am so interested in your story because as I am sure you know by now I feel very strongly about you, especially the effort that you have made in your studies with your mentors the holy sisters at the convent. I am particularly impressed that amidst all the distress that your poverty must have caused you personally you have managed to excel yourself at a musical instrument. It must be a difficult one and cumbersome to carry around with you. Oh! Please continue what you were saying about your mother though."

Donella gulped at this praise from someone who was coming to be very dear to her. She continued:

"Yes my mother would dearly love to be reinstated in her father's villa. She regrets bitterly that she ran away from home particularly as my father illtreats her shamefully. His illness is becoming worse and worse and it is only because he has to be hospitalized that she has given me permission to be here. I have told her of your connection with her father the judge and she has pleaded with me to ask you to put in a good word for her to my grandfather and use my, as she calls it graciousness to try to soften the cynical old man's heart towards his daughter. She has nowhere else to go as my father has threatened to sell his chalet if he is permanently hospitalized in the sanatorium.

An obsequious servant entered the room catching his master's attention. Viktor said:

"Dinner is prepared. Are you ready? He took her arm at her assent to his question and the manservant seated the couple opposite one another at a polished wooden table with a centerpiece of fresh flowers. They had to hurry as Donella was performing in the music ensemble that evening. She was nervous wondering what sort of reception she would receive from Viktor's sharpwitted socialite friends at the soirée. She was anticipating her arrival with Viktor. Would it set tongues wagging she thought to herself. Then Viktor spoke as roast duck and vegetables were served. He said harshly:

"This is one of the last few evenings that I will be with you at the soirées. The Kaiser and the French are at loggerheads both politically and now militarily. You do know that I am in strict army training. War could be declared at any time now. I am expecting a call from the barracks outside the town at any moment. I will be seeing the latest news about the situation in Prussia in the morning newspapers."

Donella gave a frightened start to this statement of Viktor's. Seeing that she was upset by what he had told her he said:

"I will be away fighting yes, but will be back on horseback from time to time to see to both your safety and that of my household here at my villa."

He glanced at his timepiece and said:

"We must be on our way. I hear the huskies whimpering outside. It is cold with the latest snowfall and they sense the warmth that our being on the move to reach the Judge's villa before nightfall will bring to their chilled bodies. They love the exercise."

Donella's 'cello was in the hallway waiting and she collected it as she and Viktor left the villa. When they arrived after a short journey there was a flurry of guests entering her grandfather's residence. Viktor and Donella managed to find shelter in the courtyard. Many of the visitors were just being dropped off to be fetched later in the evening but Viktor had run the dogs in their journey to the soirée with a servant to see to the animals' well being. Viktor was a popular person quite clearly as several of the guests greeted him jovially.

Viktor put his arms up to help Donella off the sleigh. Her boots sank into a snowdrift but Viktor stopped her from falling. She reached up and took her 'cello that was well protected by its leather case. They made their way inside, Donella having noticed some of the other members of the music ensemble greeted them somewhat shyly. It was obvious to all that Viktor was chaperoning her.

The women separated from the men as they all had to divest themselves from outer greatcoats and cloaks that were covered with snow flakes. Viktor was waiting for Donella an elegant sight with her golden hair caught up in a gray velvet ribbon as he had noticed was a habit of hers. She had changed her sodden boots into a pair of silver step in shoes.

It was warm inside Donella noticed and was attracted to a huge log fire in one part of the guest lounge. The musicians appeared to be assembling and were being welcomed by Herr Auberg their conductor. They made a cheerful group. Herr Auberg settled them in their places for the performance and Donella took Viktor's hand she needing his encouragement for her playing that evening.

He understood this gesture as she was uprooted from her parent's care or what care they had given her so far in her life. Viktor felt her heartbreak at her poverty stricken family background. Having seduced her mother her father had at first denied taking responsibility for the ensuing birth of his daughter Donella. Josina though with her father's stubborn nature had held him to what he had done by refusing to leave him mostly because she knew that her father would not take her back into his household had he known what had happened.

At the first interval Donella face bright and enthused by the Mozart work that had just been performed caught Viktor's eye. She knew she had to join him in the social fray. He was surrounded by expensively dressed women and their husbands and partners in dark suits and neckerchiefs. She had seen her grandfather the Judge at other soirées but Viktor had pointed him out to her this evening once again. She noticed that he was approaching the group of guests that she and Viktor were conversing with somewhat superficially. Viktor saw that she had seen the old man coming and gently taking her aside whispered:

"Now's your chance!"

As he spoke Donella's grandfather moved across to Viktor's group. He had to excuse himself as he went as there were several groups of guests clustered around enjoying the tempting edibles displayed by the servants obviously having been carefully prepared during the afternoon. It amounted to a bouffet supper. Donella and Viktor had already supped so left one another every few minutes to nibble at cheese and fruit delicately placed on chinaware on a clean white tablecloth.

The Judge was clearly aiming at speaking to Viktor. In reality he needed the company of another male at this time, particularly Viktor as it had only recently become known to him that Viktor's parents had died tragically earlier in the year. They had been close friends. Within speaking range he addressed the young man:

"Viktor my son I am so glad to be able to converse with you. I heard about your parents' ill fortune only a few weeks ago. You seem to be making a new life for yourself with this delightful young lady. I was unable to attend the funeral as was indisposed at the time. You seem to be over the worst." Viktor replied:

"Yes it was a shocking affair. I do not know how I have come through it. I am still if reminded in a state of shock."

Donella's grandfather looked down in embarrassment and then responded:

"I am sorry to bring up the subject then but I felt that I would like to offer my condolences. Is all well with you fiancée?"

Vikotr did not answer this question at first but then responded:

"No that relationship is ended now. My ex fiancée was under suspicion for a part in my parents' deaths."

Donellla was struck dumb once again at these words for Viktor had told her before now that he had ended his relationship with his past fiancée. She could see that the old gentleman was curious about her as she and Viktor had been conversing closely together during the interval it was obvious to all within range. The old man addressed Donella seeing that she was attired as the other musicians were, in black.

"You are a new member of the ensemble quite clearly. How are you finding the playing? I remember now Herr Auberg did say that there had to be a replacement of a 'cellist in the group. I am pleased to make your acquaintance."

Donella was touched at the Judge's quaint old world attempt at charm. She felt a surge of emotion knowing that he was her own grandfather did he but know it. She lowered her eyes.

"I was impressed by the Mozart work that you have just finished performing." The Judge continued:

"You seemed all of you to be expertly trained. What was you name" Viktor broke in:

"Her name is Donella. I met her at one of you soirées quite recently. We have become close friends."

At these words being spoken Herr Auberg bounced up to the group of important personages. Being a musician his sharp ears had caught Viktor's last words. He took in what was being said happy to come into a tête à tête involving Donella as he was keen to get to know her more. He was intent on keeping a contented hard working ensemble of players. He had also been struck by Donella's beauty as a young female. He was quite attracted to her in fact.

The Judge as his employer of the musicians for the evening's entertainment now became critical when Herr Auberg had joined them, and quizzically and teasingly asked him how he found Donella's standard of playing.

"She is new to our little orchestra yes, but shows much finesse in her style."

The Judge was interested particularly as he saw Victor's keen interest in the girl. He took a fatherly attitude to Viktor knowing that he had recently lost both parents who had been close friends of he and his wife. He tried to solve the relationship of Viktor and Donella, clearly close to one another. Girding up his thoughts he said to Viktor:

"This is not your fiancée surely? I have only met her once a year or so back!"

Viktor looked embarrassed for Donella's sake and explained:

"No sir. We broke off the engagement after my parents died in the riding accident that you know about. They were anxious that we marry but I did not feel she was the right person for me. My parents had been pushing me into a situation that I did not want. When they died I no longer felt tied to my ex-fiancée." Donella not having heard this part of Viktor's life felt both intrigued and interested in what was being said. Her sharp ears had taken in all that Viktor had told her grandfather.

The old man in his canny state had noticed her reaction to Viktor's words. He wondered at this but did not inquire any further into their relationship knowing that Viktor would treat her kindly whatever their future was as a close couple.

The old man of great experience in keeping his temper as well as holding his tongue did not let the information that Viktor had let out show any disturbance in himself. He showed no visible emotion. He determined to behave questioningly to the young girl at that moment in the three men's presence. He could tell of their admiration for her as it was clear that she put a lot of effort into her interpretation of the classics performed under Herr Auberg's direction. He spoke almost stuttering but in a sharp way to her:

"And where did you train in your musicianship my dear?"

Donella was not often asked this as few people were aware of the sacrifices that her mother had to make for her to learn to play the 'cello. She answered:

"An old nun at the convent here in the village taught me to play." She paused. "My mother worked to pay for my lessons. The old mother Armentia would only accept a pittance in payment for all she was knowledgeable about in music, having many years ago trained at a conservatoire before taking holy orders.' She paused again, looking sideways at Viktor to see his reaction to this reply, and then glanced at the old man to gauge his reaction, to see what his piercing eyes in his wizened old face told her.

Both of them the old man and the young girl were now aware of their superficial relationship of the present. Neither of them were in a position to shrug off propriety and one or the other throw open their arms to embrace as newly discovered family. Donella had been strictly raised in her schooling and the old Judge by virtue of what he had seen in his legal career had developed a sourness in his personality that even he hated in himself. Theoretically both wondered who the other was in a family situation but could not express it in the social position they were in.

The following months' soirées were not enough to find a suitable time to admit the entanglement of what had happened in their lives till now to bring them together. Donella was humbled by her mother's part in having left home to elope. The Judge by his uncaring attitude towards his daughter left she and her grandfather curious about one another though. All they could do in off moments when not busy were times of personal reflection of what was part of their involvement in one another's lives. Donella as a young woman would take the opportunity of following up the conversation. The Judge spoke sharply:

"Your mother worked for you? Now you are helping her I suppose."

Donella aware that she must take this chance to help reconcile a father-daughter togetherness broken so long ago, said quite firmly:

"Yes. She is desperate now to be with her father and mother. She does not know even if her mother, my grandmother is alive."

The old man glanced quickly at the young couple who were conversing with him. His work in the legal profession had brought him into contact with many different people and he could immediately vouch for their innocence and decency. What the young girl had told him in the presence of the son of old friends of his caused him to tie up their circumstances with his own.

Carefully he did not question Donella as to her mother's name. Donella herself knowing the elderly man was definitely her grandfather began to think of a way to help her mother to be reinstated at the villa. She was still very young but intelligent enough to see that the effect she had on all men was to charm them. She quickly ventured the words:

"I do love these soirées. I feel as if I live here. I feel so at home in this enormous villa. It is as if I belong here somehow."

The old gentleman with his thoughts beginning to rest on the young girl's attempt at a conversation in this sophisticated setting bowed his head as he summoned up words to answer, words gracious enough to reply to such a lovely person young as she was. He was not yet sure if she was in all honesty his granddaughter but knew that their situation in life did seem to coincide. Crustiness of years leaving his thoughts at such innocence he muttered gruffly:

"Make yourself at home then. My servants have prepared a grand spread. I have noticed that you enjoy yourself when you partake of these suppers at my soirées. That is what is intended." Donella smiled an affirmative:

"I was just thinking that I had better fetch some of the delicacies for Viktor and I to eat. Time is marching on and we still have half an evening's performance to fill in."

Viktor raised his eyebrows appropriatively as Donella wended her way amongst the guests over to the inviting spread on a white linen cloth. She and Viktor had already had supper she knew. The evening's playing had taken its toll though. Viktor was a man and she knew that he would appreciate a snack or two now just as she would.

The old gentleman, mentally applauding Viktor on his choice of companion cleared his throat as he prepared to address the Herzog Tazner, saying:

"I have not set eyes on you since your parents' passing Viktor. My deepest sympathies are with you." Viktor looked anxious but said bravely:

"Yes. It was a tragedy, my whole life was turned upside down. I have now fully taken on adulthood with no one to rely on except Donella"

Somehow she came through the exertion of the evening performance. She had just arrived with some snacks. She was deeply moved by the meeting between herself and her grandfather and longed to make herself known to him and tell of her mother's plight and need to be reinstated in her father's home. She shivered slightly as the thought of the old Judge being reunited with his errant daughter after so long. Would he take her back?

As she lay in the bed of silken sheets that night she turned on the soft pillow face pale with fear in the situation she found herself and her family to be in. She had an ally though. The door of the bedroom swung open and Viktor stood there in a braided men's dressing gown. He was fully aware of her circumstances and was deeply attracted to the beautiful young musician. Her face, pale and wan with emotion, on edge at yet another intrusion into her feelings turned to look at him, eyes deep brown in their sockets and shining gold hair in disarray.

Viktor tried to speak but the sight of her expression so moved him that he was not able to at first. Donella seeing someone familiar who had been kind to her in her life, even if only for the last few months stumbled out his name giving the young man the cue to speak. Viktor said:

"Donella are you alright? Will you sleep?" Donella answered drowsily:

"Viktor I am overcome by meeting my grandfather. From all accounts I understood that he was a harsh and grating personality. Viktor you could see I did not find him so. In fact he was quite gentle in his attitude towards me!" Viktor fobbed off her current address to him and said to her:

"Donella! May I come closer to you?" Donella with eyes huge in her face whispered in reply:

"Yes Viktor. I feel drained at the thought of my so-called family. My mother is practically destitute and my father, who is of peasant stock is at present in an asylum. I have nothing in the world except my 'cello and the ability to play it."

Viktor had reached the bed and he knelt down and took her hand that was ice cold. He had been sitting by the log fire in the lounge and his warm hand brushed her forehead. Then he held her neck intimately and said: "Donella I too am alone in the world. I am just coming out of an arranged and broken engagement. My parents have died, tragically even this year."

Donella's hand reached his behind her head and frowned slightly at Viktor's telling her this. She said sympathetically:

"How unhappy that must make you. You must still be in deep mourning for your late mother and father. Were you very close to them?"

Viktor took her hand and slid his right hand again behind her head bringing his face quite close to her anxious one. He took in the ivory color of her skin then answered:

"Yes Donella. I was greatly endeared to them both especially my mother. She was a wonderful woman fully supportive to my father in all his activities. They both worked hard for the betterment of the community and gave liberally to the poorer struggling folk in the village below the villa on the slopes of the Alps where we live. My father encouraged every performance given by the orchestra in the town nearest to us that is why I am so enthusiastic myself about the Judge's, that is your grandfather's soirées.

Of course I feel greatly privileged to have met you as a musical performer, something I have always aspired to be myself."

Viktor pulled her tousled head to his own gently and they kissed, he ardently and she hesitantly at first but later giving way to him. She was exhausted by the evening's performance but had enough energy left to succumb to Viktor's advances. His hand caressed her body and after a while he stood up and said to her:

"I must do this Donella. The servants are long ago in their quarters. No one will know."

Donella watched as if hypnotized as he shed his garments. A fire crackled in the grate at the end of the bedroom. He pulled the coverings of the bed back and then lay down next to her. They lay together touching and feeling one another for another hour or two. Donella was overwhelmed. Then Viktor without saying a word pulled up short. Then he said:

"We must sleep now. Tomorrow we will make an expedition into the town to buy you clothes. I notice that you only have a few drab garments. But to me Donella you are like a lily of the field. Why do you even need more accessories I ask myself. I suppose if you are to accompany me socially you will need to keep up with the fashions of the socialites we will be encountering together."

After they had breakfasted the next morning the servants mustered the husky dogs together to lead the couple aboard the sleigh into the village. Sleigh bells jingling and Donella laughing with Viktor in control they sped on their way. Donella tensed in the ice cold of the early morning but said:

"I have no money Viktor. How are we going to pay for all this?"

The sleigh drew in to an empty space on the outskirts of the village. Viktor gave sharp commands to the four willing hounds and panting they crouched on their haunches. A street attendant appeared and Viktor spoke briefly to him putting some silver coins into his hand so the dogs could be watched for their safety while the two shopped.

Viktor was an impressive sight as he strode up the street covered with thick snowfall from the night before. Donella had almost to run to keep up with him. She was clothed in her usual day dress of red and brown but Viktor as they walked together was imagining her arrayed in colorful seductive garments, fitting her to be with one of such high social standing as he had been born to.

They began to slow down into an ambling gait as they turned into the high street with delightful shops lining the sides. The vendors were watchful for customers. The little shops were set at odd angles one to the other alongside the pavements. Donella pulled up short as they passed by a carpenter's shop. She had seen it before as a child of only ten years, but she recognized it. She spoke hoarsely in the frosty morning:

"Viktor! Stop! I want you to see this shop that we are passing. This is where my father was employed as a wood turner craftsman. All my growing years he told me about the dear old man who employed him who owned this shop. Could we go inside there now? I would like to let the old man, if he is alive still know that I am Ernst's daughter. He will be only too concerned to hear about my father's illness and that he has been admitted permanently into hospital. That is he might have been told already but he does not know that my father will not be back, perhaps ever." Viktor though was impatient and turned, answering her:

"Another time Donella. We will be the whole morning trying on clothes for you."

Donella assented silently but as they proceeded along the side walk her spirits were cheered as Viktor halted with her outside a charming little boutique.

The proprietress was just opening the little shop. Donella looked inside. Viktor took her by the arm and they entered. There the assistant patiently showed Donella gown after gown. Donella was overwhelmed but fascinated by the beautiful and charming garments. Viktor was becoming impatient and tried to be helpful saying:

"Summer is on its way Donella. You do not have to be bundled up into too many clothes. Just choose three or four of those dresses." Donella tensed at his sharp words and asked the shop assistant:

"The dresses I have decided on are they three quarter length or ankle length? They seem so small!" The woman said:

"I have a little room at the back of the shop where I do my accounts. You can try them on there if you wish so you can see. You do not mind sir? Viktor was stamping his feet in a very masculine reaction to the cold morning. He said "Go ahead Donella. Don't be longer than you can help." Donella wafted into the rear of the boutique followed obsequiously by the assistant.

They were soon finished and Viktor made the payment for the sales. At the villa that evening Donella having bathed and dressed wearing a warm jersey attended to her coiffure. She came to Viktor nothing short of a seductress. She was quiet and composed after a filling meal was over and done with she sat close to Viktor with the log fire toasting them. They drew nearer together. Breaking the ice Viktor asked:

"Our little expedition was enjoyable didn't you find?" "Oh! Yes, Viktor. My new dresses are quite gorgeous. I will be showing them off to you until you are quite tired of the sight of me." Viktor quipped at her response: "Me! Be bored with you my dear one!" Donella felt herself blushing at his intimate words. Then Viktor said abruptly:

"Donella, we can quite easily leave the log fire to the servants and betake ourselves to the bedroom. He took her hand and led her up the carpeted stairs. They made their way to the bedroom and were soon in one another's arms with Viktor carefully undressing her.

There followed several weeks of love making every evening. They threw caution to the winds as to any serious repercussions to their actions. Then the inevitable transpired. Donella found herself to be expecting Viktor's child.

CHAPTER 11

Donella in her state of eminent motherhood was in a mild state of shock. She would have to tell Viktor no less her mother. She felt a fulfillment to her and Viktor's physical relationship, a feeling of commitment to her lover. Was this what they had both subconsciously been behaving towards with their fatal physical attraction? She spent the whole afternoon watching the snow falling outside the window of the bedroom, wondering about this.

Victor had made the room available to her. She pondered on the fact of his expecting anything like the news that she had for him. They were both in a situation of little parental guidance. Viktor's father and mother had recently died tragically and Donella's father was permanently hospitalized. That narrowed matters down to Josina Donella's mother.

Agonized Donella realized with a shudder that she had been on the point of introducing herself to her grandfather as someone close in the family. How glad she was now that she had not done this. She had also hoped with Viktor's connivance to try to reinstate her mother into the Judge's villa household. Josina was almost without means and had scarcely enough to sustain her. Donella decided that she would approach Viktor that evening.

Her whole body shaking, she desperately wondered what his reaction would be. As evening drew on she bathed and dressed as demurely as possible, on tenterhooks to know her lover's reaction with her news. Then she was ready. She left the bedroom and carefully descended the stairs. Viktor was usually in the drawing room waiting for her. He would accompany her in to the evening meal.

A little shrewdly she considered it wisest to wait until they had finished eating. Tension of hunger would not improve matters if she were to burst out with what she had to tell him. And it was good news too she thought assertively. Viktor spoke after seeing her come through the doorway:

"You are looking a little timorous and pale this evening Donella my love. Is anything untoward bothering you?"

Donella caught her breath. How could she answer him? What could she say? She must respond to his question for the meantime anyway.

"No! No! Viktor. I just feel a little faint coming from the cold outside into this lovely heated room."

They both gazed into the blazing log fire. Viktor said worriedly:

"Sit down then Donella. It's nearly time for our repast. I can hear the dishes being brought in."

Donella relaxed at the ice having been broken by his words and said, her heart thumping inside her,

"No time to rest now it seems." They went in to dine.

Donella slowly and delicately wiped her mouth when she had finished eating. Viktor had his fill of the sumptuous fare that the servants had cooked as usual. He had noticed her anxiety and knew that she had something to tell him. He prompted:

"What is it Donella?" With new vigor after the meal Donella stumbled out her words:

"Viktor I am expecting our infant in just over eight months. I am desperate Viktor. I did not know this could happen."

With shock Viktor pulled himself up and took a deep breath as he addressed her:

"Donella I know this is my fault. The members of my parents' social circle will vent bitter disapproval of what has happened should we wish to marry. They will question the whole affair wanting to know how this has come about. They will not blame me, you will be the one they will point a finger at, you will be the scapegoat. You are of obscure origins. No one in this community realizes that you are the Judge's granddaughter. I am also sure you do not want anyone to know that either in the condition you find yourself.

That I do concede to you. We have both been in a state of lacking parental guidance what with the tragedy of the loss of my own parents and your mother having abandoned you to my care, with you supposedly being in my employment as a servant." She responded:

"I will have to tell her Viktor." Donella replied in a state of tension now that her secret was out. "She will be the one who will have to guide me as to how to care for myself and the coming baby." Viktor asked:

"And are you going to tell her that I am the father off the future child?" Donella answered quickly hopeful of a permanent relationship even now marriage to Viktor to solve her problem:

"No Viktor that I refuse to ask of her. She will force me to admit the indiscretion to my father who can be very cruel to me. What has happened under our circumstances is that it will now be impossible for us to reinstate my mother in my grandfather's home. She will never be able to live down the embarrassment I may have caused. That is unless his granddaughter has a married situation." Viktor burst out:

"That is impossible in my social circle you must know that Donella, I have told you so."

Donella felt tears prick her eyelids. Then she said chokingly:

"Then only way now is for you to take me back to my mother at the chalet in the forest. She will know what to do."

Donella knew that she could have expected a worse reaction from Viktor, obviously the father of the coming child. She said falteringly:

"I will go upstairs and pack my few possessions."

Viktor nodded curtly. She stumbled up the luxuriously carpeted stairs with the change in her circumstances in the near future suddenly becoming very real to her. She would now have to leave the plush surroundings that she was just becoming used to and re-establish herself at her parents' humble poverty stricken chalet deep in the forest behind the village.

Her heart beat powerfully as she thought back on Viktor's reaction to her news. It seemed as if he was being swayed in their circumstances by society. It seemed that he would never be able to live down the situation amongst his late parents' acquaintances if they knew his secret. The thought struck her that her father was for the moment permanently ensconced in hospital so she would not have to bear the brunt of any cruel reaction from him for the present. It would be left to her mother to cope with the facts that had come to light with her state of future motherhood.

Josina would now never be able to be reinstated in her father's villa as his daughter. They had been on the point of divulging all to the old Judge, that was she and her mother's relationship to him. Now this could never be. No, not unless Viktor took the step of marrying her. She slowly bent over her mother's old packing case so as to fold and place her few clothes in it. She opened the cupboard in the room and stared at the luxurious dresses that Viktor had bought her. She decided to leave them where they were. Tears were welling up in her eyes. She brushed them away as she heard Viktor's voice, rasping now:

"Donella are you ready"? It is getting on for eight o' clock. We must leave within half an hour."

She tripped as she came to the top of the stairwell. Viktor's face was full of anger. Carefully she descended. She would have liked to throw herself into his arms but knew this was not the time or place. When that would be neither of them could tell. He said sharply:

"Don't forget your 'cello and music stand and your music case."

Donella flew to her music accoutrements. He did not help her with her load and clutching her possessions, dumfounded at what was happening they made their way through the snowbound driveway up to the waiting sleigh. The huskies were whining in anticipation of the ride. The couple with their futures now so closely intertwined yet so concerned with the present were silent. The dogs ran in front of the sleigh with Viktor's guidance.

The departure had been sudden the reaction of Viktor's at the news that Donella had given him. He was in a state of near panic. He had been completely overwhelmed by Donella's beauty and musical talent. The facts of her parentage that she had told Viktor with her father being of humble peasant stock had not worried him until this evening. Donella had seemed sure that her mother would know what to do in the event of the birth of the child. Viktor knew that if word got out about their relationship amongst his parents' peers he would be ostracized for a long while in the future.

He could only plan the coming event with Donella's wishes. And these would be guided by her mother. Donella's mother – how would he ever be able to explain away to the socialites in the community the fact that his future child was one of apparent loose morals on his side and no social planning. Victor cursed at this. His love for Donella was more than that, much more.

Viktor had felt so restrained by the situation of his former fiancée that his parents had shepherded him into that he felt in the present circumstances that he did not know which direction to take socially. He still loved Donella, what had happened to them was largely his doing. He longed for an escape out of the situation. Then he remembered just as they reached the little chalet in the woods where Donella had grown up that there was a war ensuing with gathering force in the north-west with France taking a defensive stance. He felt shut in from three quarters now. Firstly his social situation having to see Donella at the judge's soirées, then Donella's family status knowing that she was the daughter of a peasant although as well the granddaughter of a Judge, and the call to war.

Donella climbed off the sleigh when they halted and knocked urgently on the door of the chalet. She waited with Viktor standing tensely beside her. Her mother would not be expecting her. A candle glow lit the window facing them with a dim light. Donella called softly: "Mother!" Then she raised her voice: "It's me, Donella!" Her mother after a long while carefully opened the door. She exclaimed: "Donella! My child! Why are you here?"

Donella glanced at Viktor who was standing next to her at a loss for what to do next. Donella realizing that she must take control of the situation said softly to him:

"You had better leave Viktor. My mother will just be upset if you are here with what I have to tell her."

Viktor turned abruptly on his heel feeling at present no more responsibility in the circumstances, but hurt at what Donella had just said. Josina anxious now at the sudden arrival of her daughter who seemed to her to be very upset, hardly noticed when Viktor took his leave. She shook Donella by the shoulder desperate to know the worst.

"Donella child why are your here?" "Mother I am expecting Viktor's child within months. I am afraid." She said boldly then:

"I love him and he has said he will be in touch with me at a later stage when you and I have adjusted to the situation. Her mother bitter now at what had obviously happened flew at her:

"I blame you father. He was the one who involved me in all this. And now I have to forge the way ahead. I dare not tell Ernst for fear of his temper. What are we going to do? Will Viktor marry you?"

Donella answered:

"He has told me he won't for fear of social criticism with me being partially peasant born. This he says is bound to come out sooner or later if we married. I am heartbroken about it." Josina said: "Donella I think the best course to take is to have the infant adopted. I will approach the authorities within the next few days depending on the weather allowing me to go into town. You will have to help me around the chalet while you are waiting for the baby to come. I will assist you in finding a place in the hospital to have the baby but we will have to busy ourselves with the work of washing to bring in money to live in the meantime.

Relieved in the situation by the care that her mother was showing her the two set about making an extra bed ready. Her mother found some wurst and rye bread to eat with the thin gruel that she had ready to heat for herself. Donella was calm in the situation knowing that she could rely on her mother who she could tell was both anxious and angry. The physical state that she found herself in made her contented though. After the two had partaken of the meager meal her mother rasped out the words:

"It will now be impossible for me to be reinstated in the Judge's villa as his daughter. I have completely lost touch with my father. Even so if he knows what has happened he will never forgive you or I or Viktor. You say Viktor's parents were quite close acquaintances of my father's?" Donella tried to understand the circumstances. She was quiet for a few moments then spoke:

"Before this state that I find myself in occurred Viktor and I were planning and hoping to put your relationship right with your father. However Viktor now says he cannot risk the social ostracism that will happen if he and I marry. He says the aristocracy that he has been born to would be very probing as to my background. We know mother that I am of peasant stock. This is apparently unacceptable in the social circles that Viktor moves in. It could affect his whole life and possibly mine at a later time."

Her mother said harshly to Donella:

"If that is the case my child you will have to have the infant adopted. There is hardly money enough even for you and I to live on until the birth and an extra mouth to feed will be impossible."

Donella felt completely crushed. What could she say to this? Half defensively she responded:

"But Viktor loves me. He has told me so. Perhaps he still intends to marry me." Her mother said again not thinking of her daughter's feelings:

"No Donella he will not. As you know I myself was born into the social circles that Viktor moves in and it was that kind of life that I fought against that caused me to elope with your father. I now realize how foolish I was but it is even worse for you. Viktor will never marry you because it could mean that his government subsidy paid to him by the palatinate could then be jeopardized."

The whole circumstances that were developing around Donella involving people that she was close to and loved were nearly crushing her emotions that evening. Neither mother, father Viktor or even her grandfather seemed to be in a position to help her. It just seemed all so impossible so unjust. Right then her mother seemed the most concerned about her although she was the least able to help her in the long term. Josina, calming her anxiety a little now that Viktor had left began to focus on the problem. Although she was angry at Viktor for his part in the circumstances she felt that because of her own upper class heritage she could neither take advantage of his wealthy parentage or blame him in the matter of the coming birth of what would be her grandchild. Josina said:

"This has been a frightful shock to me Donella but I am sure it is just as bad for you. We can spend the next few days planning what to do both about you and I and your future child. Fortunately your father will be in hospital for some time to come so we will not have to pander to his disapproval of your physical state. He will be very angry I know but the period of his hospitalization is prolonged indefinitely so the hospital authorities tell me. I visited him last week and he seemed quite demented. They tell me that his mental state is a result of repeated family intermarriage. As one of the servant classes of society he will have respect for Viktor if he knows Viktor is the father of your infant but will have no knowledge of the correct procedures of socializing with him or any of his acquaintances."

Donella tried to understand what her mother was saying and broke in speaking her mind for the first time

"Mother it is not entirely my fault that I find myself in this state. It seems so wrong. Is there no way of forcing Viktor to take up his rightful position of father? I will plead with him if necessary." Her mother answered:

"I know for certain coming from the aristocracy as I do that an unmarried mother is quite unacceptable in these social circles. No Donella. You will have to have to have your baby adopted."

Donella paled visibly and froze with shock at her mother's decision in taking control of the situation. For someone to lean on in her circumstances she was somehow glad of an immediate solution to the coming event. Josina now involved in the whole matter now told her daughter:

"You will have to stall all knowledge of my involvement in the Judge's family. I know you were on the point of letting him into the secret of my identity as far as your grandfather and yourself were concerned in my having to do with you both. Now I am prepared to stay at the chalet with you keeping busy with the washing tasks that I earn a living with until your child is born. It is a big disappointment for me as I had hoped for some respite in this hard life of mine. Do not now under any circumstances let out my secret. Does Viktor know of my relationship to the Judge? That I am in fact his daughter?" "I don't think so, mother." Donella choked out those words. "I can't remember if I told him knowing as I did he told me, that his late parents were close acquaintances of the Judge's." Donella was not clear in her thinking as she spoke. "Good girl. A discrete attitude, you will have to take in the whole affair." Changing the subject her mother said:

"You have taken it well the fact that your baby will have to be adopted. You are quite sure Viktor has declined all responsibility of parenting his child by law or even a church marriage?" Donella said patiently:

"No mother. This will be impossible. Viktor is quite angry about the whole coming birth. He seems to blame me even though it was he who made the initial advances towards me physically. I love him but can do nothing to further a permanent relationship with him. It is impossible for us in his social circumstances with me being of peasant stock partly. He has said that at first he was quite bowled over by me but did not take into account my lowly circumstances. I do agree that my baby will have to be adopted. But what will become of me then?" Her mother took a harsh stance once again and responded quickly at her daughter's question

"You will have to enter novitiate. I have an entrée into the convent life through the Abbess where you were educated. She has powerful social connections in the nearby town and I am certain that you can be taken in as a novice."

The imparting of this last item of information moved Donella to her soul. The thought of what she had gleaned at school about the inner workings of nuns who lived in a convent lit her mind like a star exploding around her. She stumbled in her thinking. What were those words the mother superior had spoken just before she left to go out into the world to find a way of living, earning by performing as she had learnt expertly on her beloved 'cello? What had the old nun Mother Armentia impressed on those schoolmates of hers?

Yes! That was it. Poverty chastity and obedience. She would in her new circumstances have to live by those ideals. She was used to poverty, she had come from peasant origins into a desperately poor family. She would at least know what that was.

Chastity. She raised her right index finger to her temple at her head. How would her own conscience treat her with regards to the uncertain state of her virginity? Most certainly she could never love another man again. Yes, she had lain with a Viktor but surely she prayed God would forgive her if she entered the novitiate. A long dark path into the future or so it seemed to her now. That was if she followed the practicality of her mother's plans and took her vows to become a nun.

She did not think the novitiate board would even question her state of purity. The condition she would be in after the birth of her and Viktor's child would to all appearances be quite similar to the other young girls entering into a nun's life. How would she ever be able to keep her secret not tell a soul of what she had experienced with Viktor? It would be a secret that would go on for ever, seemingly.

Then again how would her somewhat temperamental musical nature seem to the Abbess' demand for obedience in the noviate, the credo for such behavior of doing exactly as told. With great uncertainty and ill ease of mind however not questioning what her mother had chosen for her to follow she drifted off into the deep slumber of a mother to be. Josina tidied a few household items away and checked the washing piled up in a corner that she would have to attend to the next day.

Ice cold shivers played up and down her spine as Donella woke to the whining of the wind outside flinging up snow particles silently against the window pane that was caked with them around the rims of the now cracked glass that her father had put in all those years ago before she was born. Josina and Ernst had eloped, that her mother had told her. As she lay there shivering she realized that all hope for she and her mother's reinstatement in her grandfather's villa as recognized members of the respected family of the Judge, had now nearly vanished. A great void faced her. Almost reading her thoughts her mother's sharp voice came to her ears:

"Donella you must get up and dress. We will have to go together to the local authorities to arrange for the adoption of your child. You are quite sure that Viktor will not commit himself in your relationship?" Donella, dressed now having confirmed her mother's words said:

"It will take time for me to adjust to the giving up of my infant but I am desperate. Viktor has told me that he cannot bow out of his social circle and accept a person of doubtful birth into his family. He says that his parents' acquaintances are already on the lookout for a match that will suit his high breeding. I will be utterly rejected in the circumstances."

Josina's hardened nature softened somewhat and she said to her daughter:

"I know you always wanted to become a member of the holy orders Donella. I feel a little guilty now because it was I who stood out against this at first. I always encouraged your 'cello studies but did not think they would lead you into a situation such as we find ourselves in."

Donella and her mother had just finished a meager breakfast of porridge and rye bread. Feeling a little calmer with the nourishment they were sipping a heated beverage of melted down chocolate Donella said nervously and despondently:

"I feel quite helpless mother. Being accepted as a nun if they will take me in as a novice seems like a long dark tunnel in the future. I wonder if Viktor even cares about what will happen to me or his child." Josina just responded with these words: "You will have to tell him my girl. There are authorities who are always available in such situations as these."

With her mother's sharp words piercing her ears cold reality struck home for the first time in her young life so far. Josina said firmly:

"We will make two stops from a sleigh ride into town. I have fed the huskies. We will have to make arrangements for the coming infant's birth registration thus giving the authorities time to find adoptive parents. If we attend to this now it will give the town council time to make arrangements for the formalities that will include your signature of permission for your child to be care for by foster parents. What would you feel about that my girl?"

Donella tensed at first at these words of attempted comfort and said face bowed in a state of utter dejection:

"I will take a while to get used to the idea mother but I can see that I will have to accept the situation. I hold nothing against Viktor. I love him and I know that he loves me. His hands are tied by social convention in this palatinate and no amount of entreaty or persuasion on my part will make him change the decision he has made regarding my self and the coming birth of his child. You see mother it is his whole livelihood that would be at stake. Viktor holds the status of a Baronetcy and is also an officer in the military mounted soldiers in this community."

At this stage their sleigh drew up outside the village council offices. They had been talking loudly over the swishing and whirring of the sled. A curious official attended to them and Donella signed where it was appropriate for her permission concerning the babe to come. The mother and daughter were ushered out. Donella spoke when they were seated on the sleigh.

"That is a great relief mother. We now have to approach my old mother superior. Once or twice I heard talk about the Abess in charge of the convent school of novices in the city beyond the village. As a scholar there was seldom a new face amongst our mentors the nuns but when a new young teacher nun appeared at the convent us pupils always tried to find out all about what it took to be accepted as a novice at the great convent where the novitiates became used to the customs of convent life.

"Yes, yes," Her mother guiding the dogs on reins seemed to know where were heading away from the city.

They saw what must be the novitiates' convent on the outskirts of the nearest town some distance that they had traveled away from the villa and forest chalet where the mother and daughter were living now that Viktor had forbidden residence at his home to Donella.

The austere building suddenly looked grim and foreboding. As the huskies pulled to a stop Donella pulled at her mother's slieve in anxiety. Josina reprimanded her daughter then in a response:

"Remember Donella. No mention is to be made of the fact that this child of your impending birth is going to be adopted Say nothing at about your condition Donella. Not a word is to be dropped with this information. We discussed all this remember?" Donella replied:

"Of course I'll say nothing. Do you think they will ask any personal questions mother?" Josina answered her daughter's tremulous question.

"From what your mother superior at the school told me they are really only interested in your scholarly record and a reference from at least one person of high standing in the community. I am intending to tell your grandfather the truth about your relationship with him one day. I intend to try at the same time to reinstate myself at his villa. I have a feeling that if I confide in him that you were the new 'cellist in his Saturday musical evenings and that I am his errant daughter of all those years ago I hope he will forgive me and take me back."

Mother and daughter walked up a grassy pathway flaked with snow. There was a bell pull for use in a cavity in the wall next to the great wooden door that was rotting slightly at the edges. A subservient young nun eased open the large door and peered out at the couple. Josina said firmly:

"The Abess is expecting my daughter called Donella."

The young woman clearly in schooling too before becoming a nun said in a low but clear voice. "Welcome Donella. And you are Donella's mother."

The novice addressed Josina who reciprocated the greeting.

"Enter the convent grounds please both of you."

The great wooden door creaked as it was opened wider by the young nun who was clearly a novice at the convent. The three persons were then together inside the convent grounds and to Donella, the novice closed the door ominously. The young girl tried to remember her schooldays those times when loving what the nuns at the convent that she had attended taught she had inwardly made a strict decision in her mind that she would follow in their footsteps.

As the three of them walked beneath the romanesque arches over the stone surface to the Abess' reception area where they were told Donella would be interviewed for acceptance as a novice. Donella's quick mind was active. No she thought the austerity of the novitiate convent made her very aware of the sort of life that she would be living if she were accepted. This was not really what she wanted for her life. She realized with a shock that she had wanted to fulfill the desire of being a performing 'cellist!

This was the musical instrument that she had studied at school with old mother Armentia. Somehow all that had changed now. She glanced to her left. There were windows in the stone wall but all she could see through them was a dark grim interior. She looked pleadingly at her mother who frowned unsympathetically. How was she possibly going to keep her secret the future birth of her and Viktor's child? Instinctively she thought to herself, her mother had been wise to see that this interview was over with before her body had begun to show that she would within some few more months be giving birth. Suddenly she was awoken from her mesmerizing as the young novice tapped her on the shoulder and said:

"Your name is Donella is it not? The Abbess is expecting you." And addressing Josina the young woman said:

"The Abbess asked me to warn you that she would be wanting to know the kind of family background your daughter comes from."

At this information Josina pulled herself up sharply as her daughter bowed her head in the shame that she had experienced at knowing this even since being a young scholar.

CHAPTER 12

The young novice knocked on the side entrance door at the end of the stone walk under the arches. She then raised her hand to halt the mother and daughter. She consulted a timepiece that she drew out of the folds of her thick cream colored robes and said softly:

"Yes the Abbess will be in the reception parlor within a few minutes. You have been most punctual in your appointment. She will be pleased that she will not have to wait for your.'

The young woman moved quickly to the firm looking wooden door. To Donella it looked awesome and imposing. At the novice's knock on the entrance door a sharp creaking voice sounded abruptly from inside the walls of the reception room. The novice with a gentle smile said to them:

"The Abbess will see you at this moment."

The young woman turned the brass handle of the door and it opened with a slight squeak. It was apparent that the quarters they were about to enter were seldom used as there was a cloying musty atmosphere inside. The novice said almost in a whisper:

"Here are the visitors Abbess. May I leave now? I have cloister duties in the prayer routines of this morning."

In her high almost creaking voice the old Abbess said:

"You may leave us now Sister Angelina. I won't be longer than an hour with our guests."

The young nun slipped out and the Abbess taking a deep breath addressed Josina:

"Your daughter I understand wishes to enter the novitiate. Does she have a calling to this holy way of life?" Josina had been expecting a questioning of some kind by the old nun. Mother and daughter had agreed that nothing was to be let out about Donella's blessed state of motherhood to be that fortunately at this present stage was not visible. Josina answered for her daughter who was completely overawed by the whole situation.:

"My daughter Donella was schooled in the convent at the foot of the Alps, we live nearby there and she has told me of her profound admiration for her teachers who like your holy order are Benedictine nuns. She has spent much time in prayer and meditation and I know she would dearly love to begin a novitiate's life in holy orders at this convent."

The Abbess who had seated herself and her visitors put her forearms on the side of the austere and uncomfortable looking chair and pulled herself up as she turned to address Donella saying in a creaking but nevertheless patient voice:

"My child why is it that you wish to join the novitiate? I do have excellent references from your mother superior where you were schooled." Donella felt panic surge in her throat. She and her mother had agreed that they would neither of them disclose Donella's secret of the physical state she had found herself in. Also her mentors as a scholar had impressed on her that she should tell the truth under all circumstances. How could she answer this awesome woman?

She thought it best to postpone her wish to enter the convent by telling the Abbess that it was not in the immediate future that she hoped to join the novices in their life of becoming nuns, something that they committed themselves to for life. So she replied with her heart in her mouth:

"Yes Abbess with all reverence I do feel called to your holy orders but in a few months' time. I wish to save money for my poor mother to sustain herself. My father is ill and will be in hospital for some time in the future and my mother has nothing but the washing she takes in for a living."

The Abbess then turned to Josina saying::

"Are you from poverty stricken peasant stock my good woman?"

Josina was not expecting such a question but felt it would enhance Donella's chances of being accepted if she told a little of her own upper class background. So she answered carefully:

"Not entirely Abbess. My father is a wealthy Judge in the nearby town."

Josina though it better not to mention her elopement with her father's servant or the fact that Donella was partly of peasant stock, not just yet anyway. So she said:

"I hardly see my father now I married beneath my station in life." With honesty she went on:

"Donella's father is a poor sick man. He is mentally impaired and will need to be incarcerated in the local hospital indefinitely. This leaves me practically a widow. Without Donella's help in her 'cello playing...." The Abbess immediately looked interested and spoke:

"Your daughter is a 'cellist" Donella stared at the bare wooden floor of the room. She thought she had better reply to this question:

"I hoped to earn a little to help my mother on her way when I left the chalet where I grew up by performing at my grandfather's musical soirées. But I now wish to join the novitiate."

She and her mother both knew that the information just imparted would go no further from the Abbess' lips. The Abbess was insistent in her questioning. Donella as she thought fitting kept her head bowed at what seemed a heartless interrogation by the old nun who seemed perturbed to hear that Donella was such a keen 'cellist. The Abbess finally stated:

"My child you will have to surrender all hope of continuing you 'cello playing. You will be constantly required to join the other novices in prayer repetition and worship during the days of the week. You will be needed in the learning of routine dressing and washing and the suitable breviaries for the time of the day. You will have to understand the activities of postulation and humility before your senior nuns who will be guiding you in this most excellent and extreme calling to shut yourself away for the years to come from humanity that as we all know is a fallen state."

Josina was becoming worried at Donella's passive reaction to the Abbess' words. She also had her heart in her mouth that the Abbess would winkle out of her daughter her true state of impending giving of birth though this did not happen. The old Abbess seeing clearly that some reaction was needed from the young girl at what she was proposing for Donella's future put her index finger beneath the young woman's chin and creaked out the words:

"Come now my child! What I have told you must mean something to you! Do you believe that you will be able to undertake the discipline that this convent gives? It will be a lifetime's sacrifice for you."

Donella's heart was pounding. She was an immature nineteen year old girl and deep in her conscience she felt quite unprepared for what she was being offered by the Abbess. She must reply but what could she say in response? She knew that she had her mother's support in whatever she would reply. She finally answered as humbly as she could:

"Yes Abbess. I will prepare myself absolutely for this life. I already know about learning in a convent as was a schoolchild there until only two years ago. Although I will be forced to forgo my 'cello playing for the time being I will sacrifice everything I know to join the novitiate. Perhaps I can teach little children the 'cello when I have reached the stage of being a fully fledged nun." At this the Abbess looked a little haughty she thought.

The few months prior to the birth of Donella's child passed quickly. Having made the excuse of having to help support her mother the old Abbess had told her that she could enter the convent when she was ready. She was warned of the rule of poverty chastity and obedience that she would have to live by. Donella whiled away a few month's practicing and playing her 'cello in the Judge's soirées. Viktor was no longer in evidence at these gatherings.

From the society gossip at intervals at the soirées she understood that he had left mysteriously one night to take part in the mounted cavalry's fighting in the Franco Prussian war. Donella's heart lurched at this information. Would she ever see him again? She had befriended an old priest who was attending the soirées regularly now that the war was likely to continue for some time to come. It would probably take her until the birth of her child. He kept her informed as the war dragged on.

Sometimes Donella despaired but persevered in keeping busy at all times helping her mother when she could and keeping her hand in at her 'cello practicing. Then it was the big event. A baby girl was born just after Christmas. Of course Donella knew instinctively what to do in the first stages of caring for the baby Ernestina. One dark evening when it was snowing heavily outside a knock came at the door.

The baby was asleep. Donella felt faint. Was it Viktor? But no it was a grim looking council nurse holding a carrycot made of metal. What an unfriendly reception for her little one. With a sinking feeling she had realized that the nurse had been sent to take her baby away for adoption as arranged. Donella felt her eyes smarting. She hugged her infant. Without a word as if the moment was unimportant or meant nothing to her the nurse took the sleeping child from Donella put her in the metal carrier and turned to leave.

Outside the dogs that would take the nurse and baby away whined in the cold. Donella watched them go having rubbed away the steamed up window pane inside with ice and frost building up outside. She sobbed quietly to herself as she fell into a light sleep that night. The day after Josina, showing no sympathy for her daughter who was floundering in her situation harshly told her to pack a small bag of basic clothing. This she did after having a small bite to eat for breakfast. When they were ready Josina said:

"The old Abbess as you remember told us to come to the convent to enter the novitiate just as soon as you were ready for it. Although she does not know about your child you will have a place in the novice's dormitory. I would consider it most unwise of you to mention the fact that you have an infant even though the baby girl is now with her adopted parents. The nurse under whose authority we took this step in the little girl's life has told me that she has a step brother and a step sister although she will not at present be told that she is not related to them by blood, or anything else about her true parents in the near future. Her step parents are well liked members of the community. You are not going to be told any more about her. You have completely relinquished any control over the little girl. Are you ready to leave now Donella?" Donella replied:

"Yes mother I am completely committed to this future life of eventually being a nun and leading the rest of my life in holy office." Desperately she said: "Does my father know anything of these matters that are happening to me?" Josina answered: "No my child. He is now not allowed to leave the sanatorium where he has been placed by the medical authorities due to an illness to do with the unreasonable and sometimes violent behavior that the malfunctioning of his brain causes."

They had nearly reached the convent outside the nearby town that they had visited a few months ago. The dogs pulled the sleigh up to the mildewed damp door. Donella carried her small bag of clothing and with her mother walked through the light snow. Her mother glanced at her daughter keenly then pulled on the entrance bell rope.

The same young novice who had greeted the mother and daughter when they had first come to the convent again received them. She hardly spoke this young nun for she was that in all semblance, a good example of her calling as they could see from the bowed visage of the young woman. She almost whispered to them:

"Come this way." Sounds of incantation floated out from the slightly opened windows. It was chill even though it was summer in the Palatinate. Even though there was an air of austerity in this as Donella thought it also had an atmosphere of holiness that would never change. Donella and her mother were again ushered into the severe old Abbess' presence. After a while the Abbess addressed Josina having studied Donella's anxious face:

"Your daughter seems committed and prepared." She turned to Donella saying with great emphasis:

"This is your first day as a novice. Even though this convent has a ceremony where the novices learning to be nuns take their vow to enter the sisterhood we will the three of us together here witness the giving over of your life to be with our Father God."

She turned again to Josina who was trying to hide the emotion that she was feeling for she knew that she would probably never see her daughter again. The old nun spoke:

"Bid you mother a final farewell now Donella."

Donella was trying to prevent her tears from smarting in her eyes. The old nun was quite unemotional quite sharp in fact. She had endured many such occasions. She said: "Sister Bella prepare to show this new novice's mother to the gate outside." Then to Josina and Donella: "So you have taken your leave of one another I can see."

Donella's emotions were swimming and it was hard for her to keep afloat. If truth be told it had been her choice initially before she had decided to make 'cello performing her living. Sadly she realized that her mother had forced this choice onto her. Soon she would be left alone with the old nun. Somehow she felt that they felt ill at ease in the situation they found themselves in, in one another's company.

The Abess was sitting bolt upright in a chair next to a small table. Two other straight backed chairs stood placed just near her. Donella wondered why they were there. The old nun rose gracefully and held out her arms in a gesture of welcome at the same time uttering with a voice creaking slightly with age:

"My child I welcome you. Be at ease please." The two of them sat quietly for some moments. Donella was clearly expected to reciprocate the greeting. She searched for words. Donella knew that she must answer, so she said somewhat naively:

"Thank you. What is your name mother?" The old nun who had turned away for a moment hearing something outside, turned again to Donella and spoke:

"The name you can all me by is Abbess Ignatia. I am the head of this novitiate convent. It is I who have the final decision amongst the novices as to when they become fully fledged nuns. You will attend prayer and study routines daily and spend at least one hour a day in absolute meditational solitude. You will also be assigned practical duties to help out in this convent community. We will rotate the duties but they include cleaning of your sleeping quarters and also kitchen duties. You will also do altar tables, candle lighting and dusting if necessary and chapel prayers three times a day When you are not occupied you will do constant prayers with the rosary that we allocate to you."

Donella was dumbfounded but tried not to show her feelings. She was clearly expected to show some reaction to all these words from the Abbess who again prompted:

"Does all this seem frightening my child? How is your physical health? And what can you tell me about your family background?"

At these last words of the old nun Donella caught her breath. She immediately remembered what her mother had told her. She must at all costs keep her secret of having a child. So she said:

"I am quite well Abbess. From what I know of my family background my grandfather, that is my mother's father, is an esteemed judge of the law in the nearby town and is well respected in his work. His cruelty towards my mother because of the constant reprimanding he had to do in his work, caused her to elope. He has cut both my mother and myself off without money because of this, for all his wealth."

The old nun was silent in compassion at the break in life of this new novice into the sisterhood. Donella's gasping breath at the reality of the life ahead of her in the step she had taken was the only sound in the austere parlor. The mother superior let the moments tick past then said unexpectedly gently:

"Compose yourself my daughter. You have taken a brave step even by coming here. From that I understand your commitment. Everything here will be quite new and strange at first but you will find others like you at various stages of learning amongst the novices. You are the youngest here. I wish you every blessing in your years here."

The Abbess took another breath in a changed mood. Then her tone was sharp;

"You realize Donella that you will be given new name in the convent that you will keep for the length of your sisterhood. Of course you know that it is not expected now that you change your mind about being a novice. We have had one or two such cases but it is highly unusual. Most of our novices absorb that holiness of life here at the convent and are deeply involved in prayers, chanting, incantation and meditation."

Donella was completely overwhelmed by the words of the Abbess and began to tremble. She thought desperately of Viktor and the fact that she would not now be able to tell anyone about her infant's adoption. How would she be able to bear it? She stuttered out a response to the crushing words of the Abbess:

"I understand Mother. What am I to do now?"

The Abbess could see the anxiety of the young girl so took her hand saying less raspingly:

"Take heart my child. You will be overcome by our rule of poverty chastity and obedience but there are a number of young women here who will echo your feelings."

Donella felt a little comforted at the old nun's speech. The old mother lifted her head in a slightly domineering way and turned to Josina:

"The noviate formalities as regards the intake of your daughter to this convent are now complete and I am satisfied with having her here with the other novices" She addressed Josina. "You may leave now." Josina took her old cape and donned it and walked slowly to the door with Sister Bella conscious painfully of Donella's deep eyes that she felt sure must be welling with tears. Then when her mother had left Donella felt that she must somehow pull herself up in selfcontrol. The Abbess saw her change of mood. Another novice silently entered acting out a small curtsey of obeisance to the Abbess who spoke with authority:

"Sister please accompany our new sister to her cell quarters near to my own cell. I would like her to be accommodated close to myself for the first few weeks of her novicehood. I will sound the convent bells in about two hours with my sequence of ringing. With the three or four new intakes the first matter we will undertake to show our new sister the way to the convent chapel.

So the Sister nodded shyly to Donella to follow her. A door at the back of the parlor opened into a sweet scented corridor of rough wooden flooring. Fanlight windows in the ceiling let in air and a little light for it was close on eleven o' clock that morning. Nearing the end Sister Bella fumbled in a voluminous pocket of her white woolen robe that she wore and produced a key.

She bade Donella halt and put the key in the lock turned it and the door squeaked open. Inside was a wooden cross above an austere bed made up with a pale blue blanket. There was also a small table and chair. On the bed lay folded two nun's habits and headdresses. Donella had wondered what she had to wear and also noticed a pair of hardy shoes under the bed.

The two novices held an almost whispered conversation. It was apparent that Donella had missed the midday meal but that there was a bite to eat at the three o'clock break in novitiate activities. Sister Bella said:

"We are called upon to observe the routine of prayer worship and learning and above all the rules of poverty chastity and obedience."

Donella looked interested in what the other novitiate had to say but was quiet, overawed so much that she could scarcely speak. She uttered hoarsely to Sister Bella:

"What am I expected to do for the rest of the day?" Sister Bella answered showing concern over Donella's floundering in a totally new situation. She said:

"Mother Superior wishes me to show you all the rooms in the convent especially the chapel here. The postulants meet there for prayer. After tea there will be something to eat. I understand you are to be invested with your new name here amongst the sisterhood."

Donella gave start. Was even her name going to be taken away from her? Sister Bella whispered:

"Put on your robes now sister and we will go in to tea. Keep close by me while we walk around the convent because it is easy to get lost here. The other novices will be surprised to see someone new but I will ask them to tell you their names that is, as they are known as novices and accepted here. Then we will go into the Mother Superior's office where you will be given a certificate with your new title written on it.

I must warn you that a couple of the nuns new to the convent have large dowries to their names. They come from wealthy aristocratic families and are inclined to be a little flighty and more than a little arrogant. I know that that Mother Superior is working all the time to improve on their personalities as regards as regards their religious calling. Come now Sister."

Sister Bella finished speaking. She had seen that Donella's thoughts were drifting. She was in the other young novice's care to accompany her to the Abbess' office and soon they were under the Abbess' eagle eye. The old nun addressed Donella:

"You are aware that you now have another name in the sisterhood. In the convent records that I supervise you will now be called by myself and your fellow sisters as Sister Winifred. I am sure that you will find this acceptable my child."

Donella bowed her head hoping that she would show respect thus while inside she was reeling. Was her very identity going to suffer? She felt suddenly that the new person that she was named would need to be acted out amongst the young women she was with in the future. Her old self had somehow vanished now. The few novices that she had seen other than Sister Bella seemed sweepingly confident.

She felt suddenly that she would experience total humiliation amongst the more experienced of them all. She wondered if it had been the choice of any of them to take on the sisterhood. She had heard Viktor talk of the wealthy aristocrats indeed those at her grandfather's soirées. To her they were uncomfortable to socialize with but not, supposedly amongst themselves. Had they been forced by their parents into this situation?

Sister Winifred as she was now wondered to herself: would taking on an earnest submission in their belief make these young women some of whom some were from wealthy backgrounds, any easier to confide in? No she reprimanded herself. She no longer had anything deeply personal to confide in anyone. Or had she? Oh! She would never forget her past life! And Viktor!

Sister Bella and Sister Winifred were told to attend vespers before an evening meal and then to settle in for sleep. The droning sound of the half chanted and half spoken prayers at vespers that evening both calmed and comforted the suddenly changed person by name now Sister Winifred.

By candlelight Sister Bella who had stayed close by Sister Winifred at the Abbess' wish. She now led her new Sister to her chamber, both lighting their way by a candle, dripping melting wax into clay holders.

"Good night Sister Winifred," she whispered to her fellow novice who could barely speak she was so overcome with loneliness. Sister Winifred turned the handle to open the sparsely furnished cell. How different she thought from the occasions that she had been in Viktor's presence.

Donella entered her cell and stood for a few moments inside feeling suddenly lonely and abandoned. She wondered how late in the evening it was. She saw a wooden cupboard and trusting that she would find nightwear inside opened it to find just that, folded up inside. She slowly donned her nightdress and turned to her bed of starched linen and rough blankets. The air was chill and it was scant comfort to climb in.

She lay there overcome by the events of the year that had led up to the situation that she found herself in. The image of Viktor's presence flashed into her mind. Tears welled in her eyes again.

Why was it that society had pulled them apart? Could it be that life as she knew it was doing this to her? She knew Viktor so well. She gritted her teeth in forgiveness as she thought of the haughty socialites who attended her grandfather's soirées. It was this sort of person who was influencing Viktor's attitude. As the tears welled in her eyes she thought: such people were more important to Viktor than herself. She felt betrayed but knew Viktor had a modicum of social etiquette to live by and that she in her circumstances could not oppose this.

She had his child though. The thought of this stunned her again as it had before since her daughter's birth She determined to herself that somehow she would see her child again one day, how she did not know. Sister Winifred as she was now then fell asleep.

A clanging bell awoke her to the presence of Sister Bella who spoke tensely:

"Hurry now Sister Winifred. We have the day's routine to follow. When you are ready we will follow what the other novices are doing. There is not too much talking allowed in the convent. Thus followed a day of prayer sometimes spoken in hushed voices in the chapel. Sister Winifred used a rosary that had been given to her. Sometimes the novices were asked to chant their prayers alone.

These activities were interspersed with instruction by the Abbess in the chosen way of poverty chastity and obedience in their behavior that in the future as nuns they were required to follow day by day. Sister Winifred clung to everything told to her by her close friend Sister Bella. Sister Winifred was guided by the austere Mother Superior the Abbess. She became one of the few in the small chosen group of fellow novices who hung back not finding that she wanted to assert herself at all in the process of a novice becoming a fully fledged nun. She had a humble opinion of herself coming as she did from a state of growing up in a hushed aura of peasantry in the little chalet in the forest. Her mother had eloped as a teenager with one of her aristocratic grandfather's servants.

She in the loneliness now surrounding her, ever more observed closely by both the Abbess and her fellow novices, became highly aware of both her fellow novices and the rituals followed by them all every day morning until nighttime. It became quite clear to her that the Abbess was having great difficulty with some of her learners. She wondered why this was at the start of her training but from the words spoken by them it was obvious that they came from wealthy luxurious homes and some of them she could tell had been very spoilt thus far in their lives and behaved thoughtlessly.

As far as the Abbess was concerned this was unforgivable though by her constant stern reprimanding their natures did after a while seem to soften a little, and they all exercised more and more selfcontrol. This made it easier for Sister Winifred to converse on an equal level of conversation with the sort of person they were.

Soon Sister Winifred became more and more accepted by the more forthright of the other novices and they were all able to perform their devotions gracefully together. The novices were questioned individually as to their talents. When it came to Sister Winifred's turn her heart rose in thankfulness when she was told that because she had an ability of playing a 'cello she might find time to keep up her practicing and even instruct pupils in the future.

CHAPTER 13

Other than the important highlights for the day Sister Winifred was told that she could continue with her 'cello studies. She was told that a professor at the town's university nearby would visit the convent to give her lessons. This would occupy her precious time. She lived now at the whim of the autocratic Abbess. When the aged nun was present in the chosen group of novices, Sister Winifred began to find the atmosphere in the convent quite suffocating indeed almost claustrophobic.

Even though she had been schooled as a young girl in a religious institution she had never found the pious life to be as real as she was finding it now. An enigmatic and eccentric figure her 'cello mentor would appear every week and torment poor Sister Winifred with his demands as to her 'cello expertise. She became the focus of attention with the more assertive and affirmative behavior of her fellow novices. Although drawing back at the more social occasions of tea breaks and mealtimes not wishing to seek attention to herself, the noisier of the group sought her out continually. Even though they were constantly reminded of their efforts to be made in holy worship and orderly behavior they obviously found this discipline to be stifling. This Sister Winifred found too as her mother had in the past allowed her much freedom by comparison.

The more daring of the little community of novices were clearly aristocratically patronized and constantly baited one another especially Sister Winifred and they did it with a wide eyed and apparent innocence. Sister Winifred they regarded as someone who was a bit of a curiosity to the wealthier dowried novices.

"Come Sister Winifred. You always hang behind when we hurry ourselves so as not to be late for morning instructions after breakfast. Why do you move so slowly?"

Sister Winifred replied humbly and defensively

"Its so that I can work on my patience as Mother Ignatia the Abbess has told us to."

The other novices in the group gave sounds of approval. They had seen that the Abbess was frowning on this treatment of the young novice who was she could see being ostracized by her fellow inmates. As the weeks then months went by Sister Winifred gradually settled into the routine of piety that she had chosen to lead as a novice. She found though that she was experiencing a feeling of desperately wishing to know how her adopted daughter was faring. She was not aware of it but her daughter as she grew into a young girl of school going age, found herself accepted into her foster family.

As time passed this child was introduced slowly to the art of music and she found the musical talent that she was born with was making her long to learn a musical instrument. Her adoptive mother had been told of Donella's gift of musicianship and began to make the earnest enquiries about a 'cello teacher for the growing girl. She was told of a nun at a nearby school who was an accomplished 'cellist and lessons began together with neither mother nor daughter realizing that they were as such related by blood.

Sister Winifred had been taking lessons herself with the music professor at the local university and had accomplished some examinations to qualify herself in the training of young 'cellists. This had been allowed her by the now ageing Mother Superior the Abbess. Sister Winifred had been seconded at the finish of her novitiate training to a nearby convent. As required by being admitted into holy orders she was not allowed to be in touch with her mother. The young nun pressed into religious service and completely obedient in the faith she was following, had one private pleasure and that was to teach her young pupils of eight, nine and ten years of age the basic elements of playing a 'cello.

One of her pupils seemed to her to be fonder of her lessons than the others and keener to please her. Sister Winifred found herself came to be more and more interested in this young girl, developing an almost anxious attitude towards her. Little did either know that they were in fact mother and daughter, by complete chance. Although the young pupil was a normal robust child Sister Winifred began to have illusions about her pupil and started to imagine her to be her own daughter, that in reality Ernestina was.

As Ernestina bent her body and mind to her 'cello playing she found her efforts in this study most rewarding. Although her step brother and sister teased her unendingly with her enthusiastic coming and going from her adoptive parents' domicile she shrugged the two's comments off and every day rushed to settle down to the practicing exercises that her mentor Sister Winifred had given her for her weekly training.

Even though she was a sensitive little girl in her musical training she, along with her brother and sister developed into a robust and healthy young girl. The hours flew by while attending ordinary school classes and the 'cello lesson was a thrilling and important weekly event for her. She had no sense of the mystery that her mentor was feeling about her that was, wondering with almost an ache in her heart whether or not Ernestina was her own child.

Sometimes when they broke off the playing, piano by Sister Winifred and 'cello by Ernestina the nun tried to control her maternal feelings of affection towards her pupil. She had no proof that this was her own daughter but found herself almost in a dream world concerning the young girl imagining how wonderful it would be if in reality this girl was her own flesh and blood. How perfect her chosen life would be if only she knew for certain this was her own child.

Sister Winifred began to study the looks and ways of her pupil thinking as she glanced covertly at the child's earnest face as she played that she could see even a faint flicker of likeness to Viktor's being her father. Surely she could even sense from the nature of this young pupil Viktor's mannerisms? Surely this was her and Viktor's child?

The young girl though had no idea of the nun's feelings towards her and as a dutiful child just followed her teacher's instructions as she learnt week by week, note by note and studied her posture as a developing 'cellist. Her 'cello was a legacy from her mother and was a cumbersome instrument and the cause of much amusement from her fellow pupils as she made her way to the practicing room after study classes were over each day.

Ernestina began to feel a little downhearted even hurt by the apparent spectacle that she half realized she was making of herself with her 'cello. She did not answer her teasers but controlled her feelings even more loving the attention that Sister Winifred was paying her. It was strange the affection that she felt for the young nun who was her teacher. Her brother and sister were a constant irritation to her in the children's free time after school. They were far more normal than she was ragging one another and boisterous in their play.

Early on in her young life she had been taken aside by her so-called mother and told that she was an adopted child. Too young to grasp fully what this even meant Ernestina at first thought that she was not really wanted and put all her energy into her 'cello playing at practice and spent as little time as she could with her classmates or brother and sister. They interrupted her she remembered on one occasion. Her brother looked into her room and looking for trouble as he usually did goaded her:

"Why do you spend so much time making those scraping sounds on that stupid 'cello? Why don't you want to play our games? Alicia and I are becoming tired of being just two together in our hide and seek. We need someone else to play with us. Why can't you leave your practicing and come and play ?"

Not wanting to cause trouble Ernestina balanced her 'cello upright leaving off her playing. She had to answer him as he was merciless in his treatment of her.

"You know I am not your real sister. What I do and it is playing this 'cello that my teacher Sister Winifred says I must, that is important to me. Why don't you go and prepare your lessons for tomorrow and leave me alone?"

Abashed at these words her brother gave a halfhearted snigger and cowed by this answer closed the door to the room careful not to make a noise doing so. As the door slowly and quiltily closed Ernsestina was left sitting in her chair in the classic 'cellist's pose that Sister Winifred had taught her. She knew that she had won yet another battle against her brother whom she knew was not related to her by blood nor was her sister as she realized because she had been told recently by her stepmother that she was an adopted child. She had not at first understood the meaning of this and had in her simple childlike way asked her mother as she had accepted her as someone kind to her always, what this meant. It was explained to her at the time of her asking that her real mother had not he money to raise her through her childhood.

This had been a shock to her and for many weeks she had mulled over this information. Now she sat staring at her instrument. The door opened again and her stepsister peered around it into the little bedroom. The apparition Ernestina saw looked slightly ashamed and spoke for the occasion the young 'cellist thought, a little timidly.

"Gunther says that he is sorry to upset you Ernestina. But we both don't know why you are so different from us. You just don't seem to like doing the same things as we do. Ernestina caught her breath. Should she tell her stepsister the true reason? Yes she would. But she would beg her not to tell her brother. Ernestina laid her 'cello down on her bed and faced her sister who had entered the room. She sensed the well meaning behind her sister's query so gathering her wits together and feeling very brave she said:

"Alicia I am different because as you say, I am not the same as you. Our mother has told me that I am an adopted child."

A rush of emotion flooded through her body. She would confide in Alicia:

"You see I am not really your sister. I have my own father and mother who are not yours. Alicia you know that I feel closer to my 'cello teacher Sister Winifred at the convent school than to either you or my stepmother who told me I am adopted."

How close Ernestina was to the truth though neither of the sisters could put a finger on, the reality of the situation. Unknowing of it Sister Winifred was in fact Ernestina's true mother. The two girls sat ill at ease on Ernestina's bed. Alicia by far the more normal and relaxed of the two could see that her sister was upset by the criticism of her stepsister and brother had of Ernestina. Alicia spoke carelessly as usual as her stepsister knew her to be

"Then if you are adopted why don't you try and find out who your true parents are? I would want to know that if I was in your shoes. Why don't you do that?"

She moved as she spoke and the 'cello still lying on open on the bed after Ernestina's practicing, shifted slightly. Ernestina quickly held her 'cello to stop it from falling and said:

"How can I find that out Alicia. You know how strict our mother is. I am too afraid to ask her anyway."

Alicia replied interested now:

"Have you no idea or no clue that you could use to find out who your parents are?"

Ernestina pulled up short and stuttered out a reply:

"But of course. My 'cello is my lead to finding out this. I now remember our mother, that is my stepmother did tell me one thing. She allowed me to continue my music studies and she said that my true mother had asked her to tell me just one answer to my personal life that I did not know."

Alicia tensed, interested and said:

"What was that Ernestina? I knew that there would be some sure way of knowing whose child you are."

Ernestina was silent for quite some moments but afterwards said in answer to the curiosity shown by her stepsister:

"It's my 'cello! Yes I remember now. She said my 'cello was a gift from my own mother. Now I know. What I am going to do is to ask my 'cello teacher Sister Winifred if she can, when she visits the stringed instrument shop the only one in town, ask if the old man there can recognize my 'cello. All 'cellos are fashioned differently. He will be able to I'm sure and will try to remember who gave it to him to sell to her. There must be a way of tracing my mother that way." Alicia said:

"But won't our mother be a little distressed if she finds out that you are doing this"? Especially if she knows that I am encouraging you in this plan?" Ernestina pulled up sharply saying:

"But I must know Alicia. I feel I am not understood in this household. I am doing 'cello studies but this is so different a pursuit to your and Gunther's activities. You do not either of you understand my art. Nor do my

stepmother and stepfather as I now know them to be."
Alicia said:

"Then ask Sister Winifred to take the 'cello there and
inquire." At a call from her brother she left the room.
The reality of her sister's last words caused her to put
this question to her 'cello teacher the next day. She spoke
softly before the lesson began hoping against hope for
some reaction from the young nun at her request. "Sister
Winifred I desperately need you help. My 'cello was the
only parting present given to me by my mother. You see
I am adopted." At these words Sister Winifred turned
sharply to her from the nearby table where she was
tidying some music scores. The nun looked at the young
girl curiously thinking to herself: I was an immature
seeking person like this little girl once. Even so, how
like me she seems. I feel for her as I would for my own
daughter. Sister Winifred's mind flew back to her early
days when she and Viktor had been so close. Yes she
admitted to herself. We were so much in love. It hurt her
to think about it.

How was it possible that society around them had
condemned their union? And this had been because
she had been of inferior birth origins. Even her Mother
Superior had known that. The Holy Orders that she had
entered as a novice had not been prejudiced against her.
She felt a strange warmth towards the young girl her
pupil.

The few times during each month that she used
a mirror caused her to come up short looking at the

anxiety in Ernestina's countenance. Was it a holiness that they both had in common or did the girl actually look like herself. The nose, straight and unyielding – how like her own. So caught up in her observance of the young 'cellist was she that he forgot that she wanted to tell her that she did want to visit the music shop herself. So then she spoke:

"Old Herr Grüssman is an old acquaintance of mine. He has dealt with many musicians in this town and has an expert memory and visual perception. I have often conversed with him and he has told me many names connected with this sort of instrument that we know. He is sure to remember the details of your particular 'cello and it's previous owner."

The next afternoon her adoptive mother had her attention taken off her children with some friends she was entertaining. Ernestina took her chance and skipped out of the kitchen door carrying her 'cello. She felt compelled to know about its donor. She felt a sulkiness pervade her thinking as she determinedly half walked half ran down the road into the town.

Yes she thought. I know Herr Grüssman's shop. I remember calling in there to buy extra strings when they broke with all the practicing that I had to do. I hope he remembers me. I didn't think at the time to ask if he remembered the instrument. She soon found herself outside the little shop with its black wooden window frames dripping wet at a sudden snowfall. The panes were frosted over. She was glad she had remembered her fur parka as a sudden chill racked her body, clothed heavily. She peered into the dimly lit little shop.

She could see a figure moving around inside. So the shop must be open so all to the good for her mission. She tried the door tarnished with age. As it squeaked open she caught the sound of chimes heralding her entrance. She levered her body around the entrance and heard the welcoming words:

"Grüsse, grüsse. Kommen sie binne."

The old man with a shock of white hair and a work like tan jacket fraying at the edges called her in. She could see that he was just finishing a bite to eat. He spoke seeing her shyness.

"How can I help you my child. Is it to do with your 'cello?" "Yes Herr Grüssman. I think, rather hope that you can help me."

She did not really know how to explain her quest to the old man but broke out scaredly because she did not want gossip about this matter to prevail in the town. "You see my mother gave me this 'cello. It is the only memento that I have of hers. You see Herr Grüssman, I am an adopted child."

The old man responded to these heartfelt words seeing her distress:

"Let me see the 'cello."

Ernestina opened up the leather case. The old shop owner could understand immediately why she had brought it to him. He said comfortingly.

"I make it my business to study closely my customers and their instruments."

He took the 'cello and lifted it onto the counter, turning it and peering at it from all angles. He said:

"They are all unique these musical instruments. Yes I remember clearly now. This 'cello of yours was bought to me by a young woman and her daughter, whose 'cello it was about fifteen years ago. Does this information help you my child?"

Ernestina was rooted to the spot in amazement. Even the chiming bell signaling another customer for the old shopkeeper did not move her. She heard the old man she had just spoken to conversing that drew his attention away from her situation for a moment but he soon again focused on his new acquaintance saying:

"Can you tell me if you can remember sir, the appearance of the young woman that you associated with my instrument that you have examined so closely? I do not mean disrespect sir but it seems so certain that my instrument is connected to someone in my family. Please, please what did she look like?"

The old shopkeeper put his head to his chest in humility remembering the occasion that the young woman had been to his shop. She had bought the 'cello in for repairs. What had she looked like? What had her appearance been? He stood pondering for a few minutes, lost in thought. Yes! He knew now. She had a slightly olive skin and had dark almost beetling eyebrows. So her hair must have been of dark complexion. This person had an almost ferret like manner as if she needled her way though life to get her own way. With her had been her daughter a pretty blond haired girl.

But this had all been some years ago. He did he satisfied himself try to make a mental note of all his customers but this occasion had stood out in his mind because usually the people that he dealt with were laiety and locals. He remembered her visit to his shop quite clearly now. He then spoke raising his eyebrows and taking in the appearance of this young girl's countenance:

"She had a look like your own my child." Then he said self effacingly:

"But all females look alike to me. I am too old to appreciate the care that they put into their appearance. And this young person that I am remembering had the innocence of a lily."

Ernestina was so struck by what the shopkeeper had to say that she did not think for two seconds that this woman was remotely anyone to do with herself. It had been her grandmother Josina that Herr Grüssman was remembering." Herr Grüssman spoke again:

"Yes, my daughter, on another occasion this same 'cello was brought in by a young nun, someone in Holy Orders."

That it had been a nun like a person she was herself being schooled by was surprising enough. But the old man had said that the young woman had even looked like Ernestina herself. She questioned the shop owner again.

Did the young nun speak much to you at the time you dealt with her? Please sir try and remember. You are certain that this was the instrument that was under discussion?" "Yes my child it was definitely this 'cello. I remember the occasion so well. I was touched by the gentleness of the young woman who was my customer. I try to run my shop with all the care and organization I can trying to please every one and that makes me remember most of my clients and the transactions I make here."

Ernestina paused impressed then said:

"You must be very clever to do that." Then changing her tactics she began to persist in her inquiry feeling that she was getting to the root of the matter.

What did this person of the Holy Orders have to do with her, Ernestina? Clutching at straws she began again.

"Did she give her name or say who the 'cello was being bought for? You do not have any record of the transaction?" "No." Answered the old man. I recall that she did not talk much at the time. She was more intent on strapping up the instrument safely and seeing that she had paid me the correct amount for the bargain. She then disappeared sweeping mysteriously out of the shop in her robes." Ernestina was totally perplexed. How could she know if this strange nun had anything to do with her life?

Meanwhile at the convent Sister Winifred was innocently unaware of what had transpired at the shop. Of course when she had become a novice nothing had been said about her newly adopted baby. No one knew in the convent anyway. Only the authorities and not even the adoptive parents would have any knowledge of the foster child's origin.

The young nun pale of countenance with the continual worship and incarceration in the convent confines said her breviary with her sister nuns day by day. Less and less frequently did the fact that she was a mother and that only known to herself come into her mind. She passed by Ernestina every day but had no idea of any relationship that she might have with the girl.

The nun and her pupil saw one another daily. Sister Winifred sometimes paused a little on her way along the cloisters when the girl caught her eye giving her mentor also a humble little nod of her head. Sister Winifred had noticed the intense piety of the young girl that was encouraged amongst the pupils. The nun after observing this young person for some time realized that something was worrying her.

She felt a strange bond between them. It was almost as if there was something more than the teacher pupil relationship that she felt towards the girl. Only the Abbess knew the family of origin of this child and Sister Winifred felt too intimidated by the effect of the severe strictness felt by the other inmates of the convent.

She had committed herself to this cloistered life that her mother and she had agreed upon after the adoption of her baby. She caught her breath as she walked underneath the arches outside. It was good to breathe the fresh air for a few minutes. The incanted prayers that morning had seemed unendurably long she had almost been unable to tolerate the hours as they spun by in the repetition of the daily word by the group of novices in the chapel.

She felt at that time a longing to see the young 'cellist that she was teaching. The thought had struck her in a kind of relief. She could substitute the companionship that she felt with this girl Ernestina for her own daughter whom she had never known. But there was more to it than met the eye. Sister Winifred hastened on as she pondered and clutched at her rosary hanging at her belt as she went a little distressed now.

The cold air of the outside as she came onto the stone balustrade outside the convent hit her face. Her head was still lowered from the piety of the incantations in the chapel that as a nun in this convent she had been obliged to take part in. As she raised her head she felt her wimple slide back a little. She put up an anxious hand to adjust it and as her face pale in the winter light tilted back her eyes fell on the much cherished young pupil that she gave 'cello lessons to. A thought struck her so that she almost gave a gasp.

She pulled in her breath tightly as she approached the young girl. The eyes that met hers in adulation Sister

Winifred realized – did they not resemble her own? She chided herself. No! This could not be. When had she last looked at her own face in a mirror? She again gave a start as she moved slowly but firmly, vestments sweeping around her nearer to the young child. The young girl Ernestina was clearly immediately humbled by the sight of her mentor. She looked as if she wanted to say something or stop in the passing by one of the other. Did she too feel a strange kind of warmth the same as she her tutor did?" The eyebrows of the girl were dark and brooding and her eyes expressed a great intelligence. Did they not look a little like her now long forgotten own mother Josina's? Or even Viktor's? But her mother Josina's eyes she remembered had been constantly darting here and there. Had those eyes of Sister Winifred's mother not been so similar even to Josina's father the old Judge's? All these memories flashed through her mind. The young girl she was observing as she walked was almost lumbering along with the enormous 'cello. Sister Winifred then recalled that this was the 'cello she had inquired about at the quaint old shop run by old father Grüssman

Her imagination took flight. She remembered the stormy night when she had delivered the old cylindrical vessel, brown with age at the edges to the monastery. A plan was forming in her head. This girl who could be her daughter, how would she live if she took on the money starved employment of a working 'cellist? Ernestina was her daughter surely! Was her life in the convent deluding her mind?

No she thought to herself. She must not allow her imagination about this child she was so obsessed with in the pupil – teacher relationship between them invade the pious life that she was living with her fellow nuns. As it was to be allowed by the Abbess even to accompany the young talented girl Ernestina on the 'cello was priviledge enough. What could she assay her feelings with? She suddenly thought, Sister Hannalene seemed very open to friendship with her.

The nuns had been told by the Abbess that they should avoid too close relationships amongst themselves. Surely the Abbess would not mind if she confided in Sister Hannalene. She turned on her heel and robes flowing in her dignified haste she went in search of the other young nun she empathized with. She found her sitting a little apart from the sisterhood. She approached carefully and beckoned to the other nun who said:

"What is it Sister? Are you in an unhappy state?" The other answered, "It is my pupil the twelve year old young girl whom I teach the 'cello." "What is it then about this?" Sister Winifred replied: "It is just that I find myself so simpatico with her that I am beginning to treat her as a daughter of my own."

Sister Winifred knew that the sister she was conversing with did not know that she was in fact a mother of a child.

Sister Hannalene countered: "It could be true sister. Did you know that I heard from Sister Maria that your pupil is an adopted girl?" Sister Winifred could not believe her ears. She looked askance at Sister Hannalene who knew nothing of the truth so far as she Sister Winifred did. Was there a family connection? Was it possible? Was Ernestina really her and Viktor's daughter?

She would have to keep this to herself because Sister Hannalene knew nothing of her fellow nun's past. So she approached Sister Winifred again. "The poor girl. To have to face a life of poverty as a 'cello teacher herself, or even a penniless performer?"

The two nuns drifted apart on this anxious note. Sister Winifred decided that she would make an excuse to visit old father Grüssman's shop. First though she would encounter the monks at the monastery, as a nun this time. She would claim the mysterious cylindrical box containing the old Vivaldi manuscripts for herself. She would explain that it was she who brought it to them initially before joining the sisterhood. Then perhaps what was in it could be revealed and if the contents were valuable they could be sold to help this poor young girl who was in the first place her pupil. Even perhaps her own daughter.

CHAPTER 14

Life within the convent walls soldiered on for the young and older novices. They were constantly being organized in the claustrophobic atmosphere amidst the cloister walls. The inmates were always aware that their life of routine piety had been forced upon them by many of their aristocratic parents in the town.

These members of the nobility had found this life a fitting one for their daughters. Some of them even had a number of girls in their family. The situation was of new intakes into another convent after the novitiate was completed. From time to time each new arrival was manipulated by the Abbess into the institution of novices.

Sister Winifred as Donella was now called by her fellow young nuns had of course been willingly admitted to another convent at first but was beginning to find the life stifling and almost unbearable. She tried to concentrate on the prayers and incantations sung in the chapel but her mind darted constantly to her only music pupil that she was teaching the 'cello. She began to be mesmerized by this young girl in her life and to delude herself that Ernestina her pupil was in fact her own daughter.

Sister Winifred was looking so distracted at times that she was pulled up on a number of occasions by the Mother Superior. She began to feel a little frantic about her music pupil. Neither of them had any basis to go on to be able to admit to one another of in reality being mother and daughter. The routine in the convent went on endlessly with meals and tea times the only break in the days with Sundays put aside for meditation.

There was no let up or relaxation permitted by the Mother Superior. Sister Winifred found herself beginning to focus her mind in the minutes that were free to her personally, on the excitement and anticipation about the 'cello lessons that she was allowed to give to her pupil Ernestina. She began to wonder too how this poor girl would be able to earn her keep one day when she left school, but then she satisfied herself that she saw the girl was highly talented and enthusiastic too about her music.

Sister Winifred went about her duties after this conversation feeling most perplexed. It was clear that although it was possible Ernestina could in reality be her daughter it seemed that neither nun nor 'cello pupil would ever know the truth. The situation weighed on her mind. What could she do in any event to help this young 'cellist whom she felt more and more drawn to. The young girl seemed to relish in the extra attention being paid to her by her mentor. Sister Winifred had no knowledge that her adoptive parents had named the child Ernestina.

Sister Winifred cast her mind back to the days before remembering the taking of her vows as a novice and then entering the full sisterhood. She recalled how she had found herself in possession of the cylindrical box, brown with age at the rusted parts meeting to enclose some item that she had not dared to pry into. Yes, Viktor had thrust it into her hands absentmindedly at one of her grandfather's soirées. She remembered her desperate dash through the snow seeking an evening's temporary asylum after ringing the rusted old bell outside the monastery.

Curiously she had been welcomed into the cloisters at the time and had explained that she would like the monks to care for the strange item that she recalled had been handed to her by Viktor that evening at the Judge's soirée where she had been performing in the little orchestral ensemble. Her grandfather the Judge, her mother Josina's father seemed unimportant to her now.

What had become of Viktor? She pondered this anxiously. At the soirée the Judge had no idea that the young 'cellist Sister Winifred had been then was his granddaughter. He had never known and now would never realize this so it seemed. Sister Winifred knew Josina her mother was tiring of her poverty stricken life. She would have liked to reinstate herself in the Judge's domestic set up, but Donella her daughter, now known as Sister Winifred would at present find it impossible to arrange what would have been a showdown for the whole family. This was because of her relationship with Viktor and the resultant birth of a daughter to them. Donella had at the time of adoption not known the name the adoptive parents had given her so was in the dark still to the very real whereabouts of her daughter.

Sister Winifred's brow was earnestly lowered in prayer. In her thoughts she could not forget Viktor. How was it that he had shown her such passion in their relationship yet had shunned her in the end when she told him that she was expecting their child? He had explained that it was because of the aristocratic values of the social circle that he belonged to. He had not come out with it but she knew it was because of her own dubious parentage. This was especially because she had told him about her father's unstable mental condition.

Her thoughts began to flash angrily around in her head and her knuckles showed white as she gripped her hands together trying to put across a placid appearance to her sister nuns as they knelt with her in the convent chapel. There was no-one she could speak to about this. This prayer hour continued in silence. She tried to focus on the young girl Ernestina that she was mentoring in her 'cello lessons. She squeezed her hands together tightly.

Yes she would claim that young girl as a substitute for her own daughter and anyway treat her as such. Sister Winifred tried to put reason and logic into her thoughts. She focused on the strange rusted cylindrical vessel that the young man whom she had seen touching his forelock, had given to Victor. Victor had then given it to her for safekeeping. The stranger though he had been so at first to her, had forced his way into the soirée and had looked so familiar.

She had just managed to catch a glimpse of him in the incident when she had come to a pause in the work of music that the little ensemble was performing. She frowned. Yes of course. It was her father. It must have been him. Then how had the strange item that she had taken such trouble to take to the monks' cloisters that night so long ago before she had entered the novitiate come into his possession? Had he stolen it? From what her mother had told her in his vulnerable mental state he could have done anything. But she knew it was for her that he had done this thing.

As the little bell softly sounded signaling the end of the prayer session she almost angrily vowed to visit the nearby monastery again and demand back the codex cylinder. She would then slip out of the convent one day in the future and take it to the music shop where she had been enquiring about her 'cello to see if the codex could be sold. And for a good price too!

Yes Sister Winifred pondered to herself trying to find a sense of identity amidst the praying sisters in the chapel. She at least knew what it was to have a child. There was a free period after this prayer session. So obsessed with the routines in the convent were her fellow nuns that she was sure no one would notice if she slipped out to the nearby municipal authorities. She must find out about what had happened to her daughter. She had given the child up for adoption yes but so frantically concerned and worried about the child's future was she now that she threw her conscience to the winds as she summarily left the group and approached the exit door.

No one seemed to notice her going. She stepped outside into a clear windy summer day. So this was what freedom was like. She remembered the way to the austere brick offices of the authorities. She entered and on making her enquiry was directed to what seemed to be an office with a nurse in uniform sitting behind a desk. Her face was flushed and with random thoughts rushing around her head at this opportunity, she put her question somewhat confusedly to the woman:

"I have come to enquire about my daughter. I was forced to give her up for adoption some ten or so years ago. Please I beg you can you give me some information about the child?"

The brazen faced woman opposite her drummed her fingers on the rough wooden desk and spoke:

"You must be aware my good woman that under only extreme circumstances can this office give out the whereabouts of an adopted child. Have you any such reason for wanting to know about this?" "Yes! Oh yes," said Sister Winifred. "I am in possession of a valuable item that can be sold to help with my child's financial future."

Here she paused realizing that she would somehow have to visit the monastery where she must ask for the cylindrical vessel that had so strangely come into her possession. It was over ten years ago that she had visited the monastery and begged that the monks would take care of it. She had not realized that it could have value then but now she was sure it could be sold to help her daughter. She would have to go to the monastery again and soon, to claim the vessel. Coming out of her brown study she pulled herself together and said again to the unhelpful nurse:

"You will help me trace my daughter won't you?

She said these words with all the trust that she could muster up. As the confrontation between Sister Winifred and the nurse continued it became clear that she was not going to get any information about her daughter from the authorities. Clutching at straws as any mother would know she desperately tried another ruse in the quest to find her daughter. So plucking up courage and hope in her effort to help in her daughter's future she pronounced:

"If I can offer the office's controlling authorities the whereabouts of my daughter, a sum of financial consideration would this place me in a better position for you to tell me something of what has become of the girl, my daughter?"

The nurse's face hardened even further and the woman spoke:

"My office can under extreme circumstances only give out information as to the banking details of the adoptive parents of the unknown child but no association between parent and child is allowed."

She became even sterner in her attitude

"You do realize Sister that this is for your and your daughter's own good do you not? It would if allowed disturb both you and your child's emotional health you see. You remember reading the rules and conditions of the giving up of your baby to another couple?" Sister Winifred breathed heavily: "Please give me the information for the bank."

Sister Winifred felt a fleeting sense of dismay. She had been caught out. A twinge of bitterness, something not condoned by the Abbess clutched at her heart. Why had Viktor allowed her to be in this situation? How could this have it happened to them. She sensed a feeling of anger towards her mother. Yes it had been Josina who had encouraged her to take on in all appearance to the members of Viktor's household, the position of serving maid at Viktor's villa.

He had also encouraged the ruse having met her at her grandfather's soirées where unknown to the old man she had been employed as a 'cellist with his villa's musical ensemble of musicians. It had also been Josina her mother who had persuaded her to have her illegitimate baby adopted when Viktor had refused to marry her.

The confrontation with the stern nurse in the cold unfriendly office at the municipality had left Sister

Winifred in a disturbed somewhat rebellious state of mind. Where was her child? Nothing the authorities could say or do would hold back any help that she could give her daughter. The nurse after some consultation with her colleagues had at last given her an account number for financial transactions. She could not continue her life not knowing that she if not Viktor at least she could give the child born of her own womb some sort of future. She rose gracefully from the seat opposite the nurse suppressing her rising anger and perspiration and left the austere office.

A breath of wind caught her face and she felt a bit better. She did not want to be seen though by any leading people of the town as she had taken her heart in her mouth by leaving the convent so, unseen by her fellow nuns who had been having a mid morning break at the time she had left.

She tried to think what would be ongoing at that moment so that she could inconspicuously fit into the routine of the day carried forward in the daily routine in the sisters' lives. Oh! Yes they would all be surely now settling into matins. She felt thirsty as the day was approaching noon and the angelus bell was sounding. She had nothing to drink since seven o'clock that morning. The door creaked open as she entered the portico of the convent.

She remembered that the door of the entrance to the chapel was kept oiled by one of the sisters so with bated breath she walked softly up to it in her soft leather shoes and clutching carelessly at the door handle in her panic she tried to pull the door open onto the group of kneeling nuns. Two or three of them stirred from their worship at the intrusion and looked around curiously at the intrusion but Sister Winifred could see that she had scarcely been noticed. She slipped into the pew and suddenly everything seemed normal again. She could not keep her mind on her devotions though and tried to plan ahead again for twenty four hours in this upset that she was experiencing. Her spirit was confused.

She thought: the nuns were trusted with access to the keys of the convent. It would therefore not be wrong of her if later that evening when all the sisters were abed she should take the keys. Yes, and she would go in search of the strange rusted brown cylindrical vessel containing parchments of musical notation, yellowed with age so as to be fragmenting at the edges. It was the item Viktor had absentmindedly given to her that memorable evening at one of her grandfather the Judge's soirées almost ten years ago. She remembered taking it to the monastery on the other side of the forest for safekeeping. Now she would go there again to reclaim it.

Somehow after what seemed an age the group prayer matins was over. It must be mid morning. One of the more perceptive of the sisters whispered to an associate as in a flutter of woolen garments the nuns left the chapel:

"It's Sister Winifred again causing a disturbance when we want to settle down to prayer." Another spoke anxiously in reply:

"I have noticed irregular comings and goings by Sister Winifred as well. I think we should report her to the Mother Superior."

The conversation whispered between the two sisters continued in this vein with the mouths of the two sisters directed half away from the poor victim they were discussing. Sister Winifred raised her chin at the covert glances. She looked through the window trying not to be anxious at the glances being thrown at her. There seemed to be gray skies building up in a stormy sky outside.

As she walked through the arched cloisters to the domestic quarters with the group her thoughts fixed on the strange fellow who had forced his way into the soirée those many years ago. The memory was so clear. He had looked so familiar, just like her father. He had touched a greasy forelock and had handed the strange cylindrical box to Viktor. Viktor had unthinkingly thrust it into her hands.

She tensed. Had the strange person been her father escaped from the sanatorium? Was the rusted container she had taken to the monastery for safe keeping all those years ago really been that valuable? She had not given it a thought at the time. Now she wanted to know for certain. Time passed as the afternoon drew on with a study period for the sisters. Sister Winifred had made her plan.

All the nuns had access to the wooden drawer where the convent keys were kept. She would use this right and flee to the monastery by night at the other side of the forest and beg one of the monks to fetch codex containing the lost musical manuscripts from the monastery attic where she had been promised that it would be put for safekeeping.

All these years she reminisced as her afternoon drew on she staying silent with these thoughts amongst her sister nuns. None of them seemed to notice her tension and anxiety. She stayed quiet over the meager supper that was usual for a repast meal. Quickly on the way back to her cell alone she planned her movements. She would have to move silently. Time passed and she heard the soft shutting of the cell doors as the nuns prepared to bed down for the night.

She lingered and then came to the door of her own sleeping quarters. It was early evening and through the tiny window of her cell she could see gray clouds being churned up by a stormy wind. She could tell this also by a tree outside being blown to and fro. Did it mean rain was on the way to spoil her plans to find her way through the forest to the monastery that evening? She would have to hurry to get back unnoticed.

She opened a cupboard where her sparse dress necessities were kept. She looked at the bottom of the cupboard and saw what she was hoping to find sturdy footwear, a pair of boots in fact. She looked again through the window but could now see snow falling outside. She was not going to give up though. She took the cape allowed to all the sisters and tucked her vestment into her boots. Nervous now at being discovered she gingerly opened the cell door and peered round it ears and eyes strained for any sound. None of the sisters seemed to be about so she quickly glided down the passage with the wooden floor and soundlessly came to the entrance hallway.

There she located the chest with the drawers where the keys to the front door and entrance gate covered with mildew were kept. She had been lucky as thus far and had not been found out. Now she must leave on her quest as quietly as possible. She opened the lock to the first door then the heavy door in the outside wall. She could not believe that she had been unnoticed in her departure.

It was urgent now. It was very real to Sister Winifred that when she had been called Donella she had been in love with Viktor so much so that she had borne him a child. What happened after that had nearly turned her mind. She was a sensitive young woman and had given in to her mother's wish that her baby daughter be adopted. Donella had no chance had not even thought to beg her father that she might keep the child of her and Viktor's union. Now that child was alive and growing up with no future except that which Donella could give her.

This was all in the child's mother's wild surmisings, yes even obsession with the age old cylindrical box that Viktor had given her all those years ago. That was even before their child had been born. By now Sister Winifred had silently and guiltily let herself out of the convent precinct and was standing in the soft falling snow outside. She took her direction in the faint light from the stars in a clear patch of sky that seemed to be clearing as she approached the forest that she would have to cross through to come to the monastery. She knew that it stood on the other side of the wood.

She breathed a sigh of relief when she became aware that the moon was out, a full moon too to light her way. There was gap in the trees. Why was this? She supposed there must be woodcutters who used the forest by day. How fortunate this was. She hoped there would be a single main path to follow not a number of crisscrossing ways to choose from

No there seemed to be a fairly broad way to follow. The snow was not too deep as she hurried along. As she walked, now slower then faster her mind fell obsessively again onto the strange container that she hoped to fetch from the monks. Surely such an item must contain lost manuscripts worth a fortune. Why had she not opened it while it was in her possession those fourteen years ago? She had then been too immature to realize this.

She vowed to take it to the old father Grüssman's shop in the town once she had claimed it from the monks. Her heart skipped a beat. Would they even give it to her? But it was hers. Viktor had given it to her. Suddenly she was out of the forest and a faint glow showed her the monastery ahead.

Sister Winifred pulled her outer cape further over her headdress because she could see the snow was falling more thickly. She had halted to do this as the faint candlelight from inside the monastery luckily fell onto the snow in her path as the moon and stars had now disappeared behind a thick cloud. She had no thought of how she would make her way back to the convent if the weather as it was at this moment should continue. She could only hope. Perhaps she could ask the monks if they could lend her a lantern to guide her on her return.

Deep bass voices chanting suddenly met her ears as she slowly and hesitantly drew closer. Then she could see a wooden door that was barred shut. She had not at first noticed the bell on a rope, a rope not as frayed as the one outside the convent. She was tense in fear of the reception that she might get but it was urgent that she ask, no demand the return of the ages old canister that she had asked to be placed in the safekeeping of the monastery all those twelve years ago or so. In a flight of fancy she was sure that it was of great value even though it might have been stolen. Even as she surmised now, it had almost certainly been stolen by her father in his worsening mental condition.

Surely no-one could have traced it to the monastery after all this time. She pulled the rope as the chanting from inside ceased. As she stood rigid in fear at what was to come, she thought again of that evening of the soirée when she had received from Viktor the item in question. The thoughts pierced her mind in a sudden realization.

Yes, it had been her own father Ernst disguised by the hat he was wearing who had forced his way into the gathering of guests, touched his forelock and proffered the old container to Viktor. Was it coincidence that this gesture all those years ago might even now benefit financially the grandchild adopted sometime after, that he had never known?

Sister Winifred tensed again taking her mind off these thoughts as she heard the thud of heavy boots approach from inside. The idea of speaking to someone from holy orders of the opposite gender sent tingles down her spine. The gap in the entrance door was dragged open creaking with a frightening sound. Someone was standing inside holding a lantern that caused shadows to fall on the snow outside.

The night was very dark now that it had clouded over and snow was falling gently. It must be one of the monks ready to speak to her. She pulled herself up wondering how she would be able to explain her presence. If she had not joined the novitiate this situation would be easier to handle. Then the monk stood there grunting a little at the inconvenience of the icy air so different from the relative warmth and shelter inside the cloisters. As she looked at him she could see his heavy brown robes fastened with a belt of thick cord at the waist. His clothing had also had a head covering like a round skull cap with no hair visible. As she looked she saw a face that was not young but ruddy and a little lined with a joviality that also told of a spirituality in the holy orders he had taken. He then spoke to Sister Winifred whose heart was panting:

"My sister what are you doing out alone in this gruesome weather? With this snow that is falling it is fit for no living being to be outside. You must come inside out of the loneliness of your pilgrimage and tell us brother monks what your quest here is. I can see that you were a sister of the novitiate. How long have you been under vow?"

As he was speaking her heart gave a jump of fear. This person was someone that she had once known and been very familiar with. But he was older now although nothing about his personality had changed. She tugged at her conscience. Why was he so familiar to her? Was it something like twelve years ago that she had known him so well? That would make him over thirty years of age. Of course! It was Viktor! So he must have survived the war against the French and with his fiancée having died, and his child by her having been given up for adoption though he did not know it he must have surrendered himself to entering the cloisters and becoming a monk.

Sister Winifred was in great fear of the monks' appearance once again since it was some twelve years ago that she was here last. She usually had a minimum to do with the opposite gender. She wondered how she would respond to the unexpectedly warm welcome that she was receiving. It was quite clear to her that the monk who had opened up the door to the cloisters was the father of their adopted child. It amazed her that the path of her life should come up against her old love even though she had been treated so unfairly. She had told Viktor that her father was of the servant class so what could she expect from someone of the aristocracy? She was nervous now that he would recognize her. He said soothingly:

"Enter into the monastery and let us brother monks do what we can to satisfy your reason for approaching the monastery on this wild and stormy night. You must have a very urgent request. Something has clearly happened to bring you into this situation that is most unusual."

As this conversation was taking place as Sister Winifred stood expectantly frozen in body and with fear at an upcoming confrontation with the group of monks. In the semi darkness with stars now shining in a lull in the weather she could hear the soft low tones of the other monks' voices inside. She tried to speak not wanting to give away her identity to Viktor, clearly quite unaware of who she was in relation to himself. Once inside there was a flurry of welcome for her. An older monk raised his hand to quieten the brothers so Sister Winifred could make herself heard. The oldest monk said:

"Don't be apprehensive. I can see that you have the same calling as we do here." So Sister Winifred plucked up courage and began to speak:

"I will explain why I am here. Some ten or so years ago I sought sanctuary in this monastery asking that a old and strange container that I had be cared for safely in the attic of this monastery. My request was granted. I was then uncertain what the item, that was an old rusting metal cylindrical box, contained. However I am sure now that it is of great financial value being an ancient and lost relic of the musical fraternity. I wish to claim it back after all these years even though it might be gathering dust in the monastery attic right now." The old monk's voice filtered into her senses:

"My sister you only had to ask of us brothers for this boon to be done for you. Nothing has changed in this monastery for centuries so the item you are describing from all of ten years ago will still be there. My brother monks and I very seldom, hardly ever venture up the wooden staircase at the back of the monastery that leads to the attic. We do not bother with dusting up there because the wooden floor is very old and from what we can see quite rotten and therefore quite dangerous. It has been left as it is for many years now so the cylindrical object that you claim to have left in our care must of a certainty still be there."

Here he paused realizing the hour was becoming late and that one of the monks would have to take his life in his hands at the request of the little visiting sister and gingerly negotiate the wooden staircase in a mission of mercy to satisfy the young nun's request. He did not quite know the nature of the object but trusted that it would be in order to return it to Sister Winifred. So he addressed Brother Viktor:

"Brother Viktor I think seeing as you were the one who gave entrance to this poor woman in her quest to salvage something she clearly thinks is of great importance, interest and value, so you should be the one to go up to the attic and see if you can lay hands on this object. You did hear Sister Winifred's description of it?"

Querulously Sister Winifred chimed in at the mention of her name:

"Yes please do see if it is still there and if I may take it away with me."

The oldest brother trying to quell the situation spoke to her:

"You must be warned my sister that by now there will be a thick coating of dust over this vessel that you have told us about and Brother Viktor here might even be troubled by spiders in the attic. Brother Viktor did not flinch at this statement. The old monk went on:

"In the meantime in this weather of ice and snow outside can we serve you a cup of warm broth while we wait in trepidation for Brother Viktor's return?"

Chapter 15

Sister Winifred was anxious on three counts now. Firstly would Viktor recognize who she was during the time of her visit to the monastery before she left? He did not seem to have the slightest idea that it was she the mother of his child who was asking for the return of the strange round box that contained something that might quite possibly be of great monetary value.

Then she found herself casting her mind back to that magical evening before she and Viktor had finally parted their life's ways. The curious person who had burst into the soirée like a thunderbolt that unforgettable evening had caused no little irritation from the guests gathered there. The memory of the man's face turned down had touched his forelock as he had hurried up to Viktor who was undeniably an important looking personage at the gathering, this thought had flashed through her mind. He was unquestionably her father. Her mother had told her that he had been institutionalized owing to the increasing poverty of the family. So he must have escaped from the sanatorium temporarily.

Had he stolen it then? Increased fear gripped her as reality came upon her in the present situation. The oldest monk had asked Brother Viktor to see if he could salvage the item. She hoped and prayed for his safety as she sipped the hot broth that one of the young monks had brought to her. She could feel the tension as the monks gathered at the door awaiting Viktor's return from the attic. As they waited she looked out of the narrow window onto the snowy night outside. She knew as they all waited that she would somehow have to make her way through the forest back again to the convent to get her night's rest.

Again terror gripped her. Did she still have the keys to the convent that she had rightfully taken? Yes she could feel them in her pocket. She must remember to put them back in the same place in the commode drawer when she returned.

Her thoughts began to be anxious again as a distant step was heard descending the stairway, and then into the passageway outside. Viktor approached the room with the dusty cylindrical vessel in his hand gripped firmly clearly having had a successful mission. Steady footsteps could be heard as Brother Viktor walked down the passage from the stairway at the back of the monastery. He had clearly had a successful attempt to reclaim the curious item under discussion by the monks and the visiting nun.

So he was safe. The weak flooring in the attic had not given way under him. Brother Viktor's face lit up with delight at being able to please this poor person who had come in out of the night outside to make such a request. As she looked around the group of monks, in trepidation that the oldest of them would even grant permission to her to take away the curious round canister her eyes met Viktor's.

He raised his eyebrows a little in questioning at the earnest look on Sister Winifred's face. Why was she staring so at him in particular he wondered? Sister Winifred after a few moments could see clearly that he did not recognize her pinched face. But their relationship went back all of twelve years. In a surge of vanity she panicked. Had she aged so much facially, was she no longer an attractive person to men? Herr Auberg the conductor at her grandfather's Saturday evening soirées had certainly delighted in her company all those years ago.

She pulled herself up into the present situation. She was a nun now and thoughts like these must be put out of her mind. Brother Viktor murmured his thankfulness at keeping safe and went into detail about his experiences in the attic of the monastery. He said:

"The dust up there is thick. There are old books and clothing lying on old broken pieces of furniture that have been discarded over the years that are thickly coated with it. It is fortunate that we had this visit to fetch the old container because we now are aware that the whole attic will have to be worked on to restore the flooring up there. My heart was in my mouth but I saw the old sacking wrapped around what was obviously what Sister Winifred was asking for because it was on the top shelf of the old cupboard. I remembered that it had been put there all those years ago."

As he unwrapped the sacking clouds of dust began to fall onto the floor of the room. The oldest monk on seeing this spoke in reply:

"Do not worry to open it Brother Viktor. Sister Winifred will be carrying it back to the convent and the snow that is falling outside will wash off what is coating the vessel. It must be what Sister Winifred is searching for, because I am fully aware of what is lying up in the attic. I have lived in this monastery for nearly fifty years up until now."

The last of the murmuring of voices of the monks died down as Donella firmly pulled the hood of her cape over her wimple. BrotherViktor was concerned that this poor person would have to brave the black night outside in her journey through the forest to the convent. He said:

"The snow is falling much less thickly now. Here – take the container in the sacking. Be careful now - do not let the dust fall onto your robes, but let it wash off while you walk a short distance. I do not think the container will be damaged when you put it back inside the sacking. The sacking is quite thick." "Yes," answered Sister Winifred, "I will let the snow fall lightly onto the container and then I will hold it in the sack under my cape to make sure no damp seeps though into the rusted metal box. I am longing to know what is inside it!"

Brother Viktor still did not know it was Donella who was speaking but both felt a strange warmth between them. Although her heart was in her mouth about this, she spoke again:

"It must be some parchments of historical interest," the elderly monk said, "yes it must be something of great historical value. It could be worth a lot of money what is inside this round box." Sister Winifred, or Donella as she had been once said confidingly, with her heart nearly breaking that she could not reveal her true identity to Viktor, also that he did not recognize her:

"Yes. I am hoping against hope that what this round container holds will be of much value, worth a lot of money. You see Brother it is mine and I want to sell it to pay for a very special child's future. This young girl is a musician, a pupil of mine. She will have a very bleak future if she has not have help in her chosen career when she is older. She is like a daughter to me. No Brother Viktor. I am just so glad that I can now reclaim it. I also feel guilty in taking it but it was given to me long ago. I have an unhappy feeling that I came by it through someone who stole it but I have no certainty about this."

Donella was referring to her suspicions that it had been her own father who in desperation having escaped from the sanatorium had given the long circular codex to Viktor, having interrupted her grandfather's soirée all those years ago, who had a little later that evening so long ago handed it to her for safekeeping. Sister Winifred turned gracefully on her heel as one of the younger monks moved to open the door to let her out into the night beyond. On peering out she saw that there was a starry patch in the sky shedding some light onto the snow as it lay heavily and thick on the ground.

One last time she looked back into the anteroom searching for Viktor. He was there and could see her earnest expression as she caught his eye. The thought struck him: why had this person taken so much notice of him during the gathering inside? He had not known what had become of Donella after he had denied her paternity rights to their child born out of wedlock to her. But this nun's face would haunt him now. He just could not place where he had seen her countenance before. He just could not connect up the present to his past. He comforted himself that her nun's wimple was disguising a very real person so he tried to let go of his feelings as she left.

Sistter Winifred was outside and making her way along the woodcutter's path in the forest. To her joy the moon came out from behind the clouds highlighting the number of stars visible. It stayed light in the dark woods until she had passed safely through. As she approached the convent she could only see a dim lamp in the window at the front of the building. Her heart was in her mouth. Had she been missed?

She clutched the sacking containing the cylindrical container. All the dust had washed off by now. She felt in her pocket for the keys. She panicked. Had she lost or dropped them? No, she felt the cold metal of the key to the outside gate a larger quite rusted one, and a smaller one to let her into the convent. She felt that it was greasy from a recently oiled lock. Now she would have to be very quiet. There was of course no sound from inside. It was late in the evening now and the nuns of habit were abed early on the cold night.

The large wooden gate was a little way from the living quarters so there was a chance that she would not be heard if the large key grated in the lock. She was right. She tried to tread softly through the thick layer of snow and silently reached the door to the interior. The keys jangled faintly as she placed the second key into the lock. She tried to muffle the slight sound with her hand.

She held her breath. Because the lock had been oiled of late there was no sound as she turned it. She chided herself for panicking that might be heard. The events of the evening spent with the monks had thoroughly thrown her thoughts of being back at the convent out of her mind. Why was this? Her thinking was half on making her way in the strange dim light of a flickering lamp on a stand near the window on the commode with the drawer where the keys were kept. That was strange. It had not been there when she had left. But visions of Viktor's appearance that she had just encountered made the blood surge to her face several times as she walked down the passage to her austere cell. The only light showed hardly visibly from the lamp she had left burning inside her room while she was out. It was guttering now.

Not a sound could be heard as she had pushed open her door. She had purposely left it slightly open before she had gone on her errand to the monastery cloisters. She knew where her candlestick holder was kept so she groped her way along the side of the bed to the little side table alongside. She was able to light the candle and put the snow damp sacking containing the sought after long round metal holder carefully under the bed right underneath at the back. The metal box scraped against the rough iron bedstead as she did so.

Then she pondered a moment. Why didn't she just open the box right now to see what was inside? Temptation nearly got the better of her but the strict discipline of her training as a novice enabled her to overcome this. No she thought, the wily old Father Grüssman at the art shop where her father had once worked would be the correct person to open it. Anyway it was clearly rusted at the top and bottom and along the side where it joined. It could only be prized open now by some tool leverage.

After her thoughts rekindling her past with Viktor had excited her she now felt keyed up once again as curiosity abounded in her mind. At that moment she vowed she could not wait another day. She would make an excuse to go to town and call at Father Grüssman's shop with the codex. Sister Winifred would have to get through the morning in her excitement before taking the cylindrical rusted codex to Father Grüssman's shop. As she racked her brains trying to sleep in what was to her something of a crisis she tried to focus on what the next day held in store for her.

Yes there would be the early morning matins, the nuns rose early to set about their duties. Then it was class for the girls who boarded at the convent. Sister Winifred eased her mind into sleep because the main task of fetching the strange object from the monastery was over. She gave a sigh of relief that there had not been a commotion caused if BrotherViktor had recognized her although she could see that he had been perplexed and puzzled at the sight of her. He had said nothing at the time she had noticed. She comforted herself that she also had kept quiet about it although it had only been that she had recognized him and not he her. She was glad that she had held her tongue about it. But that was over now.

Sister Winifred slept that night and on awakening the next morning realized that she had a weekly 'cello lesson with Ernestina her young pupil early on in the morning. She had for many months now felt a very strange emotion come over her every time that she took the young girl for a lesson. The girl seemed so familiar to the nun her mentor. She found Ernestina looking curiously at her too from time to time.

It brought to Sister Winifred's mind the thought that this pupil of hers could be of a similar age to her adopted daughter. The municipal offices had given her no knowledge of her child's foster parents or even the child's first name. Of course she did not dream Ernestina was her own child who was her pupil, nor did Ernestina have any idea that this was in reality her own mother who had at her father's rejection of her mother given her up for adoption.

Ernestina only vaguely understood that she was an adopted child. She had never been told her real surname by her adoptive parents nor ever that she was adopted. She played children's games with her foster brother and sister as she grew in years but always had a strange feeling about her family that she did not quite belong with them although she was loved enough by them all.

Today it was lessons as usual at the school but before class she hoped to take her 'cello to old Father Grüssman's shop in the village. He was well versed in his interest and love for caring and repairing musical and artistic articles and dealt with other musical accoutrements, works of art and other curiosities.

So she would have to make her way down to the shop in the village as early as possible. She hoped that she could be there as soon as old Father Grüssman opened up shop so she could find the quaint little dealer open for business. Ernestina would also have to find Sister Winifred to tell her she would not be able to attend her usual weekly lesson on the 'cello. She needed old Father Grüssman's help with her 'cello.

Sister Winifred had a restless night and after morning matins on coming out of the convent chapel she was greeted by Ernestina. Once again at the young girl's approach she had this strange sense of familiarity. Ernestina said:

"I will not be able to keep my 'cello lesson today Sister. I was unable to turn one of the tuning pegs at the base of my 'cello. It seems to have stuck fast. I am going to take it to Old Father Grüssman's shop to let him ease the peg with a little of his special oil that he keeps in stock for this. Sister Winifred thought carefully about day ahead.

She was excited now about the strange mission that she would be undertaking to take the rusted metal codex to the same shop, also on the same day that Ernestina was taking her 'cello to a little earlier in the morning. But she would only be leaving after classes were over. This suited her purposes perfectly. Blood rushed to her face as she spoke:

"Yes, yes my child. We cannot possible hold a 'cello lesson today if it is a peg that cannot be turned to tune up the string."

She said this vehemently as she was hoping against hope that she would solve a double mystery at old Father Grüssman's shop. That was that she might be able to trace Ernestina's true identity from the simple identification of the account number with the bank on the receipt for her 'cello. Also she was sure old Father Grüssman would give the number to her.

It was a small village so the account number would be a simple one. The bank would be sure to have Ernestina's real name. The solution to the problem to prove that Ernestina was her own child would be made because the 'cello was the same one that she once Donella and now Sister Winifred, had given her child hoping she would one day be a 'cellist too.

She knew that the bank had a record of this transition of the 'cello because of its worth financially and that it now belonged to Ernestina. At the time of making the gift Donella had given the bank her own name so she would be able to check the account number at the bank and thus know if Ernestina was her true child, her long lost daughter. She had always wondered about the 'cello her pupil played on.

Now she knew. Sister Winifred missed her pupil that day of the morning of the 'cello lesson that they usually had so regularly. But this would suit her purposes well because she was only taking the strange box to old Father Grüssman's shop later because there were other classes to attend to during the course of the day. The minutes ticked by as she tried to be patient during the last part of the girls' school day.

She tried to gather her thoughts together. She was dimly aware that she had seen the particular 'cello that Ernsestina used, somewhere before but could not place its presence in her memory. She would ask the owner of the little shop who undertook sundry repairs if he knew anything about its owner of previous times or even its present owner perhaps as she knew her, Ernestina.

Again she felt this drawing to herself of her young pupil but she could not explain it in her own mind.

The children in the class she had just given rose and left and Sister Winifred tidied away the last few items left lying around. She took up the basket that she had unobtrusively placed in the corner of the room and peered out of the door. It seemed that the passageway leading to the outside gates of the convent was deserted.

She moved quickly and was on her way down the road to the village within minutes. She checked the strange round codex was still in her basket. Yes it was. Her heart was thumping as she thought to herself yes perhaps two mysteries could be solved at Father Grüssman's shop. She walked down the main street of the village crowded with shoppers walking to and fro past the overhanging eves of the black timbered framed glass fronted windows of many centuries of ago.

Then immediately she became aware that she was standing right outside old Father Grüssman's shop. She recalled with a jolt that her father had once worked there. Toys and books and ornaments were displayed in the window jutting out into the street. She opened the door carefully and friendly chimes sounded. The old man came forward as she entered and spoke:

"Good day and greetings Sister,"

Sister Winifred caught her breath at this personage, someone outside her usual social activities. She questioned herself: should she even be here? Was it right what she was doing? Her conscience pricked her. She did not at first utter a word but looked into the back of the shop behind Father Grüssman. It was a small space this curious place with oddments of bric-à-brac scattered around to catch the eye, supposedly for sale. The late afternoon light fell on to an object lying on the table at the back. It was a 'cello.

She peered at it fully realizing that Father Grüssman was wanting to speak to her. She said breathlessly forgetting about the main reason for her visit, the strange round metal codex and it's as yet not fully known contents. Sister Winifred could not control herself and burst out:

"That 'cello! Whose its it Father Grussman?"

He turned around from facing her and stared at the item that he was in the process of mending. His young friend Ernestina had brought it in that morning. He faced Sister Winifred again. Impatiently now the nun questioned him again:

"Her name, what is her name, the owner of that instrument, Father Grüssman? Has she told you her full name?" Soothingly Father Grüssman answered:

"Yes my Sister she had to give me her name when she left the 'cello here for accounting and reference purposes. Her name she gave me……. Here he hesitated leafing through a book of receipts. Then he continued:

"Here it is. She was in just this morning." Sister Winifred felt a little hysterical:

"Her name Father Grüssman. You must tell me the name she gave you. You see I am her 'cello teacher."

Suddenly Sister Winifred thought this was a weak excuse and felt at a loss. How could she go into any further detail about her pupil and the 'cello without giving out the blatant truth of Viktor's and her relationship?

Father Grüssman 's words gave her a strange feeling. Then he answered, slightly nonplussed at her behavior:

"Her name she told me today but she has told me before is Ernestina. She informed me that she has an adopted mother who only very recently told her true family surname. Her full name she says is Ernestina Tazner."

Sister Winifred looked stunned. She felt faint her face whiten and she felt that the blood in her body had stopped flowing. Father Grüssman who was a sensitive old man, realized that something was wrong, put out his hand to steady her. The stiff self control that she had learned in her novitiate training gripped her and she stuttered out the words:

"No, no there is nothing untoward happening. It's just a feeling of shock being away from my usual domicile the convent on the mountain slopes where I live."

The young nun regained her composure but old Father Grüssman sensed that there was a mystery surrounding this instrument under discussion. Not only did it seem to have to do with his young client but also had some connection with this person who was asking about the 'cello. He stood back casting his thoughts back twelve years for so. Yes! He had seen this instrument before but could not connect up anything familiar about the person who had brought it to him then with the one who was inquiring about it now. Granted it was almost a disguise that she was clothed in with an inspiring headdress. His memory for faces was usually good but this pale devout looking face defied him completely now.

So it seemed that Ernestina's mother Sister Winifred was now fully aware that it was her own daughter although presently adopted, that she was tutoring on the 'cello and that the 'cello itself had once been her very own. At last she realized that she had been living under an illusion, never before knowing all these years of teaching Ernestina that she was her very own daughter, the one she had been forced to give up as a baby. But what of the young girl herself? Was Sister Winifred going admit the relationship to Ernestina? No! That would be impossible it would completely destroy her standing in the convent as a nun.

As these thoughts crowded in on her she felt a rush of emotion and needing to let out her feelings. Fortunately Father Grüssman was getting on with the work at hand. He of course had no idea of the secret that had been unearthed. He was fingering the metal cylinder nervously full of curiosity as Sister Winifred could see as she came out of her brown study regarding her newly found daughter. She had on her mind suddenly focusing on the future needs of her daughter such as any mother would like to help with, clothes, studies and such like. Suddenly the hope of value of the strange article she had handed to Father Grüssman hit home to her and she spoke:

"Do you think that this item is valuable? Will you be able to sell it?" He replied: "It looks of antique value. But I do not know what it contains." Sister Winifred answered sharply: "I can tall you that!"

The memory of Viktor's prizing open the lid all those years ago swept over as she remembered the Vivaldi manuscripts as they had shed fragments of ageing parchment, starting to fall out of the codex as Viktor had shaken it.

Donella recalled again the occasion when Viktor had opened the old metal canister those thirteen or so years ago. Father Grüssman seemed intent on seeing what was inside so as to be able to judge the usefulness and worth of the contents. He gripped the holder and tried to turn the cap of the vessel. Many winters' of lying in the damp of the monastery attic had caused rust to set in at the top where the holder of the manuscripts opened. He pulled and twisted and shreds of metal dust fell on to his spotless counter.

Father Grüssman looked irritated at this but persevered in his task. Personally he felt that there was much of value inside the item he was struggling with.

Finally in a shroud of dust the lid fell off. Father Grüssman tipped the long round holder and pieces of parchment fell out, then the whole scroll of the very very old musical compositions. Time stood still for Sister Winifred. Yes, it was exactly what she could remember Viktor holding and handling, then handing it to her at her grandfather's soirée those many years ago.

It seemed from what her mother Josina had told her that the item could quite possibly have been stolen from a neighboring estate by her own father. Josina had told her that he had escaped from the sanatorium where he had been forced by the medical authorities to live due to a mental collapse, and had then disappeared. From what she Donella, or Sister Winifred as she was now known knew of her father this was the only way he could help his daughter financially, to somehow see that she was in possession of this valuable item even if he had to steal to find it. Then she could sell it for what it was worth. Her mind flew back to the present. Father Grüssman, an old man grunted out the words:

"A gem! An absolute find a discovery! In my experience with such antique articles this item is worth a small fortune!"

Sister Winifred was becoming anxious now because her time in the afternoon was coming to an end. She said crisply:

"Then will you sell it Father Grüssman? I will leave it in your hands. I really must leave now."

Father Grüssman peered at her over his spectacles, curiously trying to connect up the story of the 'cello and the origin of the Vivaldi manuscripts in a scroll lying now on his counter.

"Yes, yes my little sister. I will just write you a bill of acceptance for this item of value that you are leaving with me." Both Father Grüssman and Sister Winifred were overcome by the opening of the old metal canister.

Its sheer age overcame the two with the atmosphere and odor of hundreds of years seeping over them.

Father Grüssman was intensely curious as many of such items found their way into his little shop and he was something of an antique dealer. Of course the events taking place at this moment in time brought back immediately to Sister Winifred's mind the occasion again of the dramatic entrance of the strange unknown person who had burst into the musical soirée that she had been performing in. She remembered that the man had closely resembled her own father as he pulled his forelock that was a habit of the servant class as he was.

As Father Grüssman handled the rusting metal holder she quickly thought back to the time when her mother had told her that her father had been admitted to the local sanatorium, his poverty having driven him to delusions. Josina her mother had told hr that he had escaped into a life of minor crime but that she had heard no more about it. She wondered then if he had indeed stolen this strange round rusting box that she and Father Grüssman were now negotiating. She broke the rather tense silence weighing on them over the deal:

"Father Grüssman I see that what you have tipped out of the holder are old parchments of original musical compositions in faded in transcriptions. I remember because I have seen them before. What is urgent to me now I need to know, if they are of any monetary worth. It is for my daughter's sake for me to know this because she has no money of her own. These ancient musical works, it appears were composed and handwritten by the famous musical person of yesteryear, Antonio Vivaldi. If they are of any great value I would like to know for my daughter who is adopted by other folk, for her sake. What is your final opinion in this matter?"

Father Grüssman looked astounded. It was no concern of his that this young nun was also a mother of the owner of the 'cello he was repairing, but he felt that he would like to help in the situation so he replied:

"Yes. To me it seems that they are very valuable. I have an acquaintance a business associate of mine who deals in publication of old musical texts. I am certain that he would be interested in this item we have before us. I will take care of it you can trust me. If you can call back here in about a month's time I will most certainly have some information about it for you."

He brushed away the rusted metal shavings from the slightly damp canister and replaced the old musical scores carefully in the codex holder. Seeing the old man's engrossment in the object that she had brought to his shop she realized she would have to say something to get his attention so she pressed him:

"Father Grüssman I must be on my way now. I am sure that I can trust the Vivaldi manuscripts to you. The old man came out of his intense concentration:

"Yes. Yes, my little sister of course." The old man was stuttering in the confusion of what he should do next. "Uh! Uh! Yes! Leave it with me. I have a contact in an old publishing house in the nearby town where I will take it to ask if they will buy this find of ours. Such a person is my colleague in this business of buying and selling of centuries old antiques. My dear I am very sure this discovery is going to cause great excitement both in the publishing world but also in the musical world. People with his interests are constantly on the watch for finds like these."

Sister Winifred looked astounded. Such matters were beyond her understanding. The one pleasure she did know in life was her knowledge, practice and teaching of the 'cello. She was finally anxious now to leave, not wanting to be in trouble by her absence from the convent. The old man's parting words were:

"Come back to the shop in a month's time if you can and I am sure that I will have some good news for you my sister."

Sister Winifred nodded and turned on her heel. The door chimed once more as she opened it and let herself out into the street where there was gentle snow falling. She pulled her cape snugly over her wimple. Inside Father Grussman wrapped the metal canister in some protective cloth and excited now that there was still some of the day left he peered out of the shop window. The street seemed deserted this mid afternoon.

He thought to himself that he would take a chance and walk quickly to the publishing house.

CHAPTER 16

The humble cleaner who Father Grüssman encountered outside the publishing house was used to such curious folk as this dapper little old man holding such a curious item. Father Grüssman queried:

"I have visited this publishing house on a couple of occasions before now in connection with old manuscripts that have found their way willy nilly into my antique shop in the town. I am aware of someone here who would be interested in ten or twelve old musical compositions that have come my way." The assistant was accustomed to such queries and had a ready answer:

"But of course. Herr Lieberman is always available in these matters. I happen to have seen him come into the office this morning quite early and I have not seen him leave. He is the person that you must speak to about this. I will quickly go and inquire if he can see you. The person put aside the broom that he was sweeping with and bade this visitor take a seat on an old but useful chair on one side. He then disappeared down a passageway.

Father Grüssman tapped his feet impatiently while he waited anxious to find out the worth of the old Vivaldi codex manuscripts. The attendant reappeared and in a voice croaking from the cold, asked Father Grüssman to follow him He said:

"Herr Lieberman will be only too pleased to see you. I have told him the gist of your query. He is very keen to see you. Come this way sir." Down a bare corridor the two men walked and then the man knocked on a door at the end. A sharp voice fell on Father Grussman's ears.

"Bring him in immediately." The cleaning person obsequiously ushered in the visitor Father Grüssman. A strange character needing a hair trim met his eyes. He could not remember in his dealings with this publishing house or if he had come across this man before. Upon seeing Father Grüssman and being aware now of the possibly priceless article that he was about to examine the old gray and longhaired publisher's voice became querulous

He was almost on the defensive and a little irritable. The peace of the afternoon in the old publishing house had been disturbed by the intrusion of the cleaner with this strange person who was claiming to have an invaluable article that he wished to discuss with his colleague.

The publisher's bifocals dropped a little down his nose as he stuttered out a response to the visitor's statement:

"What is this codex that you have brought here? Is it old tattered manuscripts inside that metal cylinder?"

His head begun to shake in excitement:

"Is it very old?" The publisher sparked the situation. This could be a valuable find, the find of the decade in the musical world in fact. "It is not every day I come across a manuscript older than a century. Although it is not my task to comment on the container you have set before me I can see that it is an antique. I would judge the manuscripts inside to be about two hundred years old by the state of the metal cylinder. Have you any idea what it contains?"

The old man was heated and curious now. This sudden intrusion into his until now peaceful afternoon could contribute financially and positively to the antique dealer and himself. The old man questioned the visitor:

"How did you come by it this article? I do not want trouble with the authorities if it has been illegally acquired. He lowered his voice covertly and said in almost a whisper:

"Has it been stolen?" He finished on a hiss.

The antique dealer could see that the other old person was working himself up in this meeting so he sought to calm him and said:

"Oh! No! This article has come by me in the most innocent way, innocent I am sure you will agree when it was handed to me by a young nun who claimed that it had been given to her more than decade ago and that it has been lodged in a monastery attic for all that time"

The publisher taking on a cynical attitude questioned further: "But where had it been before that?" The publisher was pressurizing the antique dealer who did not want trouble. Old Father Grüssman looked guilty.

"Perhaps I can explain a little to you about the four facts I do know about this obviously centuries old article. You say that you are worried that it has been stolen?"

"I cannot vouch for that sir and no authorities have tried to trace it these last twelve years or so that it has been lodged in a monastery attic and retrieved of late by a young nun now known to me. She confided that it was curiously handed to a young nobleman by a stranger who unceremoniously entered into a musical gathering at the local judge's villa.

The apparently humble servant's appearance of the entrant into the soirée was related to me by Sister Winifred the young nun I am speaking about. She confided in me that not only did he have a close resemblance to her father, but that he had also indicated desperately to the young aristocrat Herzog Viktor Tazner that the manuscripts of the codex were for a young 'cellist in the ensemble playing that evening.

You understand sir that the young cellist in question was no less than became Sister Winifred the young nun of my acquaintance as I have realized.

There was no way of knowing how he had come by the manuscripts in the codex or where he went when he left. We will just have to accept that it is possible that they were stolen from an attic in some deceased estate.

It could have been that the mysterious person was in fact the 'cellist's own father because Sister Winifred, who was the musician at the time in question confided all this in me. It all seemed very underhand.

I could understand it though because of the down spiraling poverty and poor eating and living conditions of the little family. Her father had become mentally lacking and had to be admitted to a sanatorium for his health but had later escaped and taken to thieving. You see sir it could have been that he had turned to this life of semi crime because for a long time he had been desperately anxious about the future of his daughter whom he did love."

The gray haired publisher was used to hearing such strange stories but this one was stranger than most. He frowned again at what he was being told and his glasses slipped down his nose as he first raised and then lowered his head, showing avid interest in what he was being told.

The elderly antique dealer was rambling on and on clearly relishing in the drama of the circumstances. The old publisher was clearly becoming impatient at the ins and outs of what had led up to this nearly accomplished acquisition of an obviously extremely valuable antique item. The old publisher fingered the odd iron canister and turned it this way and that. It was not an overly interesting or attractive object but he had been told of what it contained and was anxious to make a judgment of the manuscripts that the old Father Grüssman had told him were inside the old iron holder. So he interrupted the flow of words from the dapper Herr Grüssman and while twisting the lid off the holder said:

"Yes. Yes. Now I think it is about time for me to consider what is within this item. I have a lifetime's knowledge of such ancient finds and you can believe me many such old manuscripts come my way. My task is to fit them into the buying and reading and listening audiences, as in this case so that we can all reap the most profit out of the discovery of the parchments.

It seems that the person to benefit financially if she can be traced through the records in the municipal offices concerning her adoption, is the daughter of this young nun in question. I would imagine the less said about it the better. I'm sure you will agree."

He finally unscrewed the lid. Showers of dust fell onto his polished desk. The publisher frowned once more in irritation. Fragments from the manuscripts fell out too as he tipped it sideways so as not to damage what was inside the box. As the manuscripts fell out it was clear that they were in reasonably good condition.

"Yes. Yes." Said the publisher. "I will have to paint over them with a light preservative". Old Father Grüssman was becoming bored now, in contrast to the excitement that his business associate was showing Herr Grüssman had done what he imagined would please the nun Sister Winifred who had asked him to deal with the codex manuscripts. He was getting frustrated now because the old publisher could not seem to get round to terminating their interview by giving him some sort of invoice for what he was intending to pay in for what he was going about with the music scores within the codex.

It seemed that the delay was the mess that the old fragmenting scores were leaving on his once shining desk that were the problem. To Father Grüssman's further annoyance the other older man got up to call the attendant to clean it. Everything was just left lying there for a few minutes. Then the cleaner came and for some time both the old publisher and the assistant struggled to clear the dusty untidy mess and leave the fragments of manuscripts in an orderly fashion on the desk.

Giving a sigh of relief once this was done the old man spat out the words:

"Yes. Yes. Of course. I must make some sort of monetary offer to you in a sale of this codex. I will have to cast my mind back onto similar acquisitions in the past that I have dealt with."

Then almost talking to himself he began to mutter:

"Yes, true. The Verdi string works – we made a good profit in the deal. We made a fortune in deutch marks." Then that curious Mozart single work – it was printed and sold for an amount I know was a huge gain to this publishing company. I will have to make some quick calculations."

He snapped up a blank piece of paper lying on the desk and began to scribble figures on it. Father Grüssman the antique dealer was now getting more impatient than ever. The publisher looked up and then spoke:

"I will hand to you right now a bill of money for the amount that I prejudge this article's worth. See, here I have done the calculation. You will be able to deposit it in your bank tomorrow."

Father Grüssman looked carefully at the sum written on the bill of sale and a bit amazed took it and in a final effort to leave said:

"That is in order then. I must really be on my way."

The publisher summarily pressed a little bell to call for his attendant to let Father Grüssman out. Relieved after the somewhat stuffy interview he had just stepped out into the crisp cold air when he began to wonder as he walked of the procedure to follow regarding the codex's sale. When would he see Sister Winifred again? Surely she would want to know about any profit in the disposal of the codex into the music world. In the meantime he would follow the journey of the codex manuscript scores, through to music journals and orchestral libraries in the vicinity, out of interest.

This step he had taken in the sale of the Vivaldi manuscripts would surely cause a stir, more especially amongst the musicians in the palatinate they lived in. He quickened his pace anxious now about his antique shop. Yes as he approached home ground he saw a small group of people some stamping their feet to keep warm while waiting in the snow outside. He thought to himself: business was picking up for the day as usual. Embarrassed to be late he muttered gruffly:

"Yes, yes you people. My apologies for being late but I had urgent business outside the shop to attend to. Thank you all for waiting."

He smiled into his chin in appreciation of the support that he was getting from his customers for the little antique shop. He said again:

"It is still quite early. I hope the wait has not been too long." Hoping to cheer them he said:

"Here is my key."

A little put out at not being at his usual station behind his counter inside the shop he put the key in the lock and turned it. A grating squeak was heard and as of habit when the door was opened the chimes of the bell were heard from the back. How empty the shop looked but it was soon filling up with the folk from outside who spread around looking over the current wares.

Of course, Father Grüssman remembered. He had told Sister Winifred when he would be returning or roughly the hour at any rate. As surely as the thought came to him again the bell rang inside where he was just making himself a brew of strong coffee to begin the afternoon together with some suchertorten. He caught sight of Sister Winifred standing at the counter with a questioning look on her face. Surely she would not mind if he took his refreshments through to the shop's counter.

He was slowly becoming accustomed to the surrounds back in his own shop having just come from the publisher. A little nervous not wishing to keep anyone waiting in the front of the shop who might need his attention he carefully loaded himself with his coffee and suchertorten that he had prepared. He would find a moment in between the chats at the counter to indulge himself with his sustenance. Sudden hunger pangs hit him. It had been a long walk back from the publishing house.

He eased himself onto his high stool behind the counter and having put his sustenance out of harm's way took note of the folk who had honored him with their presence. Immediately to his attention came the sight of Sister Winifred. Oh! He remembered she had promised him that she would be there to hear the result of the fortunes of the Vivaldi manuscripts' sale. She was standing a little to one side but on seeing that he recognized her she moved across to him. He took the first step in the following conversation:

"Good day my Sister. I trust you are well this fine day. You have surely come to enquire as to the fate of the old cylindrical box that you entrusted to me. You were right it and it's contents are of quite some great worth. I was with the publisher who deals with such ancient findings and he has given me a bill of sale. I must tell you the value of the curious item is all yours, you having had it in your possession to trust me with it."

Sister Winifred drew herself up sharply but in a dignified way but spoke humbly in answer to this news that she had been hoping against hope to hear. If it was valuable, the codex then her new found daughter could benefit monetarily in the future and she would have her mind eased about her daughter's future. So she said:

"Yes Father Grüssman I have here the deposit number that you gave me of the local banking house that refers to my daughter's affairs. It will be quite safe to use it just as soon as is convenient to you. And Father Grüssman no one will ever know what happened to the box of famous old 'cello concertos or even where they have been these last hundred years. I only know that they were given to me by pure chance some fourteen or so years ago. I have now retrieved them."

Father Grüssman sensing her joy and relief at the feeling of security for Sister Winifred by the sale of the items joined in to respond to what she felt:

"No of course my Sister it does not matter at all where these music scores have been all these many many years. In my experience of such antique articles there is always a sense of mystery and curiosity about them. No one even knows for certain about their origin since being hand scored by the composer Vivaldi. In all probability they have gone through many hands over the time since they were created. Indeed even taken from time to time illegally. I mean to say my daughter they could even have been stolen."

Here Sister Winifred caught her breath. In what she was, a nun of holy orders, would this fact as just stated by the old man mean that she had been part of something sinful? Her mind flew back to the occasion of the handing of the rusty old box to her by her one time lover Viktor Tazner. The intruder at the time she recalled had looked so familiar. Just like her own father in fact, as she remembered. Yes and her mother had told her that in their poverty stricken household Ernst her father had been going to the bad and stealing. He was becoming deranged in their situation with less and less money to depend on.

She felt faint. How was it that in her present secure standing as a member of a convent that this might have anything to do with her? Father Grüssman's continuing words brought her out of a near sickly trance:

"It will be impossible for even the most expert antique collector to trace the path that this item has followed over the years. Humanity is just so unsteady and events happen and change all the time. No one will even know about this." Somehow Sister Winifred felt comforted by these words.

On this near bitter note of uncertainty both on her side and old Father Grüssman's sympathy Sister Winifred gracefully turned and left the little shop. The old man pondered over the conversation for the next half hour but soon gathered his thoughts together knowing that now over the following week he would like to know what was being arranged about the ancient musical compositions that had passed through his hands.

He would dearly like to know and felt in the competitiveness of his older years that he would follow up his acquaintance with the old man at the publishing house by visiting there again towards the end of the week to find out what was being done about the discovery. At least then he thought he would be able to give Sister Winifred some news about it.

She was sure she would find herself in his antique shop again in a little while. Then as planned he found himself inquiring again for an audience with the old publisher. The servant ushered him in. Both men were of a ripe old age and soon found themselves nodding and wagging their heads in gossip and conversation. But Father Grüssman's curiosity was in earnest. And he made an assertive query about the old canister that had been handed over a few day's ago. He said:

"And what my friend and brother has been decided about the article that has brought us together this day? For my own satisfaction I would be glad to know."

The other old man started shaking nervously and his mouth began to open and shut willing himself to confide his arrangements of the fate of the Vivaldi manuscripts to the newly found acquaintance of this old antique dealer. He stuttered out an affirmative:

"Yes. Yes my friend I have had them printed and the plan is that with the permission of the conductor of the local orchestra they will be handed over to the repository that cares for musical scores. That is the place that the local players use to store the scores for their weekly performances that are given for the public."

Gratified by this information Father Grüssman remained silent for few seconds. He wondered if the old publisher knew anything more about the matter. After a week or two again curiosity got the better of Father Grussman. He felt in the midst of an intrigue about what all three of them, Sister Winifred, the aged publisher and he too, knew was a vital discovery amongst the musicians in the surrounding area.

Because they were newly found and never before heard played concertos for orchestra and solo 'cello the musicians passed on the information amongst themselves. One or two of the resident 'cellists in the town orchestra egged on the conductor to make some sort of decision as to having them performed. The town leader of the orchestra took the matter up personally because of the interest that was being shown in the new discovery.

The 'cello concertos over one hundred years old had been hastily printed in the exact way that they had been written down and composed by that old master Antonio Vivaldi. The scores with copies were on sale in other towns nearby but copies were now being lodged in the little office used by the town orchestra and its conductor. All this the old publisher informed Father Grüssman who was gratified by his part in the new cultural discovery. He waited impatiently for the appearance of Sister Winifred once more in his shop.

Every time the chimes rang in the front of the shop he hoped against hope that it would be her come to the shop. Then all of a sudden one sunny day she entered unexpectedly. Father Grüssman burst out with his greeting:

"Sister Winifred my dear sister please enter." She shook the dust off the hem of her robe and came nearer. Father Grussman spoke eagerly:

"Sister I have the most wonderful news." She took her chance in replying to him as he caught his breath in his excitement. "Yes old Father I know. My superior at the convent has told me. The Vivaldi codex manuscripts have been published."

Sister Winifred caught her breath. Could it be that the old music scores that she had fetched from the monastery not so long ago were going to be valuable? Famous even? She was almost too overwhelmed to venture to speak but uttered almost hoarsely:

"Please, please tell me more Father Grüssman!"

"My dear sister the manuscripts that you brought here in the old round rusted metal container have astonished musicians and those in the magic of the entertainment world."

Sister Winifred could not contain her excitement.

"Is it really so? I can hardly believe it. What will happen now Father?"

The old man was nearly chuckling in delight at the reception his works were getting from the young nun. Then she again burst out with the words confiding her knowledge long held quiet from her fellow sisters at the convent, about her daughter Ernestina. Somehow she felt she had to tell someone the true situation, and that the old owner of the antique shop would not let her words go any further. So catching her breath again she confided:

"The old 'cello you had on the counter the last time I came here. I could tell who it belongs to because this very instrument was mine once and I gave it to my daughter." The old man looked amazed:

"Yes Father Grüssman. You must never tell her but Ernestina Tazner is my daughter although she is now adopted. But she must never know about her mother."

The old antique dealer looked quite pensive for half a minute then spoke in response:

"Yes I connect what you are saying to something I know. The young girl who you say is your daughter that I know as Ernestina Tazner is in fact searching for her mother who she has found is in holy orders."

Sister Winifred's heart thumped.

"No she must never know who her mother is! I will be in terrible trouble with my superiors at the convent. if I am found out to have borne a child and more especially if the young girl finds out that I am her mother. As it is I give her 'cello lessons and I find it hard at each lesson to keep myself from telling her the truth."

Father Grussman stroked his chin pensively. As a public figure popular in the community he had many times found himself the confidant of some curious tales. This one was intriguing him at the moment. It was clear from Sister Winifred's words that she thought Ernestina Tazner had no idea that Sister Winifred was in fact her mother by birth.

What the charming young nun did not know was that father Grüssman was in the position of being able to tell young Ernestina the truth because he recognized the shape, size and appearance of the 'cello she had brought in to be repaired as the identical one that Sister Winifred had those twelve or so years ago also brought to him for care. Should he tell Sister Winifred that he knew her secret? Fear gripped him. He did not want trouble but his conscience prevailed for the moment. So he spoke to her feeling this was the right way to handle the situation:

"My dear daughter," he began, then nervously drummed his fingers on the wooden shop counter, "do you know that I am aware that the 'cello used by the young girl Ernestina Tazner was once in your possession?"

Sister Winifred gave a start. What did this old man, until now regarding him as a friend, know about her situation as regards her daughter? No! she must never know. She would be excommunicated from the community of nuns in the little town where they lived.

Father Grüssman was now wanting to relieve himself of the burden of knowing that he was in the position of being able to inform Ernestina that Sister Winifred was in fact her mother. Could he do a good deed and tell Ernestina who often called in at his shop, the truth about her mother? His thinking at the present weighed heavily on him but he spoke:

"Ernestina Tazner is desperate to know her true parents. Would you mind if I told her? I am very fond of the young girl." Sister Winifred's heart raced. Here was the opportunity to be reunited with her daughter after twelve long years. Dare she accept Father Grussman's offer?

The following day Sister Winifred waited pensively for her pupil her own daughter, although unbeknown to the young 'cellist, to arrive. A flooding sense of motherhood swept over her all that she had missed during her daughter's growing years. Strange feelings of her memories of Viktor entered her mind forgotten experiences of the earlier years in her life. As Ernestina entered once more she watched closely as the girl walked gracefully into the lesson room.

As she bent her head and shoulders to open her 'cello case after greeting her teacher with a few words Sister Winifred's heart raced. Yes! She was Viktor's daughter most certainly, with sleek black hair and earnest almost penetrating inquisitive blue eyes.

The young girl seemed to sense the strangeness of the situation with her unknowing of the fact that Sister Winifred was her mother. Typical of a young person she shrugged off the slightly tense atmosphere and spoke breaking the silence of the curios situation:

"I did the practicing every day of those two major and minor scales that you set for me. Are you ready to hear them now?" Sister Winifred was caught off guard and stumbled out the words:

"I have the most wonderful news for you Ernestina. Do you know there has been a new discovery by someone in an old attic of some, until the present unknown, 'cello concertos by the composer Antonio Vivaldi.

Maybe you have not heard of him but he was famous over one hundred years ago as a writer of music for performance to an audience. I am told that the old box of metal that they were found in had to be most delicately handled because the handwritten musical scores were fragmenting from age.

They have now been published and now the musical fraternity is wanting to hold a competition amongst young 'cello students to make these newly famous works available for public listening in an audience."

Ernestina could not believe her ears. She burst out with amazement:

"Am I going to learn one of these works? Will you teach it to me?"

The nun answered: "Of course Ernestina. That is what I want to tell you. I have bought with me here a copy of one of the solo works taken from the Vivaldi codex manuscripts, allocated to you as one of the entrants to a competition. Ernestina could scarcely contain her feeling of excitement. A competition! Now she would be rated with other young 'cellists in the vicinity. It would be a new music score. She was tiring a little from the old familiar pieces that Sister Winifred was trying to get her to perfect. What a challenge this would be. She had always liked trying a new musical piece where possible. She spoke with great tremor in her voice:

"When will I be able to look over the new concerto that you are telling me about Sister Winifred?"

The nun was nearly overwhelmed by all this because it might mean even greater success for her daughter if she won the competition. There was also the nun was aware a handsome cash prize for the winner. There were five or six other entrants. She did not however want to load her daughter the young 'cellist she was mentoring in 'cello playing with too many details at this stage. She just said:

There have been stipulations about dress for the occasion and all the entrants will have to meet at a certain time well before the concert begins. Ernestina thrilled at the thought of the possibility of dressing up for the event so asked tentatively:

"What are we expected to wear?" Sister Winifred demure now at this question from her daughter answered:

"That is not important now but I have been told that it is a long black evening gown."

Thoughts of her own dressing up so for her grandfather the Judge's Saturday evening soirées filtered through her memory. Of course that was when she had first met Ernestina's father the Herzog Viktor Tazner. Her heart fluttered with the pain of the remembering of their forced separation. However she soon with her novitiate training came back to the present. She spoke again:

"But that is not important now. I will have the score for the competition ready for you by the next lesson we will have."

The town was abuzz one Friday evening a few weeks later. The activity was slowly centering on the town hall. Sister Winifred ushered her 'cello pupil nervously to a group of young 'cellists holding their instruments, resting them onto the wooden floor carved here and there in rosette patterns. She asked tremulously ":May Ernestina wait with you young people while I go and announce her arrival to the conductor? Which door do I go through?" They told her and she went off down a passage to the rehearsal room backstage.

Meanwhile the young 'cellists were murmuring together. Ernestina told them her name. Shyly the others told their names. Ernestina suddenly felt very selfconscious. She wondered how she looked wearing the novelty of the long black gown. Then she thought: surely Sister Winifred would have told her if anything was askew.

A bell sounded and a steward in livery appeared to fetch the group. Sister Winifred reappeared and then began to look a little lost. A door nearby opened and the sound of muted voices could be heard. Clearly this was the audience. Sister Winifred went inside and made her way to the front. On her way down the center aisle to her left she happened to notice old father Grüssman sitting quietly and alone amongst the groups of people.

The old antique dealer had noticed Ernestina Tazner's name on the program for the evening. He was thinking to himself and wondering whether Ernestina would ever know that Sister Winifred knew from seeing the 'cello in his little shop that she was her daughter. This was a mystery only to be resolved with time.

The competition commenced with the entrants lining up on stage and being introduced by name to the audience. The published concertos taken from the Vivaldi Codex that father Grüssman had handled and the Herzog Tazner before that was as much as was known about their coming to light in the musical fraternity.

The performers then pleased the audience with their accomplishments. Resounding applause was heard. It was apparent that Ernestina Tazner was one of two finalists. She came onto the stage looking strangely beautiful.

Meanwhile Sister Winifred had not noticed but the monk who had once been the Herzog Tazner was seated across the aisle from her. He had realized that this musical occasion was to celebrate the finding of the ancient musical parchments by Antonio Vivaldi that had been hidden in the monastery attic for all those years. He looked across the aisle as Sister Winifred sat down opposite him. His heart dropped as the lights were lowered and he glanced at her again and again in the strange light. Yes there she was, to him the one love of his life Donella.

CHAPTER 17

After the concert Donella sat in her cell hands to forehead in the depths of despair. Yes she had done her duty. Possibly Viktor knew now that she was now Sister Winifred. Yes that she was now a nun. But having set eyes on the presently ascetic looking Viktor she felt a surge of warmth go out of her for the one who had once been her lover. Explaining this to herself she thought: yes all those years ago and now Ernestina had reached twelve years of age.

She had until then subdued her feelings and her longing for Viktor, as a nun. Now she knew that she must leave the sisterhood with this sense of her longing for Viktor and go and find him again and persuade him to do the same. Gritting her teeth she felt he must leave the monastic orders too.

Surely what she had done for Ernestina the little girl who had not even known at the time that it was her mother who was teaching her the 'cello, would be enough to win Viktor's heart back to her. Hadn't by the glances that he had given her at the competition evening showed that he at least wanted to reinstate a friendship with her?

But they were both under vow. Although he as yet did not know that Ernestina was his daughter Donella longed to tell him and be together as a family always and from now on. Hard though it would be to reinstate themselves into civilian life she just knew from the pained look on Viktor's face that he too could see no purpose in pursuing monastic orders for himself. He had seemed delighted to set eyes on her at the concert even though the two of them had not acknowledged one another at the time for propriety's sake. Wasn't this as it should be with Donella having a child to their union those twelve years ago? Perhaps the aristocratic disapproval of her station in life could be forgotten now maybe society had changed and they could be married. Her heart thudded in her chest. She determined to seek out the Abbess the next morning.

When she awoke the next day she skipped matins and went in search of the old nun. When she understood that Sister Winifred wanted to speak to her on an urgent matter the Abbess gave her leave to be in her presence. Donella, yes Donella as she now affirmatively called herself from now on, would put her need to be free from holy orders to the old Abbess.

Another of the nuns who waited on the old Abbess personally because of her increasing age and frailty ushered Sister Winifred into her presence. The old nun, curios but with a rosy and strictly disciplined face gestured to the younger nun who had asked for an audience with her, to be seated. There was silence in the room for a few moments. Sister Winifred began to shake imperceptibly with fear at what the elderly Abbess might say in reaction to her plea.

She was sure though of her intentions though having been briefly in Viktor's presence only those few evenings ago at the concert where Ernestina their daughter had claimed a prize for her interpretation of the recently discovered Vivaldi 'cello concerto. The Abbess they knew must surely be the first to speak. Then the old nun's creaking voice seeped into Sister Winifred's consciousness.

Whatever it was that the young Sister Winifred wanted of her she hoped she could settle the matter. Sister Winifred it was known in the community was a lonesome figure amongst the other young nuns. She did not always seem to find joy and blessing as someone of her station in life should. The Abbess spoke:

"What is the matter my daughter? I can see that you look deeply troubled. Do not be afraid to speak your mind to me. That is what I am here for."

Sister Winifred let out a sigh of relief. So it was not going to be difficult to confess the truth to the Mother Superior. "Mother," she breathed out taking up courage. "I feel that I have joined the sisterhood under false pretenses." The old nun did not blink an eyelid but questioned: "But why is that my daughter? Just tell me." "Mother," Sister Winifred gasped out, "I have a child.

A little girl who is now nearing thirteen years of age. I was not questioned about that when I first joined the novitiate but feel that I must tell the truth now. All these last two years it is I who have been giving 'cello lessons to the young girl who is my daughter. I discovered the truth from old father Grüssman at his antique shop in the town. I just happened to see my own 'cello there, the one I used when I was younger at musical soirées that I played in. It was just finished being repaired and lay on the counter at the shop. Old Father Grüssman told me that Ernestina Tazner who is my daughter now uses it. She does not know that I am her mother. Oh! Mother Superior my heart is in anguish about this." The Abbess responded to this:

"My daughter, oh my daughter. You have made your confession now and it is good that you have told us the truth. It must have been weighing on your mind heavily. Yes my daughter it is not the rule of the novitiate to take in non-celibate young women but we had no way of knowing of your experience in life at the time. Yes the sisterhood has noticed over the last few years a gradual degeneration into loneliness by you, Sister Winifred. We emphasize fellowship amongst the sisters here and you were not living up to that standard. I do now see that all this is not entirely your own fault. I will contact the head of the Sisterhood and arrange for you to be allowed to leave the community of nuns here." Sister Winifred answered:

"Oh! Mother Superior I am so sorry that I did not come out with the truth about my daughter when I was first accepted into the novitiate, but my mother's influence was very strong on what I should do in the circumstances and I followed her lead. My baby had just been adopted you understand Mother Superior and I needed to be somewhere that was safe and where I would be cared for. There would not have been enough to keep me busy had I remained with my mother at my father's chalet in the forest. My father had to be institutionalized and my mother was adamant that although she liked the comforts her father the Judge offered, that she could not return to him even if she had been accepted by him at that stage in his life.

As far as I knew she remained a washerwoman at my father's chalet visiting my father, and myself in the convent from time to time. I am very anxious about her and hope that she and I can be reinstated in my grandfather's old villa, appealing to him for sanctuary as blood relations, in his old age."

The old nun had been taking in Donella's story and began nodding in agreement to Donella's plan. She spoke in response:

"It seems as if there is a chance of survival for you in the outside world my daughter. If this community of sisters can put in a good word for you to your grandfather we will do it. Go with God my daughter. You will receive a letter to free you from all obligations to the sisterhood."

Tears welled up in Donella's eyes. It had been part of her life her young life to be associated with the holy sisters. Although she had fervently joined in with the matins, angelus and vesper occasions she kept her personal affairs to herself. Words of fellowship that were spoken by her sister nuns she had responded to, but now it was the old Abbess only who knew fully Donella's story so far in her life. She had said to Sister Winifred as the old nun knew her by her name taken on joining the novitiate:

"My daughter your life with us here at the convent has been penance enough for you. You must have felt yourself bearing an overwhelming burden. I am happy for you, my child that you will be released. A life of profound religious duties is not an easy one. It seems to be that you have been guided by the Lord above in the decision that you have made to leave us."

Donella lifted her head that had been bowed in gratitude that she was going to be allowed to leave the sisters and Mother Superior and broke out with words confiding in the Abbess.

"Mother I hope to be reunited with my family, yes my mother and daughter. I have discovered that it is I myself who has after two whole years has been giving lessons in the 'cello to my own daughter. That was a long time unbeknown to either of us. This I discovered upon recognizing the 'cello as the instrument I gave to my daughter when I entered the novitiate. This was through old father Grüssman who runs the antique shop in town where I set eyes upon the 'cello again. It had been brought to him for repairs. By chance he was able to give me my daughter's name as an adopted child. I am hoping against hope to make contact again with my daughter, and also her father."

Silence fell on these words uttered with great pent up emotion by the young woman, shortly to be leaving the convent community. The old Abbess bent her head in silent prayer for the good fortune she wished on the young women. Then she said:

"Good luck and God speed my daughter. You may take your time in the practicalities of leaving, of handing in your vestments and arranging civilian dress wear."

Slowly and inevitably Donella opened a little used drawer at the bottom of her cupboard. There folded for 11 years lay her civilian clothes. They did not look moth eaten she thought thankfully. Her desperate heart gave a skip. She changed into her dress wear and shed all her nun's garments neatly onto the stiff bed of what had seemed lifetime. She folded them neatly, and packed the old case that her mother had given her with her own few drab garments It creaked ominously. Just a few toiletries she put in too. She hoped the case would hold together for lack of use.

She smoothed down her black suit bought by she and her mother all those years ago and with a heavy heart from all the time spent in the sisterhood that she had at one time once longed for, and with all the memories such as they were, lost for ever now she opened the door.

Sounds of young nuns' conversation reached her ears from up the corridor. She did not wish to be seen leaving so held her breath and took her bearing the other way towards the convent kitchen. Yes, it would be better to leave from the side entrance.

The old Abbess had not said there were any more formalities in her leave taking. She was free go to. She had the official letter allowing a release from convent life. Oh! No! Just as she started to walk briskly down the corridor with new verve a group of chattering young sisters turned the corner. They would thus be following her and would see her. With any luck they would not recognize her with her hat covering her hair that was clipped short as the rules for the sisterhood had required. Donella turned down to the kitchen, and the nuns bustled past down the passage, the swishing of their thick robes in evidence. Suddenly the hum of conversation ceased.

Donella hoped that they would mistake her for someone to do with the kitchen staff. So she averted her eyes and stood still so that they could pass. Nothing was said. It seemed that she was not to be remarked upon. She could exit the side door freely now. Donella did not know at all what to expect outside. She breathlessly opened the door. Bright sunlight nearly blinded her eyes for a moment and cold air greeted her too. She looked around suddenly feeling hopelessly lost. The security of the convent was hers no longer. She would now have to find her mother for a place to sleep and something to eat.

Donella was feeling more and more weary and depressed as the day clouded over and she entered the forest, gloomy now because of the overcast sky above. It was strange to her that it all seemed so familiar to her as she approached the chalet her home of just eleven years ago. The sisters were under obligation to rise in the mornings at five o' clock so she hoped her mother was at the chalet to give her a meal and bed to sleep on before explaining her circumstances that day. Head bowed she followed the path once known so well to her.

Suddenly she heard footsteps approaching from the opposite direction. She drew in her breath in fright. This was a lonely place. Was she in danger? She squinted against what left of the light in the sky for the day was clouding over. She tried to see who it was. It appeared to be a young man robust and with a ruddy complexion. He was carrying a load of freshly cut wood over his shoulder. One of the two of them would have to give way for the other and it was he who stepped aside. He was a respectable person and was concerned to see this young woman alone in the woods so he spoke saying:

"This is the path that leads to the washerwoman's chalet. Is that where you are going?" Donella shyly answered: "Yes that is my mother's dwelling. Do you know if she still lives there?"

The young man keen to help this poor tired looking person answered:

"No, you will not find her there anymore. Rumor has it that she left some years ago to return to her father the local judge in the town. I know this from her husband's brother. He told me that after the washerwoman's husband was institutionalized because of his illness she became so lonely that she went back to live at her father's villa. I do not know the details of her return. You are her daughter then? It was told that you joined the Sisterhood at the local convent. Is this true?" Not wanting to stop and waste time now because the day was becoming later she responded: "I will have to go back on my tracks to approach my grandfather's villa then." The young man said gallantly: "I will escort you there if you like." Thankful for his help she turned and they walked silently, she to the old ediface on the outskirts of the forest. He left her then standing knocking at the front door of the villa.

Donella was now feeling tense and miserable for the winter's day was nearly at an end in her quest to find her mother. Josina was the only contact she had of permanence in this new world that seemed to her very strange, a world she had left before being taken in by the novitiate. It did not seem much different to her she only felt very keenly a sense of time having passed. So she summoned up courage having arrived at the Judges's villa's front door. She hoped against hope that the woodcutter who had helped her had gone his way and that he had been right in saying that Josina had been accepted back at the villa by her grandfather. She stood and knocked.

It was a heavy wooden door though and her gentle hand made little impact of sound at first. So she redoubled her energy and made an angry fist and scraping her hand in the process made as much noise as s she could in the process. She banged on the door for a minute or so. Then all seemed quiet as before her efforts. Donella was desperate. Surely she had been heard by now? Oh! Why had she ever left the sisterhood? She had never felt so lonely and desperate in her life.

Then inspiration struck. Perhaps there was another door. Suddenly she remembered that there was another entrance. Yes there was a side entrance into the kitchen and servant quarters. The sky was clouding over for snowfall or rain. This was her last chance. Here was a smaller lighter door. Surely she would be heard if she knocked there? This she did her heart nearly failing. Suddenly her loneliness was appeased for someone was approaching in the passage inside. She dared not even think who it could be. She heard footsteps coming toward her from the interior of the villa. A distant, "who is it," reached her hearing.

She was dumbfounded. Must she tell this person bound to be the housekeeper or at least one of the servants, who she was? But she would have to. She watched the door open slowly as if the person opening it was afraid. Then a stern woman in black and white clothes came into sight and spoke. What she said made Donella's heart sink. "Who are you madam? We are not expecting callers at this time of day."

In the confusion Donella said: "I am looking for my mother Josina. She is the Judge's daughter. The Judge is my grandfather."

Just then it started to snow. The housekeeper as she must be, if she was to show an iota of kindness could not leave her standing outside so bade her enter. Donella was by now feeling a complete wastrel, a waif lost in the outside world that she had to all intents and purposes deserted for the novitiate some eleven years ago. It seemed like her last chance for shelter even also that this stern though kind looking woman might be able to tell her something about her mother. The person's somewhat harsh voice broke into her lonely thoughts:

"Your mother? Then are you Josina's daughter?" "Yes! Oh yes!"

Donella affirmed her voice deep in her throat.. She was clutching at straws. This woman seemed to know about Donella's mother and also was now aware that Donella was Josina' daughter. The villa from outside had seemed even more austere than the convent that she had just left, with the reception she was receiving by the person who must be the housekeeper here. It was even more startling now that she must of her own accord make contact with her own kind again after some eleven years. The woman enlightened her in her response to Donella's excitement;

"I know a little of Josina's story. We at the villa have been asked by the owner who is a Judge in the town, also a member of the nobility in this palatinate, to keep to ourselves information asked from anyone who inquires after Josina the Judge's daughter. But you are if I can take your word for it the granddaughter of the Judge. No?" The housekeeper gave Donella a forbidding look and said:

"Can I believe that? Have you anything to prove that Josina is your mother?" "Yes! Oh yes. I have madam. If you will give me a minute or two I will get my birth certificate out of my bag to show you."

Donella put her bag on a nearby table and opened the neatly packed case. Soon she found what she was looking for. On the document Josina's name was given together with her own.

Just then a sharp but altogether womanly voice was heard speaking while the person's footsteps came nearer. The housekeeper spoke:

"It is Frau Josina." Donella gasped: "My mother. My mother is here then. I can speak to her, is that right?"

The footsteps came closer and then a rather sad looking but severely dressed woman came into view. The one whom Donella could scarcely relate to seeing at present because of the lines of age in her face was clearly her mother. Josina. Josina said:

"I was looking for you Fraul Kempf. My father has a query about supper tonight." Then seeing Donella and at first not recognizing her daughter she said:

'We have a visitor? And who is this?"

After the sensitivity that the sisters had to show to one another in their fellowship and prayer life, this was rather an outspoken query. She was not sure as had only set eyes on her mother briefly once or twice during the last eleven or twelve years but she knew this was Josina her mother. She remembered that she must call herself Donella from now on. How could she make herself known to her, or rather was Josina going to take the first step in making some sort of introduction? She was right. The woman said:

"You have an air of familiarity about you. I feel faint….. Frau Kempf ….please fetch me a chair and my smelling salts.. What has happened in the past is making my head swim with uncertainty. This visitor brings back unhappy though sweet memories." She paused while Frau Kempf stroked her forehead for the person who was Josina with all her confused memories and was clearly upset. Donella's thinking at this time brought back her growing years, her short interlude with Viktor, the birth of Ernestina and the placing of the tiny baby in the metal crib when she put the infant up for adoption. Then again those selfless years as a nun, all flooded through her senses.

This was quite clearly a momentous meeting for the two women the one and the other now gradually realizing who they were. Then came the realization of the meeting in words. There was no doubt about it. Josina uttered first, weakly then louder in her speaking:

"Donella! Donella! Oh1 My daughter! How is it that you are here?" Donella lifted her head put down her case and ran with little tripping steps to the chair that Frau Kempf had put out for her. She breathed out hoarsely:

"Mother! Oh! Mother! How I have missed you and the good things of life. I have led an almost Spartan life in the convent all this time away from you! It was some eleven years ago that you and I had the meeting with the Mother Superior at the novitiate convent. Oh! Mother! I have been so unhappy so, so lonely! I have missed you even missed my father, for all the trouble he gave. But most of all I have missed Viktor."

Dimly the mention of Viktor flooded Josina's mind. Oh! Yes! He was Ernestina's her granddaughter's father. Frau Kempf seeing that something practical should be done at this emotional time, said:

"I will set the kitchen servants to prepare a meal and will myself prepare one of the spare rooms for the young lady to sleep for the night."

Josina spoke anxiously to Frau Kempf coming down to reality at last.

"Frau Kempf. Don't tell the Judge about Donella'a arrival this evening.. I will introduce them tomorrow."

Donella had been more and more distressed from the moment she had knocked on the door of the villa. Josina could see the painful anxiety in her daughter's face. She knew that Donella had been through a strained and restricted time as a nun and it was pathetic to see her daughter in such a state. Her hair was clipped short and what was left of her blonde curls clung close to her head. She was in a sorry state.

Josina sat by her bed as she lay down to sleep that night. Softly she spoke to Donella her as she gradually became a little less strained as the minutes ticked by while she grew drowsy with her mother there, and ready for sleep. Josina said to her trying to be kind:

"Why did you leave the Sisterhood Donella? You had always wanted to be part of it, it was your life's aim and ambition at one time." "No mother," Donella answered, "I saw eventually that at the time of Ernestina my daughter coming into the world that there was no alternative. But I will confide in you mother. I saw Viktor Tazner, Ernestina's father quite by chance at a concert to host a competition for the 'cello performances of some Vivaldi manuscripts of nearly two hundred years old. It was I who took them in an old codex to an antique dealer, I think you remember him, old Father Grüssman and the old codex I once had in my possession. I had retrieved it from the old monastery on the other side of the wood while I was still in the convent. There I saw Viktor once again. He thinks that I did not recognize him, that I did not realize he had also taken on holy orders.

Seeing him I knew and I think he knew too even after all that has happened that we must both leave our religious commitments after this testing time. I could see that he still loves me and always will. I am hoping to go to the monastery on the outskirts of the forest to have an interview with him and persuade him to abstain from holy orders for my sake. He will do it for me I know. Her mother chided gently:

"Hush now Donella. You must sleep. It must have been a traumatic day. I will be with you in the morning to tell my father that you are here. I have told him about you and he did express a desire to see you before the end of his life."

Donella as was wont in the convent routine had woken early the next morning. She could scarcely believe the luxury of her surroundings, the comfortable bed and soft armchair close by to sit on. She lay awake for half an hour or so wondering what the day would bring forth. She had already in the old days when she had been employed at the Judge's soirées been introduced to her grandfather. She was aware that at those times she had known his relationship to her, but that he had no idea then she was her grandchild. She had no status in the family at the villa in the few years that she had worked as a 'cellist there.

She began to hope and her hopes came to be in a small way. There was a soft tap on the door. It was her mother with a hot drink and some breakfast for her. Josina spoke earnestly:

"You must still be very hungry after the traumatic day yesterday. I don't suppose you even had anything to eat at lunchtime. You eat your breakfast now and then wash and dress. The bathroom is just opposite this room across the corridor. I'll be back after the servant has cleared the breakfast dishes. Have as much as you need to eat." Then she changed the subject, saying:

"I sympathize with you with your hair all cut short like that. But your face is shining with the abstemious life that you have led these last years within the sisterhood." Donella said:

"O! Thank you for the meal. What is going to happen today? Will my grandfather be angry that you have given me shelter at the villa?" Her mother responded:

"I will confide the answer to your question because you are my daughter. You see Ernst your father departed to the sanatorium in his critical mental state. Then there were a few years when I had to work my fingers to the bone and my back was bent in pain, my hands raw with the constant washing I had to do to earn a living, to keep myself alive There was no company, only the odd woodsman dropping by for a bowl of sustenance, or occasionally Heinke or Grisella, Ernst's brother and sister-in-law, occasionally. In the end the claustrophobia of the loneliness got me down to the extent that I became angry. So I plucked up courage one day to pack my bags and departed from the chalet to chance my luck that my father the judge would take me back into the domestic scene at his villa.

The old man had aged much in the years gone by and had softened a lot having joined the church in his retirement years. When the housekeeper introduced me to him me, most unlike him he took me back into the fold of the villa without question There was no emotional scene at the time. Sometimes he exhibits his crabbiness of the past but I am sure his heart, made cold over the years of work amongst the miscreants of the court, has softened now. I think he will be only too delighted to welcome you."

Josina waited around her daughter as she dressed, it had to be in the same black suit as she had forgone all her other clothes upon entering the novitiate. She tossed her black matching hat aside. Josina took a despairing look at the state of Donella's hair. It seemed as though huge chunks had just been cut off willy nilly all over her head. She said:

"Donella what did they do to your lovely blonde curls?" Donella answered:

"No care was given to that, it was an order of the Mother Superior. The sisters were not permitted to enhance their looks in any way. All that was beautiful in a nun was to have the shining face of a person of ongoing prayer." Josina responded to this:

"I can see that but now in the lay world you lovely blonde curls will soon take on an elfin look if gone over with by the local town hair dresser. But we will attend to that sometime soon." Josina continued in a different vein:

"I have the priviledge of half an hour or so with your grandfather the judge to let him know about your presence here and to ask him if he would like to see you today, over afternoon coffee. There will be lunch laid on first though. I will be joining you."

When the mealtime came around Josina explained a little about her old father:

"I must take his part. He was over the years that he worked at the town assizes driven nearly mad by the constant day by day flow of folk who had perpetrated misdeeds in the palatinate. As a young lawyer before he was appointed as a Judge in the town, he had to defend them verbally and such miscreants were of dubious morals, many of them without conscience at all, some of them even hardened criminals. It was not a pleasant life at all for him.

This is just to tell you what to expect when you meet your grandfather this afternoon, to prepare you. I have explained to him all about you and I must warn you he is nearly in his dotage, but all too keen to greet and welcome you in the domestic scene. He says he remembers you as the beautiful young 'cellist who played in his ensemble soirées those many years ago." Donella replied:

"Yes, I have met him before but even though I realized then that I was his granddaughter, if you recall mother, we were too afraid to make known my relationship to him at the time as he was not retired and relaxed as a once working Judge and all the crabbiness that went with it."

I am going up to my bedroom to rest now. Perhaps you would like to warm yourself in front of the log fire while the judge takes his nap in his quarters. Then I will gently knock on his door to see if he is ready to come with me to meet you. I know that he will take my arm as we come downstairs to greet and get to know you. Donella spoke outright to her mother:

"But we have met before, the Judge and I. It is just that I am aware of these many years of his existence but he has only just heard that I am your daughter, his granddaughter. In other words when he comes into the living area where you will be waiting for us it will be a huge surprise for him because I am sure the canny old man will recognize you. He might take time to focus his memory on you from those soirées when you performed for him and his guests but he will be delighted to make your acquaintance in the real here and now. I have not told him about Viktor though." Donella said:

"I intend approaching to Viktor to tell him what I have done in leaving the novitiate and ask him if after meeting and seeing our grown daughter at the 'cello competition concert, if he is going to abstain from holy orders for my sake. I know he still loves me for there was anguish written all over his face when he set eyes on me at Ernestina's concert. I am sure that he is still in love with me." Then Josina said:

"All that for another time. I did hear tell in the Judge's circle of aristocratic friends that there was a man amongst them who had secretly joined the monastic order to avoid the chidings of his fellow nobility because of a failed affair of the heart. Although recently having heard that his former lover had quitted her Sisterhood, he went on to do the same thing, abstain with the permission of the head Abbot of the monastery. That must be Viktor. He is sure to find his way here to you." A quiet peaceful joy came ovar Donella's heart.

Gracefully having said all she could to make her daughter happy, but tired emotionally from the strain of the reunion with her daughter and not only that but the coming reintroduction of Donella to her father, Donella's grandfather. She had stayed up late the night before trying tactfully to make the old man realize that there was a guest at the villa, none other that a young 'cellist who used to play in his soirées on Saturday evenings the one he had been introduced to all of those ten years ago or more, that Josina said was his granddaughter.

She had tried last night to make it clear to him that he had not known about the family kinship, that the young woman now present lying asleep in the villa having arrived that day was his daughter's daughter. The old man seemed to have found new heart to live now that he was retired and away from all the meanness that he had to endure in the assizes courtrooms

He seemed to want to take in that evening why and what Josina was trying to make him understand. Finally late in the evening in the lounge living room she got him at least to accept that there was another member of the family residing at the villa. It seemed though that it was going to be difficult for him to comprehend who it was and how the little 'cellist whom he remembered could be connected with his granddaughter.

Donella had ascertained from her father that the church's men and woman in the vicinity of the villa had been at work in the old man's later years and all knowledge of Josina's husband had been erased from his thinking in one great act of forgiveness on the Judge's part. They had persuaded him at the time to trust that he would be reunited with his daughter one day. And he had come to accept it.

Later the next day Josina and Donella sat a little nervously in the same place, the living room where the log fire was burning awaiting the presence of the old man. Josina nervously stroked her daughter's hair into place and pulled the skirts of her dress so the few creases did not show. All was quiet a quietness brought over the villa by further heavy snowfalls outside. A shuffling step was heard in the passage beyond the door. The two women tensed as the door slowly creaked open.

A cane stick could be seen manoeuvering the door open to the living room. Clearly the old man whom they were awaiting could not balance himself too well while on his feet. An anxiously high-pitched man's voice could be heard:

"Josina? Josina? Are you in there? The two women tensed at hearing the judge but his daughter nervous herself at dealing with her father's near helplessness sprung up to go to his help. A head with snow white hair clearly needing attention put a face of deep suffering ready for the rest of his way on entering the doorway that Josina was easing open for him.

He did not seem to want to let go of the door handle, an object of security that he had found in the untoward finding of his way down the drafty passages and stairs of the villa from his study. Earlier he had made his toilet with his valet in attendance. Josina gently eased his talon like hand from the knob of the door and moved it to the head of his cane stick, Josina saying:

"Come now father. Its not far now to a comfortable chair to warm yourself by the log fire."

The old man had scarcely taken in the presence of the younger women although it was clear from the expression on his face that he was aware that Donella was with them.

With a flop of his body and a scraping of his cane on the hearth, to Josina's concern he dropped his body into the chair. Clearly he was used to other people. This young person now opposite him according to his recently reinstated daughter, was apparently his granddaughter Donella. Donella looked to him a little like one of the inmates of borstal that he had to deal with in his work at the court assizes in the past, with her hair chopped off in chunks like that.

Why had Josina not told him originally that this girl was the same one as had joined his soirée ensembles all those years ago? He had remembered her clearly as he did the faces of people that he had to work with. Donella looked anxiously at her mother. Yes the Judge thought the girl's face was familiar even from so long ago. He cleared his throat.

CHAPTER 18

Donella was quite overawed by the old man in the way the young have when confronted with the aged. There was a feeling on her part of deep affection for her grandfather. Then the old man spoke peering directly at Donella having glanced at Josina:

"So you are my beautiful young granddaughter." Donella felt relieved by these words and also glad that Josina had fluffed up her short fine and curly blonde hair so she looked less of a borstal inmate, and given her some less somber clothing of her own to wear today. Her seriousness an overflow from her incarceration in the convent began to feel as if it were all flowing slowly, slowly from her. As a result she felt a more cheerful person again. The old man started talking again:

"But my dear," he addressed Donella, "we were introduced many years ago. It breaks my heart not to have known then that you were Donella my grandchild."

Donella immediately felt a deep feeling of guilt that she had not told him originally but explained:

"There was feeling of deep division between my father's household and that of my own grandfather."

Josina hurriedly put in at this point:

"You remember father we agreed to forgive and forget those past years." She glanced at her old father. Was that a tear or two welling from his eyes? He said brokenly:

"All those years Josina and you Donella. Just wasted. Wasted. Knowing you then would have made me into a caring loving father to you Josina and to you, Donella an adoring grandfather. But it was those miscreants behaving against the law that I had to deal with at the assizes. They drove me nearly mad. I grew into a mean thinking and crabby old man.

But my joy of music has warmed all that out of my system over the years. What a blessing too that you are an accomplished 'cellist my dear." Donella said in response feeling deeply for the old man, but not wanting to upset him, trying to focus on the present for all their sakes:

"Grandfather it is such a comfort to me to know you still have your Saturday soirées."

Suddenly the old man was struck by a thought and began sifting out words:

"Yes, Yes my dear,' said the Judge addressing Donella. I recall the whole period of your playing at the soirées. You stood out in the entertainment as an attractive personage."

Donella spoke wanting to humble her talent in the tradition of all musicians.

"Grandfather I must admit that I did not tell you of our relationship at the time for fear of exposing your and my mother's ill feeling towards one another at the time."

She felt that she could bring out this last state of affairs now that all seemed sweetness and light amongst the three. The old man muttered at his words. "Regrets. Regrets! I do admit them." Then he adjusted to a jauntier tone: "But you were always there for those few years. Then after some time I did not see you in you usual place amongst the musicians at the ensemble's meetings and I wondered a bit but whenever I mentioned your absence in the society gathered there, there was an embarrassed and deathly silence. It was as if you were no longer accepted here. I did not pursue the matter further. How I wish I had known then that the lovely young girl was my granddaughter." Then almost cheekily to the old man's surprise she said;

"But now I too am at the villa for good now – or so it seems."

In her overjoyed state of being accepted after her experiences in the Sisterhood and it seemed accepted into the luxury and comfort that were her right she had forgotten about Viktor showing that the thoughts behind their hoped for reunion were of a similar bent. The Judge, stuttering a little at a memory that had just occurred to him, said:

"I remember clearly those soirées of the past. I seem to remember you having a partner in Viktor Tazner, yes that you had a love affair but that it ended in tragedy and that you both look holy orders. What is the truth of that my dear?"

The Judge noticed that his granddaughter tensed a little. He wondered why. No, thought Donella desperately. I cannot tell the Judge how Viktor was not prepared to go against the general aristocratic prejudice of a child created outside a marriage bond. But Viktor when she saw him recently at the concert given to publicize the Vivaldi codex manuscript findings, she could see was clearly still in love with her. She had not known it but even when she visited the monastery during her Sisterhood at the convent Viktor who was there at the time could not take his eyes off her. Being subconsciously aware of who it was, but not realizing it in the situation at the time when she had appealed to the monks for help. Confident now in the reassurance that her grandfather was on her side she asked him if Viktor ever did priestly visits to the villa. He answered:

"Yes my dear. He comes here once a month on a regular basis. This is because I felt that I was not pleasing my holy redeemer now at the end of my life. Brother Viktor with much patience made me realize that my old age crabbiness was turning me into an even more mean person. The generosity of heart that I who was now claiming to be a Christian, I did not have. I needed to get behind me the lifetime of judgment that I had to use at the assizes and become a real loving father to my prodigal daughter. How much better I feel about this now. It has given me hope for the future and more profound willingness that I can welcome you my granddaughter.

I do pride myself that Josina who was brought strictly but well has also turned out into a good person, Donella. As a man even though he had taken holy orders, Brother Viktor confided in me that you my granddaughter had haunted him with your quaint old world loveliness. He said that he was going to sublimate his feelings in the monastic orders. He said every time that he visited here that he remembered you and the wonderful talent of your calling as a 'cellist. Yes Donella. Viktor is still in love with you. I will tell him on his next duty call to me that you are here.

Perhaps this will take a while to settle in you minds but I wonder what Viktor's next step will be now that he knows that you have left the sisterhood of nuns. For a few years now I did not realize Brother Viktor's predicament for he has also basic physical needs. He has told me that his renewed beliefs have caused a stir amongst the nobility here regarding the probable acceptance of yourself into the circle of aristocracy. You have been brought up to behave in such a way most fastidiously in your schooling at the convent. The mere fact that you are an accomplished 'cellist makes for a great step up in society."

Donella thrilled at this web of kindness being spread around her and said breathlessly:

"When does Viktor next visit you Grandfather?" The old man took his time answering after this long dialogue unknowingly trying Donella' s patience slightly:

"It could be any time now. We are nearly at the end of the month when he usually pays me a monk's visit. Yes he usually visits me to encourage my newly found faith after a time of complete involvement in the nastier side of life dealing with the odd thief or marriage infidelity, child abuse or slander cases. I know now it was not a pleasant life and in my retirement I wish to become a more believing, not such a cynical person.

This has all happened since Josina returned. In the throes of my work at the assizes court Josina once affectionately my daughter in her childhood years, I lost track of her life. It was always at the back of my mind though where she had gone to make her life of course I knew exactly where she was living. I was deferential to her choice of husband and left that part of my family relationship aside.

I felt a glow in my heart when she returned here asking my forgiveness in my old age. I was only too keen to do this as have now very little greater family left in the world. She has offered to be a companion to me in my old age telling me about her marriage over the years that I was once so against. I see now that she has offered to make up too in her understanding all that I personally had endured over the years she was away, what she should have been to me all this time. She too has had a difficult life but your pretty presence Donella has only brought joy into my life. My only regret is that I did not know that you were my own granddaughter when you were accepted as the new 'cellist at the time of the soirées.

Then there were vague rumors that you were having an affair with the Herzog Tazner that petered out from what I heard tell. I never knew why. It seems now that you say that you became a nun. Why was that Donella?" She replied hesitantly:

"Grandfather, you are a man and as a much older person you will understand what happened and forgive me. O! Grandfather do not utter a word about it but….. Viktor Tazner is the father of my child Ernestina."

The old Judge on hearing this news took it serenely enough. Donella felt she had found a friend now with his attitude to her confiding in him. The old man drew himself up saying emotionally:

"So I have also a great granddaughter." Then earnestly he said:

"You must let me meet her soon also". Donella was finding the old man had a soft heart. Of course this had to do with the fact too that she was a beautiful young girl.

The old judge however crusty and mean he had been during his lifetime of dealing with misbehavior in the court room had obviously found a new lease of life with the constant attention of his daughter who even now realized that time was approaching the evening meal. The old man was also clearly quite enchanted with his granddaughter just as Viktor had found her beauty and graciousness infused into her by the choice of musical education she had made.

The old Judge for all his calling in life was also a man and having dealt with many curious cases in his legal work did not find it strange that his granddaughter should have an illegitimate and adopted daughter of her own. He had realized those eleven or so years ago when his granddaughter Donella had been playing in the soirées ensemble of music at a time when Viktor Tazner had been very much in love with Donella who was his granddaughter.

The old man was in the courtroom for much of his life as well as following up his social life. This had left his mind quite active enough for his age. They walked down the passage in the villa to the dining room. Being seated the serving of the meal and its enjoyment began. Judge Maestricht the old man took the lead in the conversation, ever the aristocrat. He seemed very preoccupied with the fact that his great granddaughter Ernestina so he had been told was a talented 'cellist as well as his granddaughter.

Gradually the story unfolded how as a nun and unknowing as her daughter then Sister Winifred also was not aware of it for many years, and had trained her own daughter as a 'cellist. Ernestina had won the competition using a score of one of the recently discovered and newly published Vivaldi 'cello concertos. Judge Maestricht seemed very impressed but frowned a little hearing Josina's telling of the tale that the codex of

Vivaldi manuscripts that were used in the competition, had possible been stolen by Ernst her husband in his impoverished mental state. The Judge spoke:

"But surely now he can be released from the sanatorium? All these years he has been institutionalized? Isn't he well by now? Could the hospital do nothing for him?" The old man clearly felt some sympathy for poor Ernst even after their being at loggerheads over his daughter Josina all those years ago. The memory of her elopement and all that had gone before it had stuck in his mind.

Donella had a right royal feast of a meal that evening. She hardly heard the Judges words regarding her father feeling so replete in appetite. Then she realized that he was finished eating and was addressing his two newly found relations, daughter and granddaughter. Donella was quick on the uptake concerning the old man's questioning about his son-in-law Ernst. He was saying:

"Could the doctor's not rehabilitate the poor man Josina? I am all for the upliftment of such people. You do know that I worked for the interests of such folk in my career in legal circles?" Josina answered:

"Oh yes father we do know that but the doctors that we were in touch with when he first relapsed in his illness…" The Judge interrupted here because of his past employees that he took a supportive interest in. One of them was a handyman of many years ago that he had not forgotten. He called to mind that this particular young man had given him a considerable amount of trouble, embarrassing too concerning the young man's relationship with his daughter.

Yes, the old man thought to himself it was this person who had eloped with his daughter all those years ago. But circumstances had changed. Now she was back and he had invited his granddaughter, a child of this employee of the past, to live at his villa. Ten years or so ago she had been a novice and then a nun in the sisterhood at the convent outside the nearby town.

Since he had retired he had been in close contact with an old friend of his family's son, the Herzog Viktor Tazner who for some obscure romantic reason had left his family home, that was another villa nearby to take up holy orders in the monastery on the outskirts of the forest that grew near the Judge's domicile. The two men, the older with Viktor Tazner being like a grandson to him, had become very close and the young monk as he had become had been a great help to the now ageing Judge in retrieving what was left of the old man's religious feeling that Judge Maestricht had as a young man. He had confided in the young monk that the life that he had trained for, dealing with miscreants and even criminals had drawn him away from the beauty and serenity of being the deeply religious person that he had been as a young man.

Looking at Donella now seated at table exchanging conversation with her mother he tried to fix his memory on the presence of his granddaughter. He remembered that he had enjoyed watching relationships form at his hospitality soirées every Saturday evening with the little musical ensemble he had got together. And here right before his eyes, yes, was Donella that charming young 'cellist who at the time he had no idea was his granddaughter!

The old Judge chided himself for his state of mind, the cynicism that he had developed in his nature according to his training that was in the legal profession. A spark of warmth was planted in the Judge's heart now that his daughter had seen the error of her ways and in humility had come back to the old villa. Also this dear granddaughter. But who did he have to thank for the new lease of life that he was experiencing in his retirement?

It was the regular visits by the month that he was receiving from Brother Viktor once known to him as the Herzog Viktor Tazner. The two men one older and the other young enough to be a grandson to him that he never had. But yes it was not a grandson he had now it was a granddaughter. Brother Viktor had been visiting the old man for the last five years. He had confided in the old Judge that the walks through the forest gave him a sense of freedom.

The young monk was once a member of a family friend who with his wife had died in suspiciously tragic circumstances to do with the young Hertzog's fiancée. The Judge was mulling over these memories as the reunited family sat in the drawing room that morning in front of a log fire. The Judge could not get over the fact that he had a granddaughter. He broke into the feminine conversation addressing Donella:

"You still look a little pinched around the face my dear. You are so thin and slight of body. You must eat more and grow stronger. Do you not agree my daughter?" He flicked his gaze at Josina.

"You too Josina my dear."

Josina's heart warmed to her father. How was it that her father was taking a great I interest in her? Respectfully for she was still in awe of the old man she said:

"Father I cannot believe that you have forgiven me. I am unable to understand how it has come about this changed attitude towards myself."

The old man decided to explain a little of the cause of his change of heart. Brother Viktor was in fact his present religious mentor Viktor Tazner.

"My child I have a secret that I will share with you just now. Firstly I must tell you that I was also young once. As a student I was enthusiastic, and critical of the political system as it was those many years ago."

The old man looked wistful as his mind was clearly flashing back to his early days. He continued:

"Yes my dears. I wanted to fight the social structure with my fellow legal students. A better social situation was needed in the country for the poor and the miscreants. I suppose what my fellow students and I wanted was the ideal of a perfect society. Yes. We believed this was what we would achieve.

Of course as you my daughter and granddaughter know now this was an impossibility. Things did not change as we had hoped.

As I grew older and saw into the reality of what I was tackling in the court assizes the hardened minds of those breaking the law that I had to deal with, I came to know what to expect from life and my part in it. It came to the stage where with not just one but all those I dealt with I did not even expect good behavior. All my clients had some sort of complaint against the next man and my thinking grew cynical and bitter. As you know my late wife suffered greatly at the mental strain I lived with." He paused. Josina broke in:

"But you are not like that now father. Why, please tell me and how did you change?" "He replied:

"Ah! My child. I will answer you that I have a friend who is a monk from across the forest on these Alpine slopes where we live.

It so happens that his family and my family were once very close friends. Through tragedy his parents died and because of both those and other circumstances the young man took monastic orders. We have become great friends and he visits me every now and again. He has over the last five years with his superiors condoning these visits, been able to persuade me to re-embrace my religious beliefs that I held as a young person. Now my secret is this.

I have fond memories of you Donella when you were younger and playing in my musical ensemble although

I did not realize then that you were my granddaughter. I could also see that one of my aristocratic friend's son who also attended my soirées had a great attraction for you. There were rumors of great tragedy in his family of a romantic nature and the tragic death of his parents in suspicious circumstances. I missed you both when after a while you both ceased to attend my soirees. I did hear though that you both took religious orders."

There was a medley of voices outside in the hallway. The Judge was summoned to meet the company who had just arrived. Donella strained her ears. Yes she could hear the Judges crisp and creaky voice welcoming a visitor. Josina was with her daughter and could see how overcome she was. Her mother was aware of the part that she had played in separating the couple those twelve or so years ago when Donella was rejected by the Herzog Tazner's late parents' aristocratic circle of friends. Donella she could see was looking distressed at the coming meeting. She said:

"Your grandfather is welcoming Viktor. Yes Donella, it is the father of your adopted daughter. It is a strange situation but take courage my daughter."

Donella looked down at the carpeted floor away from her mother who continued soothingly:

"I am sure that your grandfather is preparing for the reacquainting of he and you Donella."

The voices in the passage continued slowly inevitably coming closer. Donella tried as her mother suggested to relax a little more and tried to hear what was being said and as she did so the door opened slowly. Her grandfather was followed in by a n ascetic and strained looking person dressed as a monk with a cowelled cap on his head. The past years told their story as the newly freed nun of twelve years standing met the eyes of the sensitive man whom she recognized as Viktor. His eyes pierced hers.

Donella's grandfather with the perspective of age and sensitive to the feelings too of his own daughter was saying as the two men walked in:

"Yes she is the person you knew so well all those years ago Brother Viktor. I have confirmed this with my daughter, her mother who knows her whole life story. She has recently left a sisterhood of nuns and will need some time to readjust to the life of us lay people. Donella my dear here is someone who is very keen to reacquaint himself with you. Are you in a ready state to say a few words to him? He would dearly love to hear your voice to know that you still exist. And exist for him."

Then Donella's heart was cut to the quick. She heard Viktor's familiar tones though clipped and restrained from the discipline that he too had undergone from being all these years also in religious orders. Then there he was the Viktor she had been so close to those twelve years past. Here was Ernestina's father, of the little adopted child whom she had not even at first recognized as her daughter while giving her 'cello lessons at the convent all those years ago. How were the three of them going to make up for what should have been a little family growing together?

Then the tumult of feelings as to the words they would speak together now in her grandfather and mother's presence. Viktor being a man albeit still at this time in monastic orders and wearing the robes of a monk was the first to speak. His words were clear but crisp. He had to remember that he was still under holy vows. He said:

"Donella my little sister, and to admit to it father of our child, to think that I have found you again. It is quite clear that you have had an ordeal. I myself have had this as well. You are shockingly enough out of it. I can see the mark of the strain that you have undergone being shut away from the world just as I have Donella. I still love you as a man loves a woman. Considering that you have had the strength of character to up and leave the sisterhood I will do the same and will speak to the Abbott post haste.

I have built up a tremendous anxiety at not leading a normal lay life. I have thought over during my celibacy what we have missed as man and wife with our talented daughter. What have you to say to me Donella my love?" She murmured "Only that I wish to be with you until the day you die after you have divested yourself of your holy orders. I am sure the Abbott will understand. After all he is a man and men understand these matters a love affair that is ours, much better than women. We are the weaker sex don't forget."

At the intimate nature of the conversation between Viktor and Donella, Josina and her father the Judge had slipped out leaving the two alone. The atmosphere between them tensed. Viktor said:

"As a monk I cannot take you in my arms Donella. But I promise you there will be other times for that together." Donella felt tears prick her eyelids at the lost years.

There was a silence between them that brought them very close together in their thoughts. Most of all they remembered all the wonderful times they had together before Ernestina had been born, the bright musical soirées that were the time and place that they had met for the first time.

The strain on Donella's countenance was changing like a vapor. There were faint lines on her face from growing just that little bit older over the last twelve years, thinking as she had then that the cloistered life was her lot until the day she died. She could scarcely believe her freedom. She spoke and broke the silence:

"When I was a novice we were mind trained never to think of ever again of being part of lay life. We had to think totally into a daily routine of prayer. It was hard and self sacrificing to the uttermost. Oh! Viktor! The tears hurt her eyelids again. I can't explain the joy that I feel at being free and liberated, not under such a strict discipline that was actually making me miserable all day and night. I did my share of crying in the holy orders."

Viktor was totally anxious and feeling guilty as well as it had been his family's aristocratic social circle that had subtly and with meaningful nuances disapproved of his relationship and his possible future marriage to Donella. He had to respond so he took a positive view as a man knowing there had been a daughter to their communing, that Donella had borne to him a little girl Ernestina. He said:

"I will now most certainly divest myself of my holy orders. We will marry Donella. I know our love is too strong to prevent that. One way of looking at our circumstances in life is that it has been a kind of testing between us we having been forced apart in our religious lives. If our thoughts have been of one another all these twelve years it only goes to prove that we were meant to be together and forever more." Donella said:

"Viktor was what we did wrong then?" He answered: "No Donella. I do not believe it was sinful. It was a love affair that the words spoken by us even now are showing our feelings one towards the other, that it is true love between us."

The couple were now alone. Donella said:

"What are we going to do about Ernestina our daughter? Her adoptive parents gave her another name that I came across by chance when her 'cello was in for repairs at the little musical instrument shop in town. There was a label of receipt lying there on the counter together with her instrument, one that was actually mine, I gave it to her for her studies long ago.

I discovered too later on that I did not even know that I was giving my own daughter 'cello lessons. I did not recognize her and she did not know who I was. I must tell you Viktor from what I have seen of her 'cello playing she is something of a child prodgidy at her instrument. I have not let her know in our regular lessons that I am her real mother for fear of recrimination from my mother superior or the municipal authorities who organized her adoption. I still have the reference number for the adoption. I needed it when the Vivaldi codex manuscripts were sold to bank the proceeds for my then adopted daughter. I hope now that circumstances have changed that we can, so to speak rescue the young girl our daughter. We must explain to her adoptive parents that we are her mother and father by blood. I doubt that Ernestina will understand but children of that age have a lot of trust." Viktor responded from his side:

"I am leaving the Judge's villa now to sort matters out to be able to abscond from monastic orders. Being men we do understand about affairs of the heart so this will not be difficult." So Donella answered: "When will you be back Viktor?" He replied: "God willing in about another month."

He was as good as his word. The couple were married post haste. After the ceremony Viktor said :

"We will have to go and see what these years away from my villa have done to the edifice that used to be my home. I have the key to the front door."

They had asked the Judge to marry them in a lay ceremony. Then the few belongings from such as had been their ascetic years were gathered in one or two bundles onto the sleigh and they set off for Viktor's home. What they saw when they arrived there was disturbing.

The whole villa had been overgrown by ivy and other creepers. There was a ghostly atmosphere about it having not been used for a full twelve years while Donella and Viktor had been in holy orders. The sleigh slid to a halt and they descended onto the light fall of snow on the ground. Viktor pulled the creeper back from the front door. His key, rusty now, grated in the lock. Then they were inside. Everything was exactly as it had been left those twelve or so years ago and they now needed the household staff to set the villa to rights. Only Donella and Viktor brightened up the now ghostly and until now deserted place that had once been Viktor's home.

Printed in the United States
By Bookmasters